AURORA

Aurora

by

Emma L McGeown

2020

AURORA

ISBN 13: 978-1-63555-824-1

This Trade Paperback Original Is Published By
Bold Strokes Books, Inc.
P.O. Box 249
Valley Falls, NY 12185

First Edition: November 2020

Credits
Editor: Barbara Ann Wright
Production Design: Stacia Seaman
Cover Design by Tammy Seidick

Acknowledgments

To my family and friends, thank you for taking the time to read *Aurora* in its early, questionable stages. The in-depth and vital feedback from all of you was never read, but thanks anyway. In all seriousness, I would be remiss if I didn't acknowledge the strong women in my life who all offered continuous encouragement when I thought very little of my writing. Thank you to Barbara, Jo, Lauren, my sisters Sarah and Bronagh, and my fiancée, Laura. Their input, help, and support got this book to a place where people in the real world would actually read it. So, blame them if you hate the plot.

To my fiancée, Laura, who always read my scribbles
regardless of how little they made sense.
And to Margot, our dog, who eagerly waited
on a physical copy of this book to bury in the garden.

CHAPTER ONE

The throbbing in my head shook every cell, with each pulse sending another wave of pain. Outside of the white noise scrambling my head, everything seemed quiet, perhaps peaceful. Well, almost everything, except for that incessant beeping provoking me in the darkness. Beep…beep…beep…

That irritating and endless beat pulled me back to consciousness and into the light. Hushed whispers surrounded me, much too incoherent to decipher who it was or even register what they were saying. I tried to open my eyes, see light, but exhaustion made that impossible as the throbbing overpowered my senses, and I was pulled back under again. I continued this dance with consciousness for what seemed like hours, perhaps days, until finally, I conjured enough strength to pull myself out of it.

My only friend in this darkness, the beeping, seemed clearer as I came around. The throbbing in my head felt angrier, and I started to feel the rest of my body with every muscle aching.

Tears of frustration formed as blurry objects appeared in neutral shades of white, pale grey, and blue, but I was nowhere familiar. I wiggled my fingers but failed to move them any great distance until I felt someone's hand wrapped around my limp wrist.

"Elena?" a muffled voice called. "Elena, can you hear me?"

I tried to answer, but it was impossible, coming out as nothing more than a mumble.

"Oh God, you're awake," she cried as the sound of her voice became clearer. "She's waking. Someone? Help!" she called into the distance as footsteps disappeared, her voice fading.

Alone again, I scanned the room, revealing more clues to my location. A TV was mounted high on the wall in front of me; the muffled British accents sparked recognition that I was at least home, though the terrible dialogue meant it was likely some tragic daytime soap. Feeling as if I was getting nowhere with sight, I tried to move my body again. It didn't budge more than an inch before pain screamed from every limb. I inhaled sharply to ease the pain only to be rudely greeted with the distinctive disinfectant smell of all hospitals. Like a signature scent of despair.

"Elena, try not to move." A voice returned, and I found its owner. By the pale blue scrubs, I assumed it was my doctor. "Can you hear me?"

I tried to answer her, but my throat felt like sandpaper. I mumbled, practically inaudible.

The doctor followed my gaze before registering my request. "Water?" After a small nod from me, she slowly brought the cup and straw to my lips.

I took a sip. It did nothing to quench my thirst but made me somewhat coherent. "Where am I?"

"You're in the hospital. Do you remember what happened?" I tried to think, but nothing seemed clear. "Do you remember anything?" I didn't have a moment to answer before the door opened.

"Hi." A man in scrubs and a white coat entered, nodding to the other doctor but keeping his distance before addressing me. "Hello, Elena, I'm Dr Greg Hall. How are you feeling?"

"Like I've been hit by a bus."

"That's oddly accurate." He quickly checked himself when he received silence from the room. "Sorry. Bad joke." He side-glanced the other doctor before rambling again. "You took quite a bump out there. Do you remember what happened?"

"Was I hit by a bus, by any chance?" I mumbled as I tried to rack my brain back to the incident but came up empty, painfully and terrifyingly blank.

"Yes. I'm afraid so." He spoke softly, with kind eyes. "You were hit by a bus a couple of days ago and have been in and out of consciousness. I will have to examine you to get a full extent of your injuries. Is now a good time?"

I gave a small nod. He poked and prodded at my feet and toes as I did the small exercises he wanted. Everything hurt, but Dr Hall, almost over-the-top polite, apologised every step of the way. His small talk and little jokes here and there made me feel more at ease, almost as if I'd known him for years.

"Everything looks good, Elena. I am very happy with your progress physically. You'll feel sore for a little while, but the pain should decrease as the weeks go on."

"Weeks? Great," I mumbled sarcastically before an element of relief washed over me. *I'm going to be okay.* "Thank you, Doctor."

"Don't thank me yet. Physically, everything is working as it should. There's just a neuro exam we have to go through. Is that okay?" he asked before side-glancing the other doctor again, who was still sitting next to me, watching intently.

"Sure, why not." I attempted to sit up straighter but failed with the lack of strength in my arms. The other doctor used a pillow to prop me up, and I sent a small smile of thanks before my attention was diverted back to Dr Hall.

"Can you tell me your name?" he asked, looking at a clipboard as if ready to take notes.

"Elena Ricci," I answered and was a little relieved to hear my voice was beginning to return to normal.

"Good. And when I entered the room, I told you my full name. Do you remember?"

"Doctor…" I paused as my mind blanked momentarily. "Craig Hall."

"It's Greg, but very close, and I have been known to mumble, so I'll let that one slide." He smiled proudly, as if I was a pup that had just learned how to sit on command. "Can you tell me where we are?"

"A hospital. Still in London, I hope?"

"Don't worry, we're still in London." He grinned. "Good. And what is this?" He held his pen in my line of vision and wiggled it.

"A blue pen."

"Good. And you can tell it's blue, which is great." He pointed behind his head but kept his eyes on the clipboard. "Now, on the TV, can you tell me what's airing?"

"Something terrible. It's probably *Coronation Street*," I mumbled, causing both doctors to laugh.

"Very good, indeed. And what year is it?"

"2010."

The room silenced as Dr Hall's eyes whipped up. He stared at me as if trying his best to hide the shock. He failed.

"What?" the doctor beside me whispered as I turned to meet her gaze.

"2010. Isn't it?" I turned to Dr Hall again as panic set in.

"Can you tell me what age you are?"

"Twenty-four." The wild eyes of the doctors told me my answer was wrong.

"And what do you do for a living?"

"I'm interning for the summer at Baker Contracts."

"Good. Well, I think that's all the questions I have right now." He jotted some notes before beginning to move toward the door. "Is there anyone I can call for you?"

"My mum and dad—" I started, but the female doctor interrupted.

"They're coming. They'll land from Sicily in a couple of hours."

"Okay. And Cat? My sist—" But again, I didn't have a chance to finish.

"Caterina is on her way." She read my mind once again, and as I turned to her in surprise, it gave me the opportunity to really look at her.

She looked to be in her early thirties, with short, wavy, dark hair swept back from her face. Although she looked worn out, exhausted from the day, her beauty was undeniable. She looked no taller than me but strong, with a hint of a sleeve tattoo peeking from under her shirt. The blue scrubs brightened her already sky-blue eyes as they connected with mine, making me feel as if I was under scrutiny. The feeling of complete vulnerability under her gaze should have unnerved me, but strangely, it didn't. She watched me with genuine concern, something that seemed misplaced, considering she was a perfect stranger.

"Can you also call my boyfriend, Tom?" I asked Dr Hall before he left. "He'll be worried about me."

"I'm sure that can be arranged," he replied. "We'll give you some time to rest and check on you again soon." He smiled as he began to leave with the other doctor.

"Thank you, Dr Hall. And I'm sorry I didn't catch your name, Dr…" I asked as she turned to look at me.

"Jax. Dr Jax."

❖

Jax

She had no idea who I was.

When Elena had been wheeled into the emergency room on a gurney, with blood pouring from her head, I hadn't realised how bad this was. Though I had been about to start the second half of a glorious twenty-four-hour split shift, all exhaustion had vanished the moment I saw her. Greg had examined her and saw she had an intracerebral haemorrhage causing a brain bleed.

Being a trauma surgeon, I had known how messy that kind of bleed could be—every second counted—but Greg Hall was not only my best friend but the best surgeon I knew. He was already more experienced and skilled than surgeons who had been in the operating room for thirty years. I had begged to be in surgery with her, but a conflict of interest meant I didn't have a say.

It had been my first experience being *the family*, waiting outside in the waiting room. After today, I would never go through another surgery without thinking of the loved ones. Their pacing, with fears and worries and agonising feelings of uselessness. It was not something I used to waste energy on. My focus was always on the patient, until today.

After surgery, I had gone through the entire procedure with Greg. I couldn't critique him, but I'd wanted to. "One more time. How far did you drill into the skull?"

"I've done hundreds of craniectomies." He'd rubbed his tired face and heavy stubble, evidence from the last three days on call.

"Fine. Then what about—"

"Jax, it's two a.m."

I'd searched for the clock in disbelief and had realised how long Greg had been sitting with me. Surgery had ended hours ago.

"You should sleep." He'd placed a hand on my knee. "Why don't you sleep at mine?"

"I'm not leaving her." Elena's beaten body in the bed seemed too fragile to be left alone.

Bruising around her face had caused swelling. Paired with the bandages and the stitches holding her arm together, my wife had been almost unrecognisable. Her usual silky brown hair had been dull and lifeless, and her beautiful tanned complexion almost yellowed under the harsh, intensive care lighting. Nothing about this battered body had resembled Elena Ricci. Even her intoxicating smell that I could never grow tired of had vanished and been replaced with despair.

Greg had watched me with wary and tired eyes. He knew me well. We used to date, studied at medical school together, and went through our training in this very hospital. We'd grown closer, almost like family, after he'd transitioned to male. He'd been there every step of my career, always a good friend, which is why it shouldn't have been a surprise when he'd sat next to me again.

"So I started with a 0.5-millimetre drill..." Greg had taken me through the surgery once again.

A few days later, there had still been no change. Everyone in the trauma department had pitched in and shared my shifts, so I wouldn't have to leave Elena's side. My friends and family had brought clothes and food and had persuaded me to sleep the odd time. I'd spent every day by her bedside, going over the last time we'd spoke—the hurtful things I'd said to her—torturing myself while begging her to wake and terrified that she might not as each day turned into the next. Until something moved in my hand.

The moment I'd registered how truly bad things were was when I heard the words *neuro exam*. Elena had awoken just moments ago, and I had been thrilled but silently keeping it together so as to not overwhelm her. Greg had to examine her before I could truly rejoice.

"Physically, everything is working as it should." I'd tuned in and out of the conversation but had watched her carefully. "There's just a neuro exam we have to go through. Is that okay?"

"Sure, why not." Elena's dry response had me smirking before she'd glanced warily in my direction.

That wasn't the first time she'd thrown me that look. Having lived with her for the past six years, I knew every one of her looks. I'd begun to think back. She hadn't been her usual warm self to either me or Greg. She had been confused and perhaps wondering why I was here.

"Can you tell me your name?" Greg had started.

"Elena Ricci."

He'd continued with questioning, and I had felt myself begin to ease. She'd recognised basic objects and could recall them, remarkable for someone with a brain bleed. Her slurred speech was likely an aftereffect of surgery. She needed time to heal, but I could help her with that as long as she was going to be all right.

"Very good, indeed. And what year is it?"

"2010."

That was all it took to cause my entire world to fall apart. I'd first met Elena in New York in 2010, a lifetime ago, really. We had been young and immature but had a connection that was undeniable. Though we'd started as friends, she was never just that to me. After a lot of denial, she'd finally accepted her feelings for me, though it had taken several more years for her to truly accept herself and address those demons she'd carried from childhood.

"What?" I'd broken the deafening silence as I'd searched her face for signs of familiarity.

"2010." She'd wrinkled her brow. "Isn't it?"

"Can you tell me what age you are?"

"Twenty-four."

My heart had stopped at that moment as Greg continued to ask questions. I'd barely heard a word as my breathing became erratic and loud in my ears.

"Good. Well, I think that's all the questions I have right now. Is there anyone I can call for you?"

I'd felt sick to my stomach as the room began to spin. Elena had asked for her parents and sister, and somehow, I'd managed to answer. My quickened heartbeat had made me tremble as my mind raced through the last eight years, something Elena appeared incapable of doing.

"Can you also call my boyfriend, Tom?" That request had been the final dagger to the chest as I felt tears begin to form. "He'll be worried about me."

"I'm sure that can be arranged." Greg had quickly moved to my side and put his arm around me. My knees had turned unsteady as I struggled to breathe with the tightening around my heart. "We'll give you some time to rest and check on you again soon." Greg finished as he began to usher me out of the room.

"Thank you, Dr Hall. And I'm sorry I didn't catch your name, Dr…" she'd asked as I turned to look at the love of my life, who had no idea who I was.

"Jax. Dr Jax."

She had no idea who I was.

Now, with the door closed, I began walking, unable to stand still. It didn't matter where, all I knew was I couldn't be anywhere near that room. Everything in my line of vision was spinning as I tried to process the situation. My sneakers squeaked on the freshly polished floors as I stumbled down the hallway, crashing into walls with no direction in sight.

"Wait, Jax. Just give me a minute," Greg called as he tried to follow. I couldn't answer. I could barely breathe as my chest tightened further as if caught in a vice. "Jax, wait. Where are you going?"

My throat was dry, my eyes blurred, and my mind spun out of control. I felt like I was being suffocated; maybe I was. Was this what a panic attack felt like or a heart attack? Maybe it was both. My stomach flipped and I felt its contents begin to surge upward.

"Jax, stop for a second," Greg called again as I burst into the washroom. He followed me there, too.

I darted to a spare cubicle and released the contents of my stomach, which was very little. I felt a hand on my back as I leant over the toilet, but Greg's caring touch felt like it was burning my skin.

"Leave me alone." I flushed the toilet and brushed past him to the sink to splash my face. I felt faint, swaying as I gripped the sink for stability. My complexion matched the tiles on the floor, a cold grey, and damp stains lingered under my arms. Even with a bad flu or hangover, I'd never looked this deathly.

"You should sit. Are you feeling okay?"

"No. Surprisingly, I'm not." I spoke through gritted teeth as I tried to walk past him, but he blocked my path. My blood felt as if it was at boiling point as I pushed him away.

"Keelin, stop," he called, and his voice bounced off the tiles like a swirl of concern I couldn't escape, and finally, I let myself crumble.

"What did you do?" I shouted, tears threatening to spill. "She doesn't remember me. She's lost the last eight years of her life. You must have done something, fucked up—"

"You know this wasn't me," he replied softly, looking offended that I could accuse him of something like this. "You don't think the bus that hit her had something to do with her temporary amnesia?"

"You don't know that it's temporary!"

"Odds are—"

"Don't tell me the bullshit statistics we give to the patient's family to give them some hope." I stormed past him, out of the washrooms and back into the hallway.

"You need to calm down." He followed, irritating me further.

"No, you need to leave me the hell alone." I turned and shoved him. He stumbled into a medical cart with a crash. Supplies clattered to the floor as nurses, some of whom were my friends, stopped at their station and watched as if fearful that they would need to call security.

I barely recognised myself, and by the look on Greg's face, he didn't either. Emotions took control with my mind unable to accept Elena's memory loss and that I could have been responsible for it.

"Don't take this out on me, Jax. I'm your friend, not a punching bag." He raised his voice, something he rarely did, before it softened again. "You've got to keep it together. This could be temporary. She could get back her memories—"

"When?"

"It could happen at any time, you know that. But we can't go in there and shock the life out of her while she's recovering."

"So we let her pretend she's living in 2010? I can't wait until she sees the news: why's that buffoon now the US president? Brexit? She will send herself into another coma."

"I don't have all of the answers, Jax. All I know is she needs time to remember who she is." As I wiped away tears, Greg nodded over my shoulder. "Besides, he needs you now more than ever."

"Mum!" My son Jamie ran toward me with Elena's older sister, Cat, trying to catch up. I lifted him into my arms and held on tight. He was like a breath of fresh air on this dark, miserable day.

"Is Mummy awake yet? Can I see her?" he asked as he pulled away, revealing big green eyes just like Elena's.

The inner turmoil I felt staring into Jamie's eyes was unbearable, but Greg was right. He needed me now more than ever. I had to be strong for him. He needed at least one stable parent as we waited and hoped Elena regained her memory, if she ever did.

Chapter Two

"Wait, so not only am I in my thirties and probably have grey hairs and more wrinkles than I know, no one can tell me anything about the last eight years?" I asked, perplexed.

"Elena, the mind is extremely fragile," Dr Hall said softly, taking the seat beside me. "Particularly after a traumatic incident like what you've been through. Patients who are overwhelmed with information all at once can sometimes regress. And like you said, eight years is a long time. Things have certainly changed. You've changed." His eyes widened, and he began to backpedal from that statement. "Probably. I mean, everybody changes over the course of their life, right? I wouldn't know about you specifically, but I'm sure you've changed too. Probably." I couldn't help but wonder if he knew more, and it frustrated me no end.

I'd aged massively overnight and was rendered with virtually no hint or explanations as to how the rest of my twenties had panned out, let alone the beginning of my thirties. There were things I'd wanted to accomplish by the time I had turned thirty. Perhaps travel a little, have a good career or be married with children. Even a pet? And then there was Tom, my serious boyfriend, but his absence indicated that was no longer the case. The holes in my mind made me feel broken and alone.

After he cleared his throat, he continued again with a seriousness in his voice. "The point is, learning all of these changes at once can actually deteriorate recovery, push patients into a state of depression, or you could shut down that part of your brain altogether. In extreme cases, it can actually decelerate the process of recalling old memories and habits, with some things never coming back."

I nodded slowly, not fully understanding. "So I'm supposed to what? Not watch TV in case I find out who's won the last eight *X Factor*s?"

"Pop culture and current events are different. Watch the news, read a newspaper, go on Facebook—"

"Facebook isn't still around, is it?"

Dr Hall watched me in amusement before starting again. "Begin to live your life again and do things that seem natural to you. Ask questions about your life, your job, family and friends. The people who are closest to you will give you the answers."

"Okay, now we're getting somewhere." The frustration eased slightly. I took solace in the fact that Cat would fill me in on what I'd missed.

"When the time is right, your memories will come back. But take it slow, Elena. Try not to be in a rush to figure it all out again." He gave me a serious look. "Eight years is a lot of time to catch up on, and you don't know how much has truly changed."

The seriousness in his tone coupled with the glistening in his eyes told me he only wanted the best for me, and that this course of action *was* best. He was my only contact to the outside world, and yet I trusted him wholeheartedly.

"My advice is to go back to your current life and just do… what you normally do every day." He smiled simply as if it was as clear as day.

❖

"Elena!" My sister's concerned voice stirred me. I must have fallen back to sleep after finding out I'd missed the last eight years of my life.

My big sister stormed into the room like a tornado, dishevelled and wild. "You bitch." She dropped several bags at her feet and ran to my side with unshed tears.

"Hey, Cat." Her arms were around me before I even had a second to wince.

I wondered again what could have driven me to step off a curb without looking. Such a basic instinct drilled into everyone as infants: *look both ways*. Then the screeching impact of rush hour traffic on one of London's busiest streets wiped years off my life.

Cat's embrace was comforting and warm. Like home. Her thick, curly, dark hair was untamed as always and attempted to suffocate me. Though her crushing strength caused pain to course through my muscles, that familiar scent soothed the agony.

"You scared the crap out of me." But she hadn't let go yet. "I thought you were dead when I got the call, and then I said to myself, if she wakes up, I'll kill her myself. What kind of Muppet doesn't look before crossing the road?" she goaded and pulled back to look me over again.

As she stared at me with something resembling pity, I took a moment to survey her. While she was still my sister and best friend, the eight years I had missed were evident. I'd been deluding myself into believing the amnesia was some sort of elaborate prank, a joke by some bored doctors who'd even printed magazines and newspapers dated 2018 to make the story believable, but looking into the eyes of someone I'd known my entire life, there was no disputing the years I'd lost.

Grey hairs peppered her roots, while creases around her eyes made her resemble our mother more than I would ever admit. Cat used to pride herself on showcasing the finest fashion trends, from high-heeled shoes to pricey designer handbags, but had transformed into someone who wore workout leggings and sneakers.

"Well, honey, you've looked better." She sighed, taking a seat on the bed. "But also, worse. Remember Nana's funeral?"

"Oh God, please don't bring that up. I'm in a hospital bed, I don't need that kind of guilt."

"You had one job, but instead, you knock over poor Nana's coffin."

"How was I going to be able to do anything after we'd finished your hip flask before we even got to the church?"

"Sambuca hardened you." Cat giggled.

"I was fifteen!"

She rolled her head back, laughing mischievously. "Well, at least you remember something." Her expression softened as concern took over.

"Yeah, it's just the last eight years I have no recollection of." I sighed as she gave a slow nod.

This was the first time I'd seen Cat, or at least, the first time I was lucid enough to remember. The nurse said the pain medicine would have that effect. It knocked me out with each additional pump.

"So what's new?" I teased as Cat picked up her several bags and moved them closer to the bed before taking a seat again. "What's been happening in the last eight years? Has that damned ash cloud finally pissed off?"

"Huh, I forgot all about that. Yes, it's well and truly pissed off, thank God, but not before leaving you stranded in New York for almost two weeks."

"I went to New York?" I asked, receiving a nod. "Did I like it?"

"It's New York, who doesn't like it?" She smiled. "It's also where you met Jax."

"Jax?" I asked, confused before the name popped into my head. "The doctor? We're friends?"

"You could say that," she replied ominously. "Wow, you really don't remember anything, do you? I actually thought you were just putting it on for attention." She chuckled as I batted her arm. "So you don't even remember about your nieces?" I gasped as I remembered she was pregnant. Pregnant eight years ago.

"Nieces as in more than one?" I beamed as she began riffling through one of her many bags, children's clothes and other items flying out of the chaotic sack.

"Why do I carry so much crap? Here." She grabbed and pulled out a slim, flat object. She began swiping and pressing non-existent buttons as I watched in amazement. "Oh, yeah." She giggled as she caught my awe. "There's a lot of new phones. Look at the size of the screen. They need to make jean pockets bigger is all I'm saying. Gone are the days of our sweet little flip-up phones."

"Excuse me? I have a BlackBerry, flip-up phones are so 2008," I joked. "Where are the buttons?"

She laughs. "Stuck in 2010. Bring back buttons, I say, much easier than all this swiping nonsense. Oh, here it is." She smiled as she handed the phone to me and revealed two beautiful raven-haired little girls. "The taller one is Abbey, and the little monster with chocolate all over her face is Kate. I swear Kate is adopted. Things were so much simpler when it was just Abbey."

She pinched the screen, and it zoomed in on their little faces. They were the perfect mix of Cat and Nick, with Abbey looking more like her mum and Kate having the cheekier features of her dad.

Having seen the picture of my sister's Hallmark-like family, complete with a golden retriever, it only cemented the time I'd lost. Cat had the perfect family, and my life was…unknown. In the past two days, I'd been greeted by two people, and one of them was my doctor, paid to treat me. I began to think I mustn't have had many close relationships.

"And how is Nick?" I asked, and I swiped to the next picture.

"He's good, worried about you, obviously. What a week for him to be hosting a conference in Milan. He flies back tomorrow."

"And did he land partner by the time he was thirty-five like he promised?" I raised my brows, knowing that Nick would be inching closer to forty at this stage.

"He made partner last year, which we thought would be great. More money, more holidays and everything, but it just means later nights working and more overseas travel." She sighed sadly. "The girls miss their dad, and I miss my husband."

I nodded as I continued scrolling. "Well, maybe he could go back to—"

The thought was lost as I stopped on one picture. I zoomed in on the image of Kate with a little boy, and I felt my breathing catch. It felt like my heart was expanding, but there wasn't enough room in my chest as I looked at this little boy no older than Kate.

"Who is that?" I asked but couldn't tear my eyes from the picture.

The little boy with sandy-coloured hair grinned at the camera while dressed in a light blue shirt which barely tucked into his grey trousers. Both children looked like they were at a special occasion, as the background captured a busy afternoon in a garden outside a church.

"Oh, that's Jamie," Cat replied offhandedly. "It was taken at Abbey's communion, and we had the kids all dressed up. Then we went for dinner at Italiano's. Kate got spaghetti all over her dress, Nick was flipping out…" She went on, but I must admit, I barely heard a word after Jamie.

"Who is he?" I asked, meeting her gaze, and that was when she fell silent. For the first time in her life. Like she was searching for an explanation but couldn't find one. "Cat?" I asked again before she blurted out a string of words.

"He's…that's Kate's…eh. He's…Jax's son," she muttered as she took back the phone and looked down at the screen. "Do you recognise him?"

"I don't know," I replied as she gave me a double take. "He probably just looks like any other kid." I dismissed but knew I had more of a connection to him.

❖

Jax

While supressing a huge yawn, the kind that made my eyes water, I stirred the pasta to make sure the tomato sauce was evenly spread out. I tried to battle another yawn just as the front door unlocked and Cat appeared.

"Hello?" she called, and I heard the girls run from Jamie's room into the hallway.

"Mummy," the girls cheered as Cat bent over and planted kisses on their foreheads.

"Did you have fun at Aunt Jax's?" she asked them as she caught me in the kitchen. "She's not trying to poison us all again with her cooking, is she?" she teased as she walked into the kitchen and toward the stove. "Go get your things, girls, and we will hit the road soon."

"I haven't poisoned anyone intentionally in a long time." I smirked, pulling out a couple of bowls from the cabinet before turning to her. "I made extra if you want to stay for dinner."

"For the third night in a row? It's okay. I've to pick up his lordship and the queen from the airport soon."

Elena and Cat's relationship with their parents was difficult, to put it diplomatically. At least that was how I'd always perceived it. As a very Catholic and Italian family, their parents lived most of the year in Sicily and flew in occasionally to visit their daughters, barely tolerating me and Nick. They were furious when Caterina had Abbey out of wedlock, and when Elena brought me home to meet them, I wasn't welcomed with open arms either. But the deep-seated issues Elena had with her parents went all the way back to her teenage years, with Elena carrying that shame every day. Her pregnancy had also caused a stir, and then my adoption of Jamie surely played a part in Stefano's heart attack a few years back. They loved their grandson now and, well, I was tolerated for the sake of Jamie.

"Your parents are staying at your place, right?" I asked as

Cat whimpered, allowing her head to fall into her palms. "And you're clearly very excited about that."

"Oh yeah, I can't wait for the judgement of how tiny my house is, how it's a mess or how I work too much and that I'm failing as a Sicilian woman because my children aren't fluent in Italian, and the list goes on."

"Don't forget having to explain Elena's zapped memory," I added as Cat groaned, banging her head off the fridge. "At least there's one good thing you can tell your mama. Elena can't remember when she turned gay and ran off with a lesbian to disgrace the Ricci name." The room turned quiet as I stirred the pot. "I'm joking." I tried to lighten the mood, but it seemed I had struck something deeper that Cat and I hadn't discussed.

"She *will* remember, Jax."

"Yeah," I lied as I tried to hide my scepticism. "I know. But for now, I'm just some doctor."

"Or her doctor roommate," Cat mumbled before darting out of the kitchen. "All right, kids, let's go."

Panic emanated from my skin as my mind raced through the implications of Elena living with us platonically. I raced after her and grabbed her before she could seek sanctuary with the children. "Hold on a sec, Cat. What did you tell her?"

"It just kinda slipped out." She shrugged. "Old habits and all that."

"So you told her she lives with me?" She nodded. "Why would you do that? And who the hell is Jamie supposed to be?"

"Don't be an idiot, Jax. He's your son. Obviously."

"Obviously?" I rolled my eyes.

"Well, I didn't lie about that. I just left out the part about who his other mother is."

The plot holes in her utterly unconvincing and reckless cover story caused my stress levels to soar, not to mention my heart tightening at the thought of burying my feelings for Elena and pretending to be nothing more than a roommate.

"Birth mother, you mean? As in, they share the same genes. Mannerisms, looks, surname. Do I need to go on?"

"Personally, I think I thought quickly on my feet." She ignored my argument and grew defensive. "We didn't establish a plan before I went in there. What was I supposed to do when she asked, 'where do I live?'"

"Well, I don't know. But you seriously think this half-assed, thrown together plan was a good idea? Really?"

"Jax, you haven't seen her. She's basically a blank canvas. She believes everything I tell her, and she's so spacey that she's literally not questioning a thing." She smiled as if proud of herself. "You got this. It'll be fine." She gave a patronising thumbs up as she called the girls again, no doubt frantic to get away from her monumental fuck-up.

"And what exactly is supposed to happen when she's discharged?" I asked as Cat scratched the back of her head. "She moves in here and what, I just climb into bed with her? And don't get me started on how confusing this is going to be for Jamie."

Cat chewed on her lip. "Okay, I'm sorry. I wasn't thinking of the bigger picture. But think of it this way, there's no better way to jog her memory than to be here with you and Jamie. In your home, together. I can already tell things are going to come back the more she's around you two."

The girls pattered into the hallway and began putting on their shoes as Cat and I grabbed their coats.

"This is a bad idea," I replied while I grabbed the girls' backpacks.

"Jax, I was showing her pictures of the girls, and Jamie was in one of them. I swear she recognised him."

My eyes collided with hers in an instant as an unfamiliar feeling of hope circled in my chest. "She recognised him?"

"Well, she didn't say as much."

I rolled my eyes as the newfound hope flew away like a bird.

"But there was something there. She just knew him. I can tell." I threw her a look before she reached for the doorknob.

"Jax, don't underestimate the telepathic vibes between me and my sister."

Cat and Elena were more than best friends, more than sisters; they'd a bond that was unbreakable. At times, Nick and I would leave them to talk at lightning speed about work, being mothers, or even just TV. It never helped that they'd speak in Italian, and occasionally, I would hear my name with zero context followed by laughing. I remember finding it intimidating in the beginning when dating Elena. Cat got a mention in every other conversation. Meeting the parents wasn't as big a deal as meeting the sister. They shared everything, so there was no point in trying to understand their psychic connection.

"Fine, but I want it on the record that all this lying was not my idea."

"It's going to work out. I promise. She will have her memories back in no time." Cat smiled before pulling me into a hug. I hugged her back as I tried to push down all my fears. "And if not, you'll just have to coerce my little sister out of the closet again," she said before making her way out the door. "Wave good-bye, kids."

"Bye, Auntie Jax."

"Bye, girls." I waved them off as I closed the door and then turned around, leaning my tired body against the cold surface.

I closed my eyes as I rubbed my face. Even after doing a graveyard shift at the hospital, I never felt this exhausted. Broken. My arms were sore, heavy from the weight of the world. Between emergency shifts, checking in on Elena from afar, and playing taxi to Jamie and the girls, it felt like every day was a hardship. I peeked as the smell of burning forced me back down to earth. Jamie was standing in the middle of the hallway, watching me.

"Hey, Jay, hungry?" He shook his head. "Yeah, same."

Making my way back into the kitchen, I put up blinders to avoid the dishevelled array of the countertops and dished up dinner. After scraping the bottom of the pot for overcooked pasta with a side of burnt tomato chunks, I threw it into the sink. Or more accurately, I placed it on top of the tower of dirty dishes built up over the last few days.

I poured us both a glass of milk but not before taking note of the scarce contents of the refrigerator. With two bowls and drinks in hand, I moved into the main area of the apartment, which consisted of the living room and dining table. Household chores, basic hygiene, and grocery shopping had clearly taken a back seat. Dirty scrubs and coats lay scattered across the back of the L-shaped couch, and the living room floor was cluttered with shoes, DVDs, and Jamie's toys. I shifted the paperwork, laundry basket, and toys to one side of the table, trying to create some sort of order and normality.

Jamie sat down opposite me and leaned back in his chair, staring in disgust at the bowl of pasta.

"You gotta eat something, Jay." I tried to persuade as he stared back at me, unfazed. "It's really good." I plastered on a big smile while trying to chow down on the minimal tasting and somewhat lumpy meal.

"When's Mummy coming home?" he asked in a small but brave voice.

He was small for his five years, but his sweet smile and big green eyes meant he'd never be overlooked in a classroom full of bigger children. From across the table, the look on his face reminded me of Elena, and my heart ached. Their features were too similar, and both possessed the power to make me do anything they wanted. Jamie asked frequently about Elena, and every day, I curved the question, but today, I could run no further.

"For every mouthful of pasta, I'll answer a question. Sound fair?"

He mulled the offer for a moment before grabbing his fork and taking his first bite. Once he swallowed, he put down the fork, crossed his arms, and asked again, "When's Mummy coming home?"

"She's supposed to get discharged from the hospital next week." His eyes lit up as he went to ask another question, then seemed to remember the game and tried to shovel a huge forkful of pasta into his mouth. "Be careful, Jamie. There's no rush."

His eyes went wide with excitement as I pushed his milk closer, and he washed down the pasta. "Mummy is coming home?" I nodded as he danced in his chair. I smiled at him sadly before his next question. "Abbey said that her mummy says that my mummy doesn't remember anything."

"Yes, that's right." He looked confused for a moment before I went on. "In the accident, Mummy lost some of her memories. She doesn't remember a lot of stuff, and the doctors don't think we should tell her everything. Not yet, at least."

"Why?" he asked as he took another mouthful.

I searched for words I strongly disagreed with. From the second Greg told me we were to keep Jamie a secret, I'd disagreed. He was her son, and Jamie needed his mother, but with Cat also agreeing, I begrudgingly decided to go along with it. Cat was quick to side with Greg despite my arguments that some studies indicated that keeping information from recovering amnesia patients could be unsettling in the long run, and in my personal view, a complete betrayal. However, even I couldn't argue with Greg's logic about how much had changed in the last eight years. Elena was an entirely different person. A married woman with a son and successful career. That would be enough to shock anyone, especially the mid-twenties party girl, *straight* Elena.

"They think it could be too much, too soon," I said to Jamie. "The doctors said that her memories can come back if she does normal, everyday things."

"Like go to work?" he asked.

"Yeah, like go to work."

"And go to the park?"

"That too." I smiled in surprise at his calm reaction to the plan.

"And drink a whole bottle of grown-up wine?"

"It's not always an entire bottle." I had to defend Elena's

fondness for good wine. With a touch of relief that he was understanding the situation, I approached the next topic with care. "But we can't tell her too much, okay?" He nodded before I took a big breath and readied myself for my next request. "And that means that, for the time being, you have to pretend Mummy isn't your mummy."

"Okay," he replied without skipping a beat.

"Now, Jamie, that means you can't call her mummy. You have to call her Elena."

"Duh?" he said with his mouth full. "I'm almost six, I know how to pretend." I smiled at his tomato-covered face, amazed at how easy this conversation was, something I had dreaded for days. "Does that mean she doesn't know you're married?"

I took a shaky breath as I tried to get the words out through an aching chest. "That's right. As far as your mum…Elena knows, we're just friends. So you think you can keep it a secret?"

Jamie nodded excitedly, almost as if it was a fun game played at the expense of his mum. "You're gonna have to hide that, then." He pointed over my shoulder as I turned and followed his gaze to our wedding picture on the side table.

Our wedding day had been one of the best days of my life, a close call between that and the day Jamie was born. It had been a small gathering of family and friends on a summer's day near the beach in the south of England. There was no reason to make a big fuss as we'd already been happily together for several years.

My eyes travelled around the house as I nodded again. "There's a lot I'm going to have to hide."

CHAPTER THREE

"Darling?" the voice cooed in my ear. "Elena? Bella?" I almost opened my eyes before a harsh voice butted in.

"Mama! Don't wake her. She had brain surgery, for Christ's sake."

"Language, Caterina," my father scolded. "You have daughters of your own. You cannot use unladylike words like that."

"Sorry, Papa." Cat groaned, and I could practically hear her eyes roll.

Mother and Papa had been beyond strict when we were growing up. Of course, that was whenever Papa was in the country, and whenever Mother wasn't having a long wine lunch with the neighbours. Our only role model for years was our British-born au pair, Lily. She couldn't have been any older than her early twenties, but she cooked, helped us with homework, taught us English, and tucked us into bed at night; most days, we saw her more than our own parents.

Hence why I was a little surprised my parents flew to London in the first place. They hated Britain. In fact, every time we visited, they would try to persuade me and Cat to stay in Sicily. Sure, the wine and weather would be better, and being able to speak fluent Italian would make it a simple transition, but London was my home. I went to high school and university in the UK, and to me, this was home.

"Look at the state of this dump." Mama's disgust would be written across her face, which was why I kept my eyes closed, to avoid her disdain. "It's a wonder she's still alive."

"She's fine, Mama. The NHS is taking good care of her."

"Ha. The NHS. Useless, broken system," Papa barked, followed by the unforgettable rustling of a newspaper he was no doubt behind, his favourite hiding spot from responsibility.

"And what about that nurse? Where is she?"

"Jax is a surgeon, Papa. I'm sure she will be up soon. She's probably just working."

"I'd rather she didn't," my mother muttered. Her comment stirred a defensiveness in me that I couldn't quite comprehend. "And so she can't remember a thing?"

"Not of the last eight years, no." By Cat's exhausted tone, I knew this was not her first time explaining my amnesia.

"Nothing?" My mother's shrill voice had me wanting to roll my own eyes. "Very strange. And so she doesn't remember anything. What about our thirtieth wedding anniversary at the Fairmont?"

"No, Mama, she doesn't remember your gala ball or, you know, the last eight years of her life."

"And we're supposed to just not tell her?"

With a long drawn out sigh, Cat replied, "The doctor said it's best that she goes back to normal, everyday life and that eventually, her memories will come back."

"That sounds absolutely ridiculous. What kind of doctors does this country have? Riffraff from off the street."

"Can I get anyone tea?" The familiar sound of Nick's smooth voice made me want to smile before I remembered I was faking sleep.

My memories of Nick were filled with carefree bliss. He was like the brother I'd never had, which I guess made him my brother now, considering Cat and Nick were married. He adored my sister. That was the only reasonable explanation as to why he would put himself through a weekend hosting my parents.

"Yes, make yourself useful and get some coffee. Not everyone is obsessed with tea like you Brits." My mother stroked my forehead, leaving her cold touch behind.

The door shut quietly before Cat spoke up again. "Please, do not order my husband around," she said through gritted teeth. "You don't talk to your own husband that way, so refrain from speaking to mine like that."

"I will never understand what you see in him."

"Mama!"

"Don't raise your voice to your mother, Caterina," my father barked as the room turned silent.

And at that moment, guilt overwhelmed me, knowing that I got to hide behind closed eyes, but my sister was stuck in some sort of beratement hell.

"She's waking up." my mother said as she stroked my forehead, and I blinked, adjusting to the light. "Hello, darling. Mama and Papa are here now."

I fully opened my eyes, and all I could see were my mother's obnoxiously large diamond earrings. The familiar and overpowering smell of Chanel No. 5 filled my nostrils, making me feel queasy. She pulled back and smiled. Well, it looked like that was what she was trying to do, but the sheer volume of plastic surgery in her face made it unmoving and stiff. It almost looked like she was in discomfort.

"Hi." My voice cracked before Cat moved to the water station and grabbed me a cup. As I took a sip, she mouthed a thank you, to which I shot a quick smirk. "Thank you for coming all this way, Mama and Papa."

My father lowered his newspaper and moved to my side of the bed, brushing Cat out of the way. His pale grey suit was pristine, with a sharp white collar, making his white stubble even more noticeable. He scanned the length of my battered body and offered a small smile.

"Of course, darling. How are you feeling?" He kissed the top of my head.

"I'm okay. Sore but okay. I just can't wait to get out of here. I've been here for like—"

"Six days," a voice interrupted. All heads turned toward the entrance of my room. "Hello, Mr and Mrs Ricci." Jax gave a small nod.

Jax's eyes never left mine as she moved farther into the room, toward me. However, my gaze was rudely blocked when Mama began stroking my head again, more affection than I'd ever received from her.

"You've been in this hospital for six days, and you're still not out of this bed. Terrible. Why don't we see about getting you moved to a real hospital?"

"If I may, Mrs Ricci," Jax said, but my mother refused to even look at her. "Elena has made terrific progress. She's moving around and even walking unassisted in physiotherapy, despite the somewhat verbal resistance."

I grinned, one which Jax returned. She must have spoken to my physiotherapist, and although my walking was still slow, my profanities were in excellent condition.

"We have some of the best hospitals in Sicily. All it would take is a phone call," Mama almost cooed into my ear.

"She's doing great here," Jax tried but was silenced again.

"Elena is our daughter. I think we would know best." My mother's glare was like a dagger as the room turned silent.

I'd experienced her haunting stare on numerous occasions, usually during times of disobedience, but sometimes just for existing. I would cower away from that glare, and yet, Jax stood tall, almost unfazed. This clearly wasn't her first encounter with my mother. Strangely, seeing Jax stand up to her made me want to do the same.

"I'm not going back to Italy," I said before my mother could sling another demand into the room.

"But, darling," Papa tried.

"I'm not leaving." My voice was stern, and it made me feel powerful, like how I imagine my mother felt.

"Who wants coffee?" Nick sang, arriving with a tray of cups. "Hey, Elena's awake. How you doin', kid?" He beamed at me, and I smiled back. Nick was quick to take in the tension of the room. "What'd I miss?"

"Mama, let's go see the kids at the house. They're excited to see you both." Cat tried to usher them out, but they seemed apprehensive. Eyes darting between each other, unsure if they should leave me alone with Jax.

"I have a physio appointment now anyway," I lied.

My mother nodded. "We will be back tomorrow, bella. *Ciao*." She kissed my head again as she collected her Prada bag and fled the room, allowing the temperature to rise again after her icy departure.

❖

Jax

"Your physio isn't until tomorrow morning." I raised a brow once we were alone. "Lying to your parents, not very Catholic of you."

"Call the pope." Elena tried to lift herself up in bed, but she winced and gripped her arm in pain. I moved to her side to help prop her up. "Besides, it was either that or throw myself out that window. How is it possible that my parents have become more intolerable with age?"

"They're a picnic, that's for sure," I muttered, placing an extra pillow behind Elena's back.

My heart rate picked up as I breathed in her scent. Cat had delivered some of Elena's things a few days ago, and Elena was beginning to smell and resemble her old self again, the woman I had fallen in love with. She smiled politely, and my chest ached when I remembered she had no idea who I was.

I created some distance and crumpled into a nearby armchair, feeling the full weight of exhaustion after the last ten hours on my feet.

"I'm sorry about what they said. How they spoke to you."

"Consider it forgotten. Trust me, that's not the worst they've..." I had to stop myself. Elena couldn't remember the countless arguments we had with her parents about our relationship or my adoption of Jamie. Elena scrunched her brow in confusion as I attempted to correct my faux pas. "That's not the worst thing I've heard from a patient's parents. Nothing is ever quick enough when it comes to recovery." She nodded, seeming to accept the slipup. "For what it's worth, I'm glad you're not leaving...for the best hospitals in the world."

She rolled her eyes. "My delightful parents, ladies and gentlemen." She shook her head dismissively. "Are your parents as bad as mine?"

I inhaled sharply, a knee-jerk reaction to being asked about my parents. When I'd entered the room, I'd made the conscious decision to keep the conversation light and avoid divulging anything too deep. Not until Elena was better.

She seemed to pick up on my mood shift. "Sorry if that's a bad topic." She needed to feel comfortable around me. We were supposed to be friends, after all.

"No, it's fine." I pushed through the discomfort. "My mum is a complete headache and tries to get involved in my life constantly. You think an Italian mother is hard work? Try dealing with an Irish mammy. *No* is not in her vocabulary. But she's always been there for me no matter how many times I've messed up. She's pretty great. I don't know what I would do without her."

I wanted to mention my dad. He was an important part of my life before he passed away recently, but my emotions were already on the verge of collapse. I took the safer option and shut my mouth instead.

"Sounds like you've a close relationship with her." Elena smiled, but it didn't reach her eyes. Mainly because she had no idea what a happy relationship with a parent looked like. "Has your shift just started?"

"Just ending." I welcomed the change in topic, rubbing my face.

"You look tired."

"It's been a long week."

"Tell me about it," she quipped. "Any plans for a wild Saturday night in 2018? Still so weird that it's 2018."

"I have a very special and perhaps sexy date tonight." Elena raised a brow. "Yes, with the on-call room. I think things could end very well."

She played along. "Do you think you two will go all the way tonight?"

"Well, between being paged by interns unable to place a catheter and patients trying to die, I'll be lucky if I get more than forty-five minutes of sleep. Besides, the on-call room is such a tease."

She giggled, and it was like music to my ears. "But what would your husband say?" She continued the joke, but the change in my facial expression must have caused her to recant. "Oh, sorry, the wedding band. I thought you were married," she said as I looked down at my hand. I usually removed my wedding band when working, but today, it had escaped me. "Sorry for assuming."

"Don't worry about it, and please, stop apologising. You can ask me anything you like." I smiled, but the tension remained. I changed the direction of conversation to a lighter topic. "How are you feeling?"

"A little sick of people asking me that. But I guess it comes with the territory of being stuck in hospital. My head is still sore, but Greg, I mean, Dr Hall said that will likely continue for a while."

"You can call him Greg. I think he prefers it. So no dizzy or fainting spells?"

She shook her head, "Just some strong symptoms of mind-numbing boredom."

I chuckled. "Hospitals are like that. It's how we get people to leave. A similar technique they use for prison. So let's say you weren't imprisoned. What would you be doing right now?" I asked as a small smile graced her lips.

"Eating pizza, drinking wine, and watching a horror classic."

"With Hannibal Lecter?" I rolled my eyes.

"You read my mind."

"You're such a freak."

"It's one of the best films ever made," she argued. "Who doesn't want to watch Anthony Hopkins lust over fava beans?"

"Most people," I said. "You love those thrillers, even if you don't get a chance to watch them as much anymore."

She tilted her head at my response, and I realised I'd shared too much.

"That's right, you've a son." My eyes connected with hers, hopeful. "Cat showed me a picture."

"Right." I nodded frantically and tried to wipe the optimism from my face. "Yeah, Jamie. He's quite the handful, so scary movies are left to after the watershed. But he's a sweet kid." She smiled warmly at me, prompting me to say something deeper. "He's really looking forward to seeing you again."

Her eyes lit up, and at that moment, I felt hopeful for the first time in almost a week of gloom. Although Elena didn't remember me, that might not be the case for Jamie. There was something in her expression, an excitement about seeing him. Perhaps an emotional bond to her son even if she couldn't remember him. That thought created optimism. He could be the beacon of light that would bring back her memories.

CHAPTER FOUR

Over the last couple of weeks, I'd had the short-term memory of a goldfish. My life consisted of seeing the same handful of people on a loop, where they'd ask me the same questions in the same hospital room.

Rehab was a continuous uphill battle which took dedication. At least, that was the bullshit my physio doctor spouted. The first couple of days were what can only be described as some form of torture. I was in agony and fatigued, and the doctor sadistically offered words of encouragement, like that would help. But alas, it was what I deserved for playing chicken with traffic.

Rehab meant I got to leave my room, though, out of the pit of despair I'd been trapped in for the last two weeks. My head pounded when I used too much energy, and then the doctors raised the stakes by weaning me off my pain medication. Eventually, each step became easier, and this morning, I was finally signed off to be discharged. I had check-ups every week for the next six weeks to track my progress, but as Cat put it, I would have a doctor for a roommate keeping an eye on me.

Along with Cat, my parents, and nieces, Jax had also called by to visit a few times. It seemed strange that I would soon be living with her. A stranger. A pleasant stranger but a stranger nonetheless. However, I'd take somewhat awkward conversations with Jax any day over the tedious exchanges with my parents.

They complained about the nurses, the coffee, the cafeteria

"slop," the lack of medical expertise, and "third-world" hospital beds. It took very little convincing from me to encourage them to return to Sicily before my release. I was flattered they had flown to London after my accident, but the older they'd gotten, the harder they were to please, and I saw the physical strain it was having on my sister and brother-in-law.

"I just dropped them at the airport." Cat breathed relief down her end of the phone. "I can literally taste freedom."

"I bet, and this is coming from a girl about to be released from hospital." I packed a few of my belongings while we talked.

"You're released tonight? I thought it was tomorrow. I wanted to be there when you got out."

"It's not prison, Cat. Besides, you've had to host Mama and Papa for the last week, which I'm sure felt like prison, so you're taking a night off. Go home, order takeout and open a bottle of wine." She tried to object, but I cut her off. "This is not a request, it's an order. You've been running around for me for weeks, but that's over now." At that moment, Jax walked into my room with a large bouquet of flowers. I felt a blush creep onto my face that I wasn't expecting. "Besides, I have an escort home, so don't worry. Brunch tomorrow? I'll give you a call if I can ever figure out how to dial a phone with no buttons." I said my good-byes with my eyes glued to the flowers.

"Happy discharge," Jax said before grimacing. "That sounded a lot less gross in my head." With a small head tilt, she handed me the flowers.

"You didn't have to do that. Thank you." I smiled back and studied the flowers closely. "I love sunflowers."

She returned a small smile. "All set to go?" I nodded as I grabbed one of my bags, and Jax grabbed the other without invitation, almost as if it was second nature.

I signed a couple of papers and said my farewells to the nurses who worked on my floor before I left the building. The cold bite in the air stung as we set out into the chilly night. It was mid-autumn, but I wasn't expecting it to be quite so cold. It had never looked this frosty from the safety of my hospital room window. Once in Jax's car, I quickly found the heating and turned it on full blast, surprising her when she turned on the engine.

"Make yourself at home, why don't you?" she said with a chuckle.

"It's freezing."

"It's twelve degrees Celsius."

"More like minus twelve," I mumbled as I wrapped my arms around myself.

Jax reached behind me and offered a cardigan from the back seat. I quickly wrapped it around me, and without intending, I took in a deep breath; the smell of sandalwood filled my senses. The distinct smell, not unfamiliar, caused my mind to cloud over, transporting me to a past memory.

It was like a flashback, a gateway to my forgotten past. I was in this same car, but I was comfortably wearing the cardigan rather than using it for warmth, and I wasn't in the passenger seat. I was driving with the windows down as a cool, summery breeze rustled my long hair, causing it to dance around my face. Adjusting my sunglasses, I turned to the person beside me with a contented smile, but I couldn't make out who it was. Where I was driving to or from didn't seem important. The feeling of complete happiness filled my body and warmed my soul. I was free. A hand laced mine on my knee, and everything felt right.

A second later, I was released from the blissful flashback.

"Is this mine?" I asked, causing Jax to hit the brakes slightly.

"Why do you think that?"

"It just feels very familiar." She stifled a smile as she looked straight ahead. "What?" I asked as she tried to hide her smile even more. "Jax."

"All right, all right. It's not yours, but you have borrowed it on occasion. And by on occasion, I mean, you take it all the time."

"Oh, it's yours?" We must have been super close if I took her clothes—I didn't even do that with my friends in college. The familiarity with the cardigan was both relieving and concerning. "Is home far?" I continued to stealthily inhale the cardigan in the hope that it would spark more memories.

"Not at all. We passed it a couple of minutes ago. I just have to make a stop elsewhere first, if that's okay." I nodded. "Cool. I was going to get a pizza for me and Jamie, if you'd like to have dinner with us too?" she asked quietly as she pulled up outside of a row of grand town houses along a quiet street.

"Sure."

She disappeared from the car and went across the road. She waited a few minutes after knocking on a large red door before it opened, and an older woman ushered her inside. She emerged a moment later carrying a little boy who slept soundly. The older woman watched from the doorstep with a wistful smile and her grey hair tied neatly in a bun.

I jumped out of the car as Jax approached, and helped her place him in the back seat, something which felt natural, and Jax didn't seem to think it out of the ordinary. Maybe Dr Hall was right, getting back to my new life would rejog my memory.

Jax closed the door and waved at the old woman before making her way to the driver side again. I gave a small smile as well to the woman, who watched me closely with curious eyes, a similar hesitance I'd witnessed with Jax.

"Is that your mum?"

"Yeah, she watches Jamie sometimes. She said he's been passed out for a while. I'm not really surprised," Jax whispered as she started the car. "He didn't sleep much last night." She began driving again.

"Is he not a great sleeper?" I looked over my shoulder at the cutest little boy sleeping in his school uniform.

"He's usually fine. I think he was just excited."

"Excited? Excited to see me?"

Jax nodded sheepishly before it was time for another stop. As she hopped out of the car, the door slammed, stirring Jamie.

"Mummy?"

I turned to see him barely open his eyes. "Hey, your mummy has just gone to get pizza. She will be back soon." I smiled as his little eyes fluttered closed again.

"I missed you." Three tiny words, no more than a whisper, echoed in the still car. The words stirred something in me that caused my stomach to lurch and limbs to feel shaky. He'd missed me. Me? I was a combination of humbled, touched, surprised, and concerned all at once.

❖

Jax

"This is why I have dreams about building a snowman." Elena laughed as the movie credits began to roll. "Those kids next door in the hospital played this movie every damn day."

"Kids today love *Frozen*. Jamie makes me watch it at least twice a week," I replied as I checked between us and found him clutching my side, fast asleep. "Looks like the excitement was a little too much for him. How long do you think he's been out cold?"

"Judging by the drool, I'd say a while." I followed her gaze and rolled my eyes at the wet patch on my side. "Do you need help?" she asked as I began to lift him.

I shook my head but smiled at her eagerness to help, just like old times.

She'd surprised me multiple times this evening. From the second I picked her up from the hospital, little things had jogged her memory, not the complete picture, of course, but a little snippet of her previous life. When she'd asked about my old cardigan, I had to laugh. I'd had it since university, and she used to always steal it. In fact, she had it on her again as she moved into the kitchen to pour another glass of wine.

"This wine is so good," she'd murmured through mouthfuls of pepperoni pizza earlier this evening. "God, this pizza is the best." She'd almost moaned.

As if I wasn't going to pick up her favourite flowers, stock the fridge with her favourite wine, and buy her favourite takeout. She didn't have a clue who I was, but I knew every like and dislike, preference, and pet peeve of hers. After putting Jamie down, I emerged into the living room again to find her back on the plush couch, surfing the channels with another glass of wine for both of us.

"I took the liberty of topping up," she said as I took a seat next to her but kept a far enough distance so I wouldn't slip into old habits.

Jamie had been my sole focus the second we got home, and any conversations throughout the evening had been tailored to the five-year-old, but now I was nervous. Particularly since this was our first time completely alone together, in our home, starting on a second bottle of wine. I found myself second-guessing everything, having to check myself before I did something wife-like.

"What do you usually watch on a Friday night?" she asked as she flicked through the channels.

"Whatever is on. Usually we're…" I stuttered before correcting myself. "I'm watching a boxset, and so maybe I'll watch an episode or two."

"What are you watching right now?"

"*Orange Is the New Black.*"

"Never heard of it. Is it a fashion show?"

"Definitely not." I chuckled. "It's a show about a female prison."

"Sounds dreary." She cocked her brow at me. "I'll have to give it a watch." I nodded along with her, even though we'd already watched four seasons together. "Do you go out much?"

"Not really. I'd need to get a babysitter. It's just a lot of hassle."

"Where's his dad?" Her question, as innocent as it was, caused me to panic internally as I tried to come up with an explanation.

"He's not around."

"Why?" she asked absentmindedly, staring at the TV, but then caught herself. "I'm sorry, that's way too personal." She jabbered on frantically as I watched a blush appear. "Next, I'll be asking if you have a boyfriend." She chuckled to herself before she took a glance at my wide-eyed expression. "I'm on a roll with these personal questions."

"It's okay, Elena." I tried to calm her nervousness as her eyes danced anxiously around the room. This wasn't the reaction I wanted. She should ask questions. I wanted to make her feel more comfortable. "Jamie's dad just didn't want to be a part of his life. Work was more important, and he never wanted to get to know him. Jamie used to ask about him, but now he's accepted it. As for a boyfriend, no. I don't have the time, and even if I did, well, I'd still give a hard pass." I took another swig of wine, spotting Elena's bewilderment, which prompted me to elaborate. "Given that I'm gay and all."

"Oh, I didn't know. So no girlfriend then."

She showed no signs of awkwardness as she pulled her eyes back to the television. My eyes stayed glued on her as I let a breath exhale slowly. No to the girlfriend part, but I could offer a wife that hadn't a clue.

"Asshole," Elena blurted out of nowhere.

"What?" I tried to follow her train of thought, but all I found was an inoffensive advert on the TV. "Not a fan of bleach?"

"Not the advert," she teased. "I was thinking about your ex, Jamie's dad." She thought for a moment. "What kind of person wouldn't want to be around that little boy?" she asked, as if it was the most ludicrous thing in the world. I gave a shrug as my response.

Although I was fully aware of what had happened between Elena and her ex-boyfriend, it was not my story to tell. How

Jamie's father had told Elena he wanted nothing to do with the baby. Elena and I hadn't been friends very long before she'd fallen pregnant. At the time, she had still been trying to make things work with her ex-boyfriend, Tom. The same Tom Elena had asked for in the hospital. I'd never met the guy; he'd been too busy in Nottingham, sleeping with every paralegal in a short skirt. Elena used to travel to see him every second weekend until they'd finally decided to call it quits. Then she'd found out she was pregnant. Only years later had she filled me in on the horrible things he'd said to her, accusing her of cheating and claiming the baby wasn't his. He'd even tried to pressure her into getting rid of it.

In the end, she'd left him and had decided to raise Jamie herself. She was the strongest woman I'd ever met. It was the thing I loved most about her. The reason I'd fallen in love with her. It was only during pregnancy that things between us had started to change. From then onward, we'd gravitated toward each other, even if Elena had to shut me out for a while to figure out who she was.

"Do I have a boyfriend?" She perked up, pulling me back into the room again. "Cat said that me and Tom are no longer together and haven't been for years, but is there anyone else?"

"Uh…"

"Do I date? At all? I must date sometimes. Please tell me I haven't turned into some kind of loser hermit?" Her voice turned high-pitched in panic.

"Of course you date. You've dated. You date all the time." Her eyes widened in surprise, causing me to dial it back. "You date like a normal, regular amount. You don't have Tinder or anything but—"

"What's Tinder?" She tilted her head.

"It's an app on your phone."

"For dating?"

"Yeah, I think it's used for dating or more like casual hookups," I babbled. "Not that there is anything wrong with one-night stands. It's just I don't think you really do..." Feeling as though I was digging a hole filled with lies and indirectly causing Elena to question herself, I curbed the direction of the conversation. "It doesn't matter. The point is, you're not a hermit. You date, yes, just not right now."

She seemed to accept my ramblings, and I gave a small exhale of relief. The light at the end of the tunnel.

"Okay, good."

"Good?" I asked, perplexed.

"Well, yeah. Imagine if I had been dating someone, and then I wake up and literally don't even know who they are. How awkward would that be?"

"Totally," I mumbled polishing off the remainder of the glass.

CHAPTER FIVE

I jolted upright in bed, clutching my rapidly heaving chest. After a fumble in the dark, I reached for the bedside lamp and was a little shaken when I realised I wasn't in my familiar, yet depressing, hospital room but in my unfamiliar, but actually very real, bedroom.

I couldn't exactly recall the nightmare that had me in such a state, but it felt like one of those dreams where I was falling from a building and had hit the ground with a bang. This dream wasn't uncommon for me these last few weeks, although I foolishly thought that once I was released from hospital, perhaps the dreams would stop.

My gaze travelled around the bedroom as I took a minute to try to remember it. Last night, my head had been a little too fuzzy from the wine and too comatose from the mountain-sized pizza to really take it in. I'd simply crawled into bed, barely shedding my clothes, and had fallen asleep the second my head touched the pillow.

My old bedroom at Cat's place, when we used to live together, had been completely different. I had a collection of mix-matched, second-hand furniture, with an entire wall plastered with pictures. Looking back, it had been a collage of my youth, with photographs from college, old school friends, and family vacations in Italy. That room had been an extension of who I was, like a hall of fame of my adventures, but here…

The furnishings were finished in a dark chocolate wood and felt as smooth as caramel to the touch, not like the IKEA classic I was accustomed to. Other than that, the room stood relatively bare. The only things cluttered on the dresser were some makeup and lotions. Two lonely photographs sat on the dresser too, one of which was me and Cat, which looked as though it had been taken recently, and the other was of me on my graduation. Where were the rest of my memories?

The bed sheets were crisp, soft, and expensive. A beige theme was noticeable throughout the room. Unrevealing, just like the rest of the apartment. Last night, after Jax had driven me home, I'd walked through, hoping it would jog some morsel of a memory, but nothing. No memories. It was as if I was stepping foot inside it for the first time. And now, being in my bed felt bare. The bed sat intimidatingly large in the centre of the room, resembling a king-sized bed in a posh hotel.

The apartment slept soundly. I could tell by the stillness on the other side of the bedroom door. I pulled myself from the warmth of the sheets and spotted the alarm clock, revealing it was only 7:15 a.m. The autumn mornings ensured that even the sun got a longer lie-in than me. In the hospital, the nurses would begin rounds at this time, making it impossible to consider a lazy snooze. The bedroom felt cold, prompting me to snatch the dressing gown from the back of the door and shuffle into a pair of fuzzy, well-worn, and perfectly fitting slippers.

Before leaving the bedroom, I decided to check myself over in the floor-length mirror, the first chance I'd had to do so since the accident. As I studied my frame, I realised that, in this light, I had nowhere to hide.

The bruising along my jaw and cheek had started turning an unflattering yellow, but as Jax reassured, it meant the injury was healing. With a good foundation, I could easily hide it, and thankfully, with no man in my life, I could safely hide the nasty bruises still lingering on my hip and thigh. A jumper would be necessary to hide the six inches of stitching on my bicep, but thankfully, it wasn't summer anymore. I pulled my hair back to reveal the bald patch and stitches from surgery. No date in the schedule to get them removed just yet.

Aside from the injuries I was still tallying up, there were clear and indisputable signs of aging. The few wisps of grey hair would need a trip to the salon, and for the beginning stages of aging on my forehead, there was always Botox, I teased myself. I reached to the hem of my tank top and pulled it up to inspect my tummy, which was, surprisingly, sporting several stretch marks that were becoming more visible as the bruises faded. I had never had a weight problem, but I must have had at some point in the last eight years.

I made my way into the living room, which was spacious and warm, with splashes of navy, grey, and a mustard theme running throughout the living room and dining area. The apartment tour last night didn't include Jamie's or Jax's bedrooms, and I was oddly curious about Jax's sleeping quarters. The decor of her apartment seemed very clean, polished, and modern but didn't appear to have many personal touches. It made sense, considering she leased out her spare room.

The thought had never occurred to me to ask who owned the apartment. I just assumed I was a tenant, considering she had a child. Besides, I couldn't imagine ever owning, or more importantly affording, a place of my own in London. A three-bedroom apartment must have cost a small fortune, and although Jax was a doctor, she obviously couldn't afford it by herself. But then again, could I really afford to rent in this location in my line of work? Did I even have a line of work?

"Morning."

I jumped. Jax supressed a smirk from her position against the kitchen door frame. Her hair was a little wild, and she sported slouchy jogging bottoms with a dark capped T-shirt revealing several tattoos on her biceps. Strangely, I found myself caught in a gaze as her eyes playfully danced around the kitchen countertops.

"I see you found everything okay." She glanced to the bowl in my hands.

It was then that I noticed I was in the middle of preparing pancake batter. I had somehow managed to find the ingredients and equipment for making breakfast without even thinking.

"Weird."

"What is?" she asked as she moved farther into the kitchen and pulled a carton of juice from the fridge.

"I didn't have to think twice looking for all of this." I motioned to the messy kitchen countertops. "Which I will clean, of course, but it's like my hands just knew where to find everything. And pancakes? I never make pancakes." I trailed off as I finished the last of the stirring and began to heat the pan for frying. "I just have a craving."

"Doesn't surprise me," she replied. "The mind works mysteriously and is essentially powered by habit. Plus, pancakes are Jamie's favourite. You make them most Saturdays for him." Her eyes lingered on mine for a moment, and I felt myself being pulled in like a magnet. Jax broke her gaze first as I busied myself with pouring the mixture into the pan. "Speaking of which, he's usually up by now. I rarely get a lie-in."

"Would we class before eight a.m. as a lie-in?" I teased.

"It is for a five-year-old. Well, he won't be five for much longer."

"When's his birthday?"

"First of November."

"Just after Halloween? That's rough."

"Tell me about it. Sweets, cake, and chocolate for days." She pinched the bridge of her nose as she began to make coffee. "Last year, he puked all weekend. I could have killed your sister for letting him have two slices of cake."

"Do you and Cat see each other a lot?" I asked, feeling increasingly curious about their seemingly close relationship.

They mentioned each other a lot, and it was strange. Maybe

it was just a mum thing that I wouldn't get. They both had kids around the same age, but they seemed super close.

"Ye…ah," she stuttered nervously. "Cat watches Jamie sometimes, and the girls are here all the time." She trailed off before adding, "To visit you, mainly. Because you're their aunt, right?" she clarified bizarrely as she handed me a cup of coffee.

Nervous energy from Jax was equal parts strange, considering she seemed like a fairly confident and assured person, and kind of cute. Her brow creased, hands couldn't still, and a subtle blush appeared on her cheeks. I took the cup, grateful for the distraction, and couldn't help but notice how soft her hand was for the brief moment we touched. She moved to the breakfast bar to take a seat, leaving me wondering if I had even asked for this coffee or had she even offered? It was just like second nature for her to make me a cup with extra milk, exactly how I liked it.

"Watch they don't burn," Jax said, motioning to the pancakes as she caught me staring into space. I quickly flipped the pancake, only to reveal that my absentmindedness had caused the damn thing to burn.

"And so, how'd we meet?" I tried to change the subject but was met by a soft thud from somewhere else in the apartment. Our eyes sprang to meet each other as little pitter patters could be heard.

"That'll be the prince." Jax hummed as she went back to her coffee and flipped through the old magazine on the bar.

"Prince?"

"That's what you call him. He gets whatever he wants." She rolled her eyes as the little boy came dashing out of his bedroom.

"Mum," he shouted.

"Jamie, there's no need for all that shouting." She hushed as she lifted him onto her lap, allowing him to see over the breakfast bar.

He smiled mischievously at me as Jax's eyes found mine,

and she planted a soft kiss to his head. Oddly, I felt a warmth spread across my chest, a feeling which caused the corners of my lips to melt.

"Only little boys who use an inside voice get pancakes." I threw a wink at Jax. "You want to help me flip this one?" I didn't need the response as he practically jumped from Jax's arms, eager to help.

We were just finished with breakfast when Jamie perked up out of nowhere. He had been eating pancakes, chatting about his school friends, but the conversation had quieted down until his next question.

"Can I have another, Mummy?" I looked up and was surprised to see he was staring at me. "Mum?" He turned to Jax, who was seated beside me at the circular dining table.

"Sure," Jax replied in a voice almost two octaves higher than I'd ever heard before. Normally, her voice was deep and almost raspy. It was one of the first things I'd noticed about her, but now it sounded like a teenage boy.

"So what are your plans for today?" She changed the topic at lightning speed as she fetched Jamie another pancake from the pan, and I followed her into the kitchen, clearing some of the plates from the table.

"I was supposed to see Cat, but she texted earlier to say she needs to reschedule. Something about the girls' recital."

"Ha. Say no more. Ballet is something Abbey takes very seriously. Well, I was going to take Jamie to Camden Market and the park if you'd like to join us," she said almost nervously while she looked at the stove, avoiding my gaze. "Jay loves the market and watching the boats. Don't feel like you have to."

"I'd like to go." I cut off her mumbling, causing her to stop and meet my eyes. "Really, that sounds great." I turned toward the sink to wash up, shielding myself from the unbreakable trance she had on me.

"No way," she said. "You cooked. I'll clean up."

"I don't mind." I tried to argue until her hand engulfed mine. The contact felt like an electric shock.

"Listen, I didn't want to do this but I am much stronger than you. I will overpower you if you argue, and let's be honest, you're missing half a brain. I think you've suffered enough." She spun me on the spot, hands falling to my waist before nudging me forward, sending my body tingling from the contact, and out of the kitchen. "I'll clean up and get Jamie ready, and then we can go." I headed to my bedroom, smiling the entire way, until her voice stopped me. "And Elena." I turned as she smiled genuinely at me. "Thank you for breakfast." My eyes were trained on hers for a moment before I escaped behind the bedroom door.

❖

Jax

For the first time in weeks, it felt like she was back. I hadn't seen a bigger smile on Jamie's face since the accident as he grabbed Elena's hand and led her through Camden Market as if she hadn't visited the market a hundred times before. Elena threw me glimpses where I had to pinch myself, reminding me that she was different from the woman I married. For someone who couldn't quite remember, she fell in so naturally with our family.

"Mum, look at me," Jamie yelled at the top of his lungs from the largest slide in the park.

"I see you." I waved with a mumble under my breath. "For the eighth time."

Elena chuckled at my comment as she drew the hot coffee to her lips, and we watched Jamie play. We were seated at a nearby bench as the cold damp air settled around us. Winter had come early this year, leaves continuing to fall from the trees with each light breeze.

"He's sweet." She smiled, letting out puffs of warm breath while snuggling under her scarf.

"He's a pain," I said as I stole a glance or two at her. "But he's my pain."

It was rare we both got a weekend entirely off. Either Elena was working or I was on call at weekends. It was sad really. But seeing her now was like meeting her all over again and acted like a bit of a silver lining. Elena not working herself into the ground was a freer and happier woman. Working less agreed with her and us, if there still was an *us*.

"What did you think of Camden Market?" I asked.

"It never really changes, does it? Not even in eight years," she mused. "It was nice going with Jamie, though, felt like going for the first time again." He waved before running around to climb the slide steps again. "Does that sound weird? I've been there countless times, but today was one of my favourites."

"No, not at all. I feel that way all the time with him. Children have a way of bringing out our inner child and making us see things for the first time all over again." I shrugged but turned to look at Elena in time to see something in her eyes. I might have missed it if I hadn't caught her off guard. She had a special glint in her eyes, one I liked to tell myself was reserved for when I was being particularly thoughtful. "What?"

She shook her head, supressing a smile. "Nothing." I nudged her slightly, causing the smile to grow affectionately large. "It's just…that was just very sweet. I never pegged you as the sweet type."

"What type am I?" I asked, perhaps flirted, as I turned to face her, moving closer. Her breathing turned uneven as her eyes darted to my lips.

"I didn't…I just…" She stuttered as she gulped audibly. "I just thought…"

"Mum!" Jamie's shouts pulled me from Elena as I waved at him again.

A weird tension lingered between us with no one willing to speak up after the flirting. I was just about to change the topic, but it was Elena's turn to catch me off guard.

"Can I ask you something?" She watched me nervously, and I found myself incredibly intrigued. "Did I ever talk about anyone?"

"You talk about a lot of people," I said, evoking a small smile. "Anyone in particular?"

"About Tom?" she blurted quietly.

I swallowed the bad taste in my mouth before answering. "Your ex-boyfriend?"

"Yeah. So..." A silence fell between us as she sipped her brew.

"Was there something you wanted to know?"

"No." She shook her head frantically before biting her bottom lip. "Well, yeah, kind of." She played with the rim of her cup before a small smile broke out across her face. "Have I...do I talk about ever...Do I ever talk to him?"

"I'm not sure." I managed to keep my face neutral as my chest started to tighten. "Why?"

Her face continued to show this strange teenage puppy-love. "Well, I was thinking of calling him. I don't know, just to catch up, maybe. I mean, he was my boyfriend. I loved him at one time. I'll admit, I do feel some disconnection from him now, but maybe if I was to see him again. You know?" I nodded along and forced a smile to mirror her excited expression. "I have been thinking about him a lot lately and wondering what happened. Between us. We used to be so happy, and then it ended, and I'm not even sure why. Cat said we broke up years ago but..."

"That was before your accident," I whispered.

"Right?" She smiled as if relieved that I was following her train of thought. "I'm so glad you get it. I'm different now, and maybe he is too. You know? Maybe he changed, and what broke us up doesn't matter anymore. Maybe he misses me too." I nodded as I tried to even out my breathing, but with every inhale, it felt like it was cutting my insides. "What do you think? Should I call him? I mean, you're my friend. Do you think old me would think I was crazy for wanting to talk to him?" She looked at me as I thought for a long moment.

I wanted to tell her everything. Scream that he wasn't worth an ounce of her time. Tell her how many other women there had been for months while they had still been together, tell her every terrible thing he'd said to her after they'd broken up and when she'd found out she was pregnant. I wanted to tell her that letting him pull her in again would be the worst mistake. Hell, I wanted to kiss her. Spark something in her, remind her of who she was. But as I stared into her eyes, I realised something heartbreaking. I wasn't her wife right now. I was her roommate, a friend, someone to confide in during this extremely turbulent and confusing time. With that in mind, I swallowed all the pain rising in my chest.

"I think I can't make that decision for you. I only knew you briefly when you were with him. Even then, all I know about him is what you told me. I can't tell you what to do." She nodded a couple of times, accepting my answer as I took a deep breath to stop the pain in my heart.

CHAPTER SIX

My knees bobbed up and down with every bump on the road as the bus battled through rush hour traffic. Today, I would return to work. It was part of an "easing back into work" programme which consisted of a half day in work every other day. I was ready for the change of pace. A few weeks of moping around the apartment had me crawling the walls. At the same time, I was incredibly anxious. The last time I remembered setting foot in Baker Contracts, I got coffee and scanned invoices. Cat said my role had evolved significantly since then. In fact, I had an assistant who got me coffee, a strange turn of events.

I'd progressed from receptionist to assistant to customer support, and then last year, I was promoted to customer support coordinator, where I managed my own team. It felt surreal, considering I'd no idea what I was supposed to be doing.

My stop flashed on the board above my head, and I departed. A drizzle lingered in the air, not enough to make me reach for my umbrella just yet. I walked the short distance to the large estate which held Baker Contracts, but when I reached the door, I realised it was locked with a keypad.

"Well, look what the cat dragged in!" The familiar voice caused me to spin to face the woman behind me. "Please, tell me you still remember me?" The dark-haired woman bit her bottom lip anxiously as she stood under an oversized umbrella.

"As if I could forget you, Kim," I said, and she pulled me into a hug. She'd started as an intern with me on my first week. "You still work here? You hated this place."

"Not as much as you did, honey. What can I say? It pays the bills, and that's enough for me, especially with another one on the way." She pulled back, hand on her pregnant belly, and entered the code in the keypad.

I struggled to keep my mouth from falling open in shock at her small bump. Kim was a party girl with pink hair who never wanted to settle down, was drunk most of the time, and jumped from a bad relationship to the next. She now stood before me, a woman wearing oversized glasses in sensible footwear with a "Best Mummy" travel mug.

"It's two-two-five-three, by the way, considering your head is emptier than it was before the accident," Kim joked as we stepped into the foyer of the building and out of the rain.

"Hey, at least I show up to work sober," I said and was happy to see she remembered just as clearly as I did.

"Remember how wasted we used to get at lunch and then roll back into the office?"

"Those happy-hour shots were never a good idea. It made Walker so much easier to deal with, though."

"Thankfully, he was fired."

"He was?" I beamed with glee. "There is a God. And who took over for him in finance?"

"You're looking at her." She chuckled. "I know, I used to hate it, but now I call the shots, and frankly, everything is so much smoother. Wow, you really don't remember anything, do you?"

"Annoyingly, no. Last time I laid eyes on you, you had pink braids and a nose ring," I said as she giggled. "And now…"

"I'm a mummy with my third on the way." She patted her round tummy as I caught sight of her large engagement ring and matching silver wedding band. "Things certainly change." Kim nodded toward the elevator. "Come on, I'll show you to your office. You'll be wandering around the corridors for the rest of the day if I don't."

"Did they renovate?" I asked when nothing in the building looked familiar.

"Yep, expanded the whole division. Big investment from our US partners."

I nodded along with her as my gaze travelled around the modern and sleek office. My memory of the space was old, dull, and outdated, with computers and boxes of invoices lying around. Now the office was full of young people in casualwear hooked up to laptops and drawing on whiteboards. Gone were the big honchos in expensive suits acting as dictators, and now it looked like Google's headquarters, with a few of the young employees waving and welcoming me back, unaware that I had no idea who they were.

"How are you feeling, by the way?" Kim asked as we stopped in the kitchen, and she poured me a coffee from the machine.

"Good, physically. Most of the cuts and bruises are practically gone, and I got the stitches out of my head and arm a couple of days ago."

"And mentally?" she asked.

"Not a fucking clue." Kim cackled, spilling her tea on the counter a little. "Seriously, I have no idea who any of those people were out there. Caterina calls me a vegetable." I shook my head while Kim composed herself.

"Give it time, honey. Soon enough, you will be calling the shots in here." She winked before leading me out of the kitchen. She nodded down the hall. "You're just down there on the left. Your assistant's name is Tansy, and she will be expecting you." I took a deep breath as I followed her eyes down the hallway. "If you need me, you remember where finance is?"

"How could I forget?" I rolled my eyes before saying my good-byes and making my way down to where Kim had pointed.

When I came to the open door, I saw four desks all facing each other with soft music playing in the background. I looked around the small, quirky office space where colourful posters hung on the walls, and there was a mini fridge stocked with beer in the corner. Two people were frantically typing, seemingly unaware of my presence. I cleared my throat, but neither of them budged. It wasn't until I moved farther into the room that one of the guys jumped to his feet, yanking the headphones from his ears.

"Elena, you're back." He looked shocked as the other worker who'd had his back to me also jumped up and smiled brightly.

"Hi," I said to the two twentysomething guys who stared back at me expectantly. "I'm sorry, I don't—"

"Damn, Tansy told us you wouldn't remember our names. I'm Sam, and this is Chuck."

"Charles, actually." The man who'd had his back to me corrected as he pushed his glasses farther up his nose and straightened his shirt.

"His name is Chuck ever since he dropped his laptop in the foyer fountain," Sam said as Charles rolled his eyes.

"She doesn't remember that, dumbass."

The two began arguing as I silently watched their bickering. Then I remembered I was their boss. I couldn't be that strict if they felt comfortable enough to argue in front of me. I took solace in that before I interrupted them.

"It's nice to meet you both. I was told to look for Tansy."

"She went to the bathroom, I think."

"Okay, and where do I normally sit?" I asked as Sam slapped his head.

"Right, duh!" He thumbed over his shoulder. "Your office is back there." I smiled before making my way toward the small office at the back of the room. "Can I get you anything?"

"I'll be okay, thanks…"

"Sam," he finished for me with a soft smile as I willed my mind to remember it.

"And Chuck." I pointed to the other employee, who nodded, accepting that Chuck was his name for the rest of eternity.

I closed the door, leaving the boys to bicker, and was surprised to find my office so spacious. Not enough to do kickboxing, but I had enough room to have two people seated comfortably with me. I'd never had my own office. Although the space was simply decorated, there was a warmth to it that made me feel at ease, familiar in an unfamiliar way.

The window behind my desk overlooked the carpark, not exactly an inspiring view. But a park in the distance had some children playing, and I found myself smiling, thinking back to Jamie, wondering how he was getting on at school. I took a seat at my desk and spotted a couple of picture frames. Surprisingly, there were more than in my own bedroom.

One was of me, Cat, Mama, and Papa. It looked like it might have been taken in Italy, as my tan glowed, and Cat was darker than I had seen her in a long time. Both of our complexions always took so well to the sun. The second photograph was a picture of me, Jax, and Jamie at some sort of carnival. As I looked at the picture closely, a bright flash passed before my eyes.

"Mum, can we go on the Ferris wheel again?" Jamie asked with his hand in mine as he pinched some pink cotton candy from Jax.

"Again? We already went on it twice," Jax whined playfully, helping herself to some more cotton candy. "And you know I don't like heights."

"I'll protect you." He beamed at her before tugging on my hand until I dropped to my knee, meeting him at eye level. "Oh, please, oh, please, can we?" His shimmering green eyes crumbled me like they always did.

"Okay, but this is the last time," I replied, feeling my heart expand as he jumped with excitement and began running to the nearby Ferris wheel.

"We wouldn't dream of denying Prince Jamie a royal request," Jax teased as she pecked me on the cheek, her lips lingering.

"Elena!" A young girl burst through the office door, pulling me from the flashback. My heart rate remained heightened, and my hand still lingered on my cheek from where Jax had kissed me. "Bullocks, I'm so sorry. Are you okay? Did you get lost? Trish on reception was supposed to call me when you got in." The twentysomething girl spoke at the speed of light, making it difficult to keep up, particularly when my head was still reeling from my flashback. "And then Trish said that Kevin said that Manjit said you were already here, and then I went looking for you, and Mike said he saw you in the kitchen, and then—"

"Tansy, I presume?" I interrupted as she breathed a sigh of relief and nodded. "It's nice to meet you, well, for me at least. Why don't you sit?" I suggested as she struggled to carry a small stack of folders.

"Thanks," she murmured, proceeding to pile the folders onto my desk, knocking over the infamous carnival picture. "Sorry, I just wanted everything to go smoothly today. It's not every day your boss comes back to work with no idea what's going on." She shrugged as I picked up the picture and tried to fix some of the new chaos on the desk. "Not that you don't know anything. You know stuff. Right? Like, some stuff. You can still speak, right? Because my friend Janice's cousin once got a glass bottle to the head in this nightclub—Malibu Blue, it's in Manchester—and he was in the hospital for like two months, and he had to learn—"

"Tansy?"

"Yeah?" she asked, wide-eyed.

"Are you a little nervous?"

"Completely shittin' it."

I chuckled. "Me too." I watched her relax a little. "To be honest, I'm a little out of my depth. Last time I remember being here, I was Trish in reception."

She nodded. "I know. You're the one who saved me from reception. Remember?" she said and then corrected herself. "That's right, you don't. My bad." I chuckled as she gave me a reassuring smile. "I wasn't sure how much you remembered, which is why I made you these." My gaze followed hers, landing on the coloured folders as she went on to explain, lifting each folder as she spoke. "Green is the projects we are working on right now, in detail. The white folder is a list of the company's clients and their engagement surveys for the last twelve quarters, along with each presentation summarising the findings. Blue includes the overseas consultancy projects for the last year, our analysis, and the findings. Purple is the company structure, the food chain basically. Directors, employees, our team, who I think you basically met. Chuck and Sam?" I nodded as I watched her in surprise. "And red is a basic background on the company for the past eight years, the usual stuff like the people you like and don't like, who you eat lunch with, who's great for office gossip, and who's a giant asshole to avoid—"

"Tansy?" I interrupted again. "Did you make all this for me?" She nodded as if it was no big deal, despite the folders being full of notes, charts, graphs, and sticky notes. "This must have taken you forever."

"It did, but you're a great boss." She smiled genuinely, and I felt my heart warm a little. "And it can't be easy for you. I just wanted to help."

"Thank you. This helps a lot," I said before she relaxed more into the chair, making herself comfortable.

"How's home life?" I barely knew her, but I felt like we shared more than just work problems. She had a welcoming aura surrounding her. I could tell she cared about my answer rather than just asking an empty question like an artificial colleague. It was what prompted me to be candid.

"Strange. Everything is new, and I don't know where things are, and I'm just hoping things will fall back into place but they're…well, kinda not." I laughed lightly, even though it was a great concern of mine.

"It will, with time."

"It's just taking so long. Longer than I think everyone was

expecting." Disappointing people was one of my biggest fears, but I didn't voice that.

"At least you have Jax to keep you on track."

I nodded with a small smile as I thought of my roommate, who had been increasingly consuming my thoughts lately. Her thoughtful gestures of including me in everyday tasks and even intimate occasions like evening meals didn't go amiss. We clearly were very close, and even her son had been great at helping me adjust to my new life. I didn't think I would have been coping as well living alone.

"And how's your little man? Making sure Mummy gets better, I'm sure. He's such a sweet boy."

"Wait, what? *My* little man?" She looked at me as if I had two heads as my heart began to race. "Jamie's not my son."

"Oh, my bad," she said. "Jamie is Jax's son. I always thought you had him. He looks just like you." The phone started ringing loudly outside my office. "Sorry, I have to get that. The boys never answer the phone, drives you cray." She dashed outside to answer the call but not before berating Sam and Chuck.

I sat gobsmacked in my chair. Why on earth would she think Jamie was my son?

❖

Jax

"Anyone home?" I called as I closed the door behind me before removing my coat and scarf.

"In here," a sea of voices called.

"And where is here?" I played along, taking off my work shoes and removing my backpack, ignoring the aches in my tired muscles.

"My room, silly," Jamie called, though I was already going that direction.

When I reached his door, I found Jamie, Abbey, and Kate playing with one of his dollhouses, and a swarm of action figures sprawled out across the floor. To my surprise, Elena was lying on Jamie's bed with her head resting in her hand, watching them. She smiled, and in that moment, all exhaustion vanished, and I forgot I'd just worked a double shift.

"Hey, girls." I smiled at the kids before my gaze naturally found its way back to Elena.

"Will you play with us?" Kate asked, giving me her best toothy grin despite missing her front teeth.

"Sure. After I make dinner," I said before Elena rose to her feet.

"It's in the oven. I better go check on it." She made her way toward me. "Girls, make sure to finish your homework before your mum gets here."

"We will, Auntie Elena," they sang as she brushed past me and moved to the kitchen. As she passed, her perfume lingered in the air. I couldn't help but breathe it in. Her scent still did things, even if she was oblivious of the effect it had on me.

"Caterina called earlier and said she couldn't collect them today," I said before adding an apology. "I'd no idea she was going to ask you to watch them all afternoon. I'm so sorry. I would have called my mum or tried to get cover if I'd—"

"Jax, it's cool. It was really nice getting to spend the afternoon with my nieces." She smiled warmly as she stirred the pot of rice before placing the lid on top. Delicious smells wafted from the oven, and my stomach growled. Elena was always a much better cook. "Besides, it gave me something to do. All afternoon, I sit about or go for walks or clean or cook. I'm bored out of my mind." I chuckled as she checked on the curry cooking in the oven. "They won't even let me log on to my emails outside of work, it's bullshit."

"You've only been back one week, Elena," I said, grabbing two beers from the fridge and passing one to her. "How are things at work? Tansy still being a scatterbrain?"

After her first day of work, she'd come home and told me Tansy thought Jamie was her son. I'd almost choked on a mouthful of mashed potatoes. Elena just thought her assistant was a bit of an airhead and got confused, so thankfully, our cover wasn't blown. I'd called Baker Contracts the following day to explain the situation.

However, as the weeks rolled into months, the guilt at having to continuously deceive and in some cases, blatantly lie, to Elena was becoming unbearable. There were far too many mistakes, and I was struggling to keep track of all the lies. I only agreed to keeping who me and Jamie were a secret in the short-term. Had I known Elena's memories would still be foggy, I would have never agreed. She deserved to know the truth, and it wasn't fair on Jamie.

"At least from now on, they've agreed to let you work every day, Monday to Friday," I replied, squashing those thoughts.

"For three and a half hours." Elena tutted before taking a gulp of beer. "I'm not allowed to work past lunch. I was still in my office today at one p.m., and Kim called security." I tried to hide my laughter, but it only seemed to frustrate her more. "It's not funny, Jax." She whipped the tea towel playfully at me, causing me to raise my hands in surrender.

"Okay, okay. But look at you, you survived your first week back at work," I said as she pulled the heavy pot of curry out of the oven and placed it on the countertop. "Soon, you'll be wishing you only did half—"

Elena stumbled backward, clutching her head. I rushed toward her in an instant, trying to steady her.

"Head rush," she mumbled, but her eyes were unfocused, sending me into a slight panic.

She slumped, barely keeping herself standing, which prompted me to lift her so she was sitting on the counter. As I stood close, studying her facial expression for signs of stroke or fainting, I reached into my scrubs pocket and pulled out my pen-light.

"Elena, look at me." She met my eyes, and I began moving the torch in front of her line of vision.

"I'm fine, Jax," she replied, resisting the bright light.

"You nearly fainted." I made my voice insistent and stern as she huffed, following the light with ease.

"See, I'm fine. Just hungry. I haven't eaten since breakfast." She rolled her eyes as she tried to jump down, but I stopped her, holding her thighs in place.

"You're not fine." Despite trying my best to hide it, she must have seen the worry on my face. My rapid heart rate also made my voice quiver, or perhaps that was my fear of Elena relapsing coming to the surface. "You had brain surgery only a few weeks ago. You can't rush your recovery. You could make yourself really sick if you overdo it. I need you to take better care of yourself."

"I'm sorry I scared you," she said, placing her hands on my shoulders. A comforting wave crashed over me as I exhaled. "I will take better care of myself. Take it slow and be bored." I had to smile. "Happy?"

The front door swung open, and Cat tore into the apartment like a tornado. She froze, eyeing me in between her little sister's legs. "Am I interrupting?" She tilted her head as I jumped at least a foot backward, and Elena slid off the counter and walked toward her.

"Hey." Elena smiled. "The girls are in Jamie's room." She nodded as she led the way.

"I'll be right there," Cat replied before rushing into the kitchen within whispering distance. "Were you just doing what I think you were doing?"

"No! I thought she was going to faint so I—"

"She fainted?"

"No, but I thought she was going to."

"So you took it as an opportunity to get between her legs? Nice."

I moved past her, choosing to give up on this conversation

and stir the boiling rice. "I want my key back," I muttered, taking a few desperately needed gulps of beer to calm my nerves.

Cat proceeded as if never hearing me. "This is great, though. There's chemistry, right? I mean, that *definitely* looked like chemistry. I can't remember the last time Nick had me up against the—"

"Dear God, please stop talking," I almost shouted. Cat shrugged, unfazed, before I continued. "Maybe there is some mild flirtation going on between me and Elena, but we've got bigger problems," I said seriously, and the mood changed in an instant.

"What do you mean?" she asked, folding her arms as concern washed over her face, likely a mirror image of mine.

"A couple of nights ago, Elena called Tom."

"Are you frickin' kidding me? That spineless dog, that asshole." I cut her off with a low shush. "I can't believe she called him. We had lunch yesterday, and she didn't say a word."

"Because you hate him. You don't even try to hide it. Elena won't tell you because she knows you'll only disapprove."

"But she talks to you about her ex-boyfriend?" The irony was not lost on me either. "Was it a long conversation?"

"Long enough," I said as she looked genuinely concerned. "I know I shouldn't have, but I overheard some of it. She explained that she lost her memories, and then he talked for a while, but from what I gathered, the conversation sounded like it was mainly chitchat. Catching up."

There had been a lot of giggling coming from her bedroom, and it had made my heart ache. Even Jamie had heard her laughing when I was tucking him into bed, but I'd pawned it off, telling him she was only talking with Cat. The sinking feeling that I was losing her was all that consumed my thoughts these last few days. They'd been texting as well, not that I was looking at her phone, but messages had popped up a few times during dinner. The smile on her face when she read his messages was the hardest, but I'd pretended everything was fine. Deep down, it felt like I'd been kicked in the gut.

"I'm so sorry, Keelin." Cat gave my arm a small rub. She'd only used my first name on a handful of occasions. I ran my hand through my hair with my eyes squeezed shut, unable to meet her sympathy.

"She still doesn't remember us." I was already being pulled into a warm hug before I could open my eyes. She held me for some time, until I heard someone emerge into the living room, coming toward the kitchen.

I composed myself as Cat took the lead. "It smells amazing in here, Elena. What did you make?"

Her response faded out, and I joined the children in Jamie's room. I tried to inject some life into my body to play, but my mind was elsewhere, plagued with the guilt of lying to Elena. Surrounding her with family and yet keeping her so unbearably in the dark, at arm's length. It had been weeks without so much as a morsel of memory resurfacing. The memories she managed to regain were fragmented, and I appeared to be absent from them.

The appearance of Cat at Jamie's door pulled me out of those thoughts, and I followed her into the hallway and out of sight of the children.

"I just wanted to make sure you're okay before we go." She brushed my arm soothingly.

"I'll be fine Cat, thank you." I nodded before catching her off guard. "But I think it's time." Cat frowned but she quickly followed my train of thought. "It's time to tell her the truth."

"I don't think that's a good idea," she said without considering the options. "She's still recovering. It'll be better to wait a couple of weeks, see if her memories come back on their own."

"Hold on a second. You're not the one lying to her every day. I'm walking on eggshells in my own home and having to be a single parent to Jamie." I hushed to avoid anyone overhearing. "This isn't your decision to make." The flick of her brow, like a cat ready to attack, was a warning. "Look, I want us to be on the same page. You're her sister. Once she knows everything, it'll be you she comes to. I'm no one to her."

"Jax, you're not no one." She sighed, but it was a weak argument. "I hear what you're saying, I do. But I don't want you to tell her yet. I just want to protect her until she's strong enough. She almost fainted tonight. Can we just give her a week or so?" I sighed in defeat, knowing that I couldn't tell Elena without Cat on board. "I want us to do this together too. Tell her when the time is right, but I also think that Elena talking to Tom might be the reason behind speeding up this decision."

"Well, yeah. Can you blame me?"

"No, of course not. I'm not happy about it either, but Tom can't be the reason we tell her, especially if she isn't ready."

I rubbed the back of my neck in thought. Begrudgingly, she'd won me over.

"I'm not saying never. Just give it some more time, Jax."

Cat pulled me into a hug as I caught a glimpse of Elena eying us from the parting in the kitchen wall. She studied us cautiously, hesitantly, no doubt without realising I was watching her too. The thought occurred to me that perhaps she was listening, or maybe it was just my seemingly close relationship with Cat that caused her concern.

Once Cat and the girls were gone, I made myself busy cleaning and spending time with Jamie. Talking to Elena felt forced during and after dinner. I wanted to reconnect with her, but the constant texting, granted it might not always be with Tom, created friction between us. The wedge only continued to push us further apart over the course of the next couple of weeks, and it made coming clean all the more difficult.

CHAPTER SEVEN

"I'll have the goat cheese salad, please, but no capers." I smiled my thanks to the server as Kim perused the menu a little more.

She hadn't changed one bit, not in eight years, her indecisiveness only growing worse. She'd asked me several times what I was going to order, even though we both knew she was going to make a hasty snap decision. She thrived on pressure. For that reason, it shouldn't have surprised me that she was now in charge of managing multimillion budgets as Head of Finance.

"Sorry," she mumbled to the server, who politely smiled but let out a heavy sigh. After an excruciatingly long moment, she was ready. "Okay, I'll have the lasagne, but instead of the shitty salad, can I get gravy chips and a side of cheesy garlic bread?" She handed the menu to the server as they jotted down the order quickly, and although there was no obvious judgement, she felt the need to say, "Baby cravings."

"Can I also get a glass of merlot?" I added as Kim threw me a look.

"One of those lunches, is it?" She chuckled before resting her elbows on the table and leaning onto her palms in anticipation. "Tell me all."

"There's nothing to tell. It just feels like an abnormally long week."

"Honey, I told you it was too soon to go back to five days a week."

"There's work to do, Kim. There's a lot to catch up on. I was basically non-existent for a month there, and then the board meeting is next week."

The monthly board meeting was fast approaching, and even though the senior team insisted that I didn't need to present our findings this month, I was eager to prove myself. I already felt out of my depth in my personal life. I wanted to feel like I wasn't a huge failure in work too.

"Hey, this is not the kind of stress you should be putting yourself under." Kim rested a hand on mine. "And this is coming from a pregnant woman, okay? After all, you were in the hospital last month. Cut yourself a break."

I shrugged and thanked the server when the glass of wine was placed in my hand. I took a big gulp as Kim thought for a moment before probing again. "Is something else bothering you?" she asked. "Something at home?"

"No. Everything is fine. Just fine." I dismissed the conversation and tried to redirect. "How about you? You've your six-month scan tomorrow, right? Do you both want to know the sex?"

"Did you not see my lunch order? It's clearly going to be a boy. They always make me pig out on everything in sight. But I think we will leave it a secret. It's always more of a surprise that way. Besides, my money is on a boy, Nicola is sure it's a girl, and if I win, she's taking me on a spa weekend to Barcelona."

"And what does Nicola get if she wins?"

"I'm having her baby. That is her prize." I giggled as she patted her belly.

"I'm still adjusting to all of that." I waved at her pregnant belly. "I never would have pegged you as the 'mummy' type."

"Neither did I." She chuckled before she looked off into space thoughtfully, and a content smile came over her face. "You remember me back then? I was a party girl, last one to leave the club and always searching for the after-party. But, and I know it's a cliché, and I hate myself for being *that* girl, when I met Nicola, everything just slid into place. She made me want things that I never even thought I'd get to have. As I fell in love with her, I wanted a family, and I knew she was the only one I wanted to share that with."

Her voice faded as I found myself getting lost in my own thoughts. Her words shifted something in the pit of my belly, and all I could think about was Jamie and more alarmingly, Jax. I could somewhat rationalise why Jamie appeared in my head. When I thought of having a family in my future, I hoped for a child as lovable and sweet as him. But with Jax, I felt something else. It was like a comfort and warmth which I couldn't explain. Even while raising a small child, she was concerned with me and my health every day. Jamie even watched me as if it was his job to make sure I was taking care of myself. The thought made me smile.

"What?" Kim's voice pulled me back to her.

"I've just never heard you talk like that before. I'm really happy for you."

"And I'm really happy…that our food is here." The server appeared and handed the plates toward us. Miraculously, Kim was already eating before it touched the table. "And don't think I didn't notice you dodging my question earlier."

"There was no dodging."

"You practically jumped to the next table."

"I may have sidestepped slightly."

"Well, slide back and take a seat, honey," Kim retorted as she shovelled garlic bread into her mouth. "Spill. What's going on at home?"

"Nothing is going on, it's just…" I rolled my eyes as I tried to push the thoughts of paranoia out of my mind, but with Kim's eyes bulging in anticipation, I decided to divulge. "It's Jax. She's been a little distant lately."

"Oh. But last week, you raved about her. How great she's been at checking in with you and—"

"That was last week." Kim frowned, prompting me to explain. "There was a moment, an awkward encounter a few days ago, and ever since, Jax has been really weird with me. We aren't watching TV in the evenings, she barely talks to me at dinner, and sometimes it feels like she's actively avoiding me." I pushed the salad on my plate as I felt my appetite disappear.

"Well, what happened a couple of days ago?" she prodded as I felt the temperature in the room rise.

"It was stupid." I shook my head as I took another gulp of wine for encouragement.

"So stupid that you're blushing."

"It's warm in here," I argued, rolling up my sleeves. "They should open a window."

"It's practically winter," Kim said, waving her scarf. "And you're avoiding again."

"Fine. It's not even a big deal. I was cooking last week, and I felt a little light-headed, and I guess I lost my footing because next thing I know, I'm sitting on the kitchen counter with Jax in between my…and her hands were all over my…my…legs. And then my sister walks in." I stuttered shamefully as Kim raised her brows with a smirk to follow. "It's not a big deal. It's just a little awkward now, even though it was all perfectly innocent, and nothing was going on at all." My tone was so transparent that even I was sceptical.

Kim processed the dribble of words, leaving me to force down half my glass of wine in the deafening silence she'd exiled me to. "Back it up, why was Jax between your thighs in the first place?"

"She was checking my eyes."

"More like checking you out."

"Kim!" I batted her arm. "It wasn't like that. In the beginning, she really was just checking to make sure I was okay but then…I don't know." I thought for a moment as Kim held on to my every word. "Maybe it was something more. But it was stupid, and now she's been really awkward with me ever since."

"How'd you feel about it?"

"Well, her awkwardness is making me feel awkward."

"Not that, Elena. How'd you feel about the moment?" Kim asked as I frowned at her. "Did you want to kiss her?"

"What?" I laughed loudly. "Kim, come on, you know me. The amount of times you've thrown yourself at me and nothing." She nodded. "The bottom line is, I'm not gay."

"You don't have to be gay to want to kiss another woman, Elena."

"Okay, well bisexual or whatever." The word "bisexual" caused my heart to skip a beat. Like a jolt that made my breathing uneasy and my emotions unsettled.

"Or sexually fluid?" she asked as I returned a blank expression. "Sexual fluidity is a real thing and more common than people think. Research shows that while some are straight or gay or whatever they want to identify as, a lot of people fall in this grey zone of fluidity. I believe sexuality is more complicated than just gay or straight. People can't be defined in categories like they have been for centuries. In fact, people just are who they are."

"I'm not sure I follow."

"Just because you've always drunk orange juice doesn't mean you can't wake up one day and want apple juice." Kim winked while munching on a chip, but the comedy was lost on me.

"This analogy is really bad, Kim." The bite in my response seemed to cause her light demeanour to change.

"Fine, then, I'll be blunt. Just because you've always screwed men doesn't mean you can't be attracted to a woman. People fall in love with the person, not the gender."

"I'm not in love with Jax." My words came out more defensively than I'd intended. I tried to brush it off but the wave of fear crashed around me at the mere suggestion that I could be in love with Jax. *I'm not gay*, I repeated in my mind, something I used to have to do continuously at St Catherine's Boarding House. *I'm not gay. I'm attracted to men* repeated again and again as my high school experience surged into my frontal lobe, and I struggled to focus on Kim.

"I didn't say you were," she said carefully. "What if, maybe in that moment, you felt something toward her, and maybe, just maybe, you liked that feeling, even if it did scare you a little. And maybe she's awkward because she felt it too." I stared down at my half-eaten salad, letting her words sink in. "Or maybe I'm just full of shit," she added playfully.

I shook my head and drowned out those thoughts. Thoughts that frankly were preposterous, considering I wasn't inclined that way. I changed the topic soon after and refrained from thinking too much about the subject again.

❖

Jax

"Ma," I called as I used my key to get into her house. The huge red door struggled to open fully, a stack of mail and subscription magazines blocking its path as Jamie and I slid in before it shut with a bang behind us.

"In here, love."

"Go say hi to your nan," I said as we navigated our way through my mother's unorganised heap of a hallway.

I gathered the stack of mail from the worn hardwood floor and set it on the workbench where old photo frames sat cloaked in a light layer of dust. At least twenty coats, all shapes and sizes, hung on the near-collapsing coatrack as newspapers and magazines lay in a heap under the staircase. The woman who'd raised me had always had a place for everything. After a hectic week, like any other home, a bit of dishevelled chaos would build up but never more than a few days before she would reorganise everything again.

However, my childhood home had looked chaotic like this for the last eighteen months. I lifted a pile of the letters, swiping through some of the mail as I heard Mum and Jamie giggling from the living room. As I made my way down the hallway, I stopped at the same spot I had been for the last year and a half.

"Hey, Dad," I whispered, looking fondly at the small portrait on the wall. I remembered the exact day it was taken and what had led to such a rare picture of my dad looking truly elated.

"Siobhan, you've been with me through thick and thin, and we've been married thirty-eight years, so you know by now, I hate *getting my picture taken." He growled as I moved the camera away from my face, and he threw his newspaper at the wall, fed up.*

"Catch yourself on, Bert," my mother shouted from the kitchen. "We had a deal, you remember. If the cancer came back, I get a decent photo of ya, and look where we are now? So sit down."

She appeared with a plate of biscuits and a tray full of cups of tea, not that I wasn't still drinking the last cup. That was how Irish mothers worked: when dealing with a tough situation, there was nothing a good cuppa tea wouldn't solve.

"Maybe a picture of you and Siobhan could be better," Elena suggested with her hands on her hips as she moved behind the tripod to get a look at the last few snaps. "And maybe we should work on your smile, Bert."

"You look miserable, Dad," I added while swiping through a couple of the last shots.

"Oh, for Christ's sake, Albert." Mum tutted after peeking at the pictures. "You look like a dry shite."

"This is shite. I'm not doing it," he shouted while climbing out of his chair.

"What are we supposed to do at the funeral, just not have a picture of you? People won't know whose funeral it is. Albert Jax is common as muck. I know at least two." The sarcasm in Mum's voice was lost on my fed-up father.

"Jesus, Siobhan, people will know it's my funeral. Sure, it'll have half of your family Irish dancing on my English coffin."

"I'll be the ringleader, leading them like Michael bloody Flatley at this rate. Now, sit down and take a picture." He grumpily stared at my mother as she challenged him with hands on hips.

Elena and I held our breath, not knowing which way this was going to go. My mother and father were always very, to put it diplomatically, passionate people. They shouted and argued all day, but they loved each other with a fierceness I'd never witnessed in two other people. My dad always said as long as you don't go to bed angry with each other, a marriage will last a lifetime.

I used to think my mum and dad were extremely unhappy with the way they argued, and then there would be mornings I would catch them sitting at the breakfast table holding hands for hours on end while reading the morning newspaper or when my mother cuddled against him as they watched TV. After almost forty years of marriage, that was the kind of love I aspired to have.

"I'll sit down if we can have fish and chips for tea," Dad bargained. "And I get to watch the grand prix tomorrow." The room was tense and silent. These bargains usually went one of two ways: either they would settle an argument or erupt a new one.

"Aye, all right," Mum said as she handed him his tea and pecked him on the cheek. Dad took a sip and grinned happily before plopping down on the armchair again.

"Great cuppa tea. I knew there was a reason I ran off with you." He winked at me and Elena behind the camera. "Not a bad arse either."

"Bert," my mum screeched in a scold as my dad roared with laughter.

And one snap later, we had the picture.

I smiled to myself as I looked at that picture. My dad's thinning hair and rosy cheeks would be how I'd always remember him as he laughed with a glint in his eye. He'd never looked happier than when he was winding up my mother.

"You all right, love?" Mum asked, leaning against the door frame as she watched me staring at the picture of Dad. "He was an old bastard, wasn't he?" she asked as she joined me, looking up at him. "But he wasn't a bad lad."

"I miss him too, Mum," I whispered, wrapping my arm around her shoulder.

"If he was still here, he'd tell us to give over and put on the kettle." Mum tapped me on the bottom before steering us toward the kitchen. "Do you want a sandwich with your tea?" Jamie was in the living room watching TV as I slumped at the kitchen table.

"I'm good with just the tea. We'd lunch earlier."

"It's only a wee cheese sandwich, love. I'm making one for the little prince too. I may as well," she said, pulling out biscuits and snacks from the cupboards and putting them onto a plate.

"No biscuits for Jamie, Ma."

"But he's hungry."

"He just ate."

"Aw, a biscuit won't hurt." She brushed me off as she walked into the living room with a plate of treats. I rolled my eyes and got up from the table, finishing making tea for her.

"How are you, Mum?" I asked, taking a seat at the table again as I watched her potter about the kitchen.

"Grand, love. Just back from Belfast. Your aunt Eileen was asking for you. And your granny wants to see you all over before Christmas this year." Mum slid a handful of envelopes across the table before whispering. "And a few cards from your aunts and uncles for Jamie's birthday in a couple of weeks."

"Thanks, Mum, but I think our annual family trip to Ireland will get a miss this year," I muttered, taking a gulp of the hot tea and then regretting it when it burnt my tongue.

"But I thought Elena was getting better." Mum passed a sandwich to me. It didn't matter what I told her. Somehow, something to eat would appear with a cup of tea.

"Physically, she's fine. Greg said she's doing great, which reminds me." I stopped midsentence and pulled a foil-wrapped loaf from my satchel before handing it to my mother. "Greg baked it this morning before his shift at the hospital. Your favourite."

"Banana and chocolate chip bread." My mum peeled back the aluminium foil and breathed in the freshly baked goods. "You see, if you had just married him back when he was still a woman, then I'd have fresh banana bread all the time."

"And divorce would have followed once Grace became Greg, Ma! Besides, he's just trying to butter you up because now that you're single, he might actually have a chance."

Mum blushed before taking a sip of the brew keeping her hands warm. "Greg's a handsome man, but I don't think he could handle me."

"Ma!" I rolled my eyes, taking a bite of the sandwich.

"Back to Elena, has she had any more memories come back to her?" She took a nibble at my sandwich before giving a quick look over her shoulder to make sure Jamie wasn't nearby. "How's he taking it all?"

"Jamie's been great. I mean, he's slipped up once or twice, but Elena is completely oblivious." I rubbed the back of my neck. "And yes, memories are coming back to her. She will remember where a bar is, or she will put on a new movie and remember she's watched it before. So things are coming back to her, but I just thought that by now…" I trailed off with a heavy sigh.

"She would have remembered you," Mum finished as she

took my hand. "It's still early days, love." I nodded but didn't believe her. "Don't lose faith. That girl loves you and Jamie like crazy. Just because she's lost sight of that doesn't mean those feelings aren't still there."

"I don't know."

"Why would you?" Her question threw me. "Well, it's like this. Do you remember your first crush?"

"Ah yes, Rosie Enderby."

"And do you remember how you reacted when you realised you liked her?" I frowned, unable to recall over twenty-five years ago. "Well, I do. You were six at the time, and for months, you two were inseparable, playdates and doing your homework together every day after school and sleepovers, you name it. It was coming up to Valentine's Day, and you wanted to get her a card, which I thought there was nothing wrong with. I always knew you were gay." I stifled a grin as my mum continued telling a story I had no recollection of. "A day or two after Valentine's, I found that card in the bin in your room, and I remember asking why didn't you give it to her, and you said, because she wanted to get a card from some boy in your class."

"Jonny Sutherland," I muttered with disdain.

"That's right, little Jonny, who if memory serves me, is now the lovely Tiffany Latoya, starlet of London's drag scene."

"How on earth do you know that?"

"I know everything," Mum finished with a wink. "But when I asked you why you couldn't give a card to Rosie as well, you said, because she doesn't like me." I tried to remember this conversation, but it was lost on me. "And then, just like that, you stopped seeing Rosie. You got awkward around her, stopped having sleepovers and speaking to her."

"Is there a point to this tragic walk down memory lane?"

She smacked my arm. "My point is, when you have feelings that aren't reciprocated, you close up. You have always been that way. Even when you brought home your 'friend,' Elena Ricci.

You passed her off as just a friend, but I knew you were madly in love with her, and as soon as you realised it too, what did you do?" She waited, but I didn't want to admit there was some truth in her theory. "You stopped talking to her." She raised her brows as I avoided her knowing look. "Just like you did to Rosie when you were six. Thankfully, the silent treatment didn't work with Elena, and you got together, but the bottom line is, you do this every time. When you can't handle your feelings, you run away. When you think you might be losing her, you decide to run first." She rubbed my hand as she dipped her head to meet my eyes, which had fallen to a tea stain on the tablecloth.

"But what if I can't…" I trailed off, my voice small like a six-year-old's who just got their heart broken for the first time. "What if she wants someone else?"

"You're afraid of an ex?" Mum exclaimed. "The same ex that Elena left for you?"

"She didn't leave him for—"

"That arsehole doesn't stand a chance next to you." She continued dismissing me. "She fell in love with you once before, didn't she?" I looked up as I percolated what'd she said for a moment. "He was around then too, but that means nothing when it comes to love, the real kind of love that you two have." Her next words hit home again. "But she'll never have a chance to fall for you again if you keep closing yourself up."

As always, she was right. I had been colder to Elena recently, fearful that she was drifting further from me and closer to Tom.

"Thanks, Mum."

"What are mammies for?" She smiled, rising from her chair and walking toward the living room when I followed her. "As for grannies, we usually forget what we left on the telly for our grandchildren."

"Is that *Game of Thrones*?" I screeched when I arrived in the living room, about to witness the infamous and gruesome red wedding murder scene.

"I'm sure it's nothing he hasn't seen before." She shrugged, petting his head as he stared almost traumatised at the television screen.

"Ma!"

CHAPTER EIGHT

My phone buzzed on the kitchen countertop as I pulled the cookies from the oven. With one hand still clinging to the baking tray and the other covered in flour, I managed to somehow catapult the phone to my shoulder to answer. "Hello?"

"Buzz us up, it's freezing out here," Cat yelled as my nieces chattered in the background.

"Coming." I raced from the kitchen after throwing the burning hot tray somewhere on the countertop. "Jamie, are you dressed? Kate and Abbey are almost here," I called before pressing the unlock button on the intercom to grant entrance downstairs.

"Yeah." He ran out of his room. I barely caught a glimpse of him before he tripped on his jeans, which he hadn't pulled up fully. The loud thud caused me to jump out of my skin, and his crying followed soon after.

"Jamie, what happened?" I panicked, running to him as he lay facedown on the carpet. He cried loudly, and I wished Jax hadn't left for work just moments ago. "You're okay, Jamie. It was just a bad fall. Let me see your head."

I lifted him onto my lap as he gripped his forehead. Wails bounced from the walls, making me think the worst as I tried to soothe him. I had to try a few times to pry his hand away until eventually he pulled it back, revealing a raw carpet burn across his cheekbone and forehead.

"Shit," I let slip, which happened to be the worst thing I could have said. His eyes grew wide in panic as he surely began to think the worst and followed it up with louder crying.

"It stings," he wailed, filling the apartment.

"I know. It's okay. It's just a little scrape."

I shouted a string of profanities in my head as I tried to think of anything to calm him down. I lifted him onto my hip and brought him into the kitchen to clean up his head. At that moment, Cat waltzed into the apartment.

"Anybody home?" she called as the girls ran straight for Jamie's room.

"In here. Quick," I pleaded, but she was already headed in my direction. I dabbed at his forehead, which only caused him to scream louder.

"It's bad," I said in Italian so Jamie wouldn't understand. "I've maimed him. Shit, Jax is going to kill me." I looked for a first aid kit. "What kind of doctor doesn't have Band-Aids in the house? I'll cover it up. Is there a cream I can put on it? Shit."

"Oh, that is bad. Yep, that's going to scar. He will have that for the rest of his life," she replied in Italian.

"Oh my God. Really?" I shrieked as Jamie stopped crying, startled by the volume.

"No!" Cat hit me on the back of the head. "It's a graze. He has a new one every week." She rolled her eyes and turned back to Jamie. "Do you think some cookies and ice cream might help with the stingy cut?"

He nodded slowly as the tears subsided almost instantly. Cat kissed him on the forehead next to his cut and helped him off the countertop as I uselessly stood in the corner still clutching an unopened first aid kit.

"Okay, Jamie, go pick a movie, and Elena and I will get the ice cream and cookies. And for being such a brave big boy, you get an extra scoop." He flashed a toothy grin before he darted out of the kitchen.

"I need a drink." I slumped against the counter as I ran my hand through my hair. Cat laughed as she started to clean up the shambles of a kitchen. "Jax left literally twenty minutes ago, and I destroy her house, almost kill her child and—"

"Relax, Elena."

"Are you kidding? He was screaming the house down. I didn't think it was ever going to stop, and there's flour everywhere, and I burnt the cookies. Who burns cookies? It's a disaster. I don't know how people do this whole *kid* thing."

"With help." She winked as she handed me a glass of wine. I gave her a double take. "Hey, it's five o'clock somewhere. Besides, wine is half the fun of playdates, and Jax always has the best wine. Why do you think I invited myself here?" She took a swig of her own wine. "Well, that and my thoughtless husband has been on a conference call since nine a.m."

"Who works at nine a.m. on a Saturday? Well, apparently Dad does too. Mama called this morning."

"Ew. What did the dragon want? A pound of flesh?" Cat spat as she scrubbed the dishes in the sink.

"Just checking in. As she does. Twice a week."

"Guilt will do that to you." I didn't miss the dark underlying tone in her voice.

"What has she got to be guilty about?"

"I wouldn't even know where to begin." She tutted, and I frowned. "Hold on, you and Mama talk twice a week?"

"Yeah." The bewilderment on her face made me question the frequency. "Is that a lot?"

"Considering you were barely talking before, yeah, it is." I went to ask why we weren't speaking, but she beat me to it. "What exactly do you two talk about?"

"I don't know. Stuff, the weather, work and…" I trailed off, but it only seemed to ignite a fierce curiosity in her.

Cat didn't know I was speaking to Tom again, and frankly, it was for the best. Mama had been trying to help, giving me some good advice, like perhaps I should explore my feelings for him again. To communicate these ideas to my sister would have been a mistake. Cat had never liked Tom. She'd called him a piece of shit the first time they'd met, and he'd referred to her as a stuck-up bitch. It had been a train wreck and had caused a rift between me and my sister the entire time we'd dated. Until I could figure out my feelings for Tom, it was best she knew nothing.

"And about her new face-lift," I finished.

"Ha, I wonder if next time they can inject her with some humanity. She's seriously lacking in that department."

I tried to change the topic. "Who was Nick on the phone with?" Cat's harsh words about our mother surprised me. I remembered them being closer, even closer than me and Mama, but something must have happened in the last eight years that caused this serious breakdown in their relationship.

"Japan," she said, taking a bigger gulp of wine as she leaned against the counter to watch me finish cleaning. "This is his first weekend home in three weeks, and I had to take the girls out of the house because he has work."

"That's not good. Have you tried talking to him?"

"What a great idea, Elena." Cat sarcastically clicked her fingers. "Why didn't I think of that like three months ago?" I gave a sympathetic smile as she dropped her head into her hands. "I'm sorry, I don't mean to take it out on you. I know you're only trying to help. And you are helping. Thank you again for taking the girls tonight. Nick and I just need some time to…"

"Screw?"

"As if. We'd have to stop arguing long enough for that to happen. Although angry sex has been strangely satisfying." She nodded as if deep in thought before her demeanour changed. "But I miss just normal sex and not arguing via text and whatever else married couples do. It's been so long, I forget."

"Well, hopefully, tonight will be your lucky night."

I tried to cheer her up, but I had my doubts. I always looked up to Cat and her relationship with Nick. It was the kind of loving and supportive relationship I wanted with Tom, but he kept falling short. The fact that this conversation was not the first time Cat had divulged their marital problems concerned me greatly, and it was clearly having an emotional toll on her.

"Maybe." She nodded, but I knew she wasn't convinced. "And how are things with you?"

"Good. Work has been kind of hectic but in a good way, and things are slowly but surely coming back to me. I now need minimal supervision to find my own files on my desktop."

"Groundbreaking." She winked as we clinked our glasses in cheers. "But I was more interested in knowing how things are with Jax?" Her staring intensified as I gulped. I'd dodged one delicate topic already; it was unlikely she would let me off the hook this time. "Quite the interesting position I walked in on last week. We never talked about it."

I knew she wasn't going to let that go without an in-depth analysis, and yet I was painfully unprepared, despite my conversation with Kim yesterday. The moment between me and Jax repeated on my mind for reasons I wasn't entirely sure of, and therefore was most certainly not ready to talk to anyone else about.

"Yeah. It was pretty weird. No more skipping lunch for me, light-headedness is a bitch." I took another drink as I tried to excuse myself from the conversation. "I should go check on the kids."

"They're fine, Elena." She leaned on the doorway, preventing me from leaving. I couldn't make eye contact, and my hands were twitching, no doubt making me look guilty as sin. "You're not uncomfortable talking about Jax, are you?" She raised her glass but didn't take a sip, studying me over the rim.

"No, of course not. We're friends." I shook my head rapidly, feeling the blood rush to my cheeks.

"Because the other day, it looked like Jax was in between

your legs." I could feel a blush heating my face. "You two were super close. Almost as if you were about to kiss."

I tried to keep my cool, but it was impossible. I detested that Jax was causing this strange reaction in me every time I thought of her. Cat's line of questioning shouldn't have been causing me to blush. That would only be happening if I *liked* Jax, which of course, I didn't. We were friends, good friends. I could think about my friends sometimes, like on my way to work or sometimes late at night, in the shower. Jax was like some kind of plague that caused a fever across my skin, and I wished more than anything that it wasn't happening, not again. I feared I was falling into the "promiscuous tendencies" that I worked very hard to fix, correct, and rehabilitate years ago.

Cat's hand on my arm stopped my brain from racing, and her warm eyes connected with mine, calming me. "It's okay." A bang came from the living room, causing us both to jump. "What's going on out there?" she called in her best mum voice, but she held my gaze.

"Nothing," the three children chimed angelically.

"Nothing, my ass," Cat muttered as she started walking into the living room to investigate. "You get the ice cream. I will tame the children." She moved toward the doorway but stopped and looked over her shoulder. "You know you can tell me anything, right? Any time, any place. You know that, Elena."

"I know." I smiled in the hope of reassuring her. "Now go, there could be a fire in my living room."

The breath I was holding slowly released as she disappeared. I pushed my thoughts of Jax deep down where they most definitely belonged and began searching through the cupboards for ice cream bowls.

In the process, I stumbled onto a strange makeshift filing cabinet. A dozen letters, bills, and other paperwork fell onto the counter. I shuffled it all together and shoved it back in the cupboard, afraid of prying into Jax's privacy, but I spotted something on the floor. An old plane ticket stub. The instant I touched it, I found myself being transported back into a memory.

A long, heavy sigh escaped me as I stared at the airline board in the departure lounge of JKF airport. A long list across two screens of international cities all blinked red with cancelled flights. I wasn't the only one who was frustrated. Other angry passengers were shouting at various airline employees. I stared at my phone, ignored the countless texts and missed calls from my mother, and dialled the only person who might answer at this hour of the morning. I was disappointed when all I got was her voice mail.

"Hey Cat, it's me. Again." I sighed down the phone as I checked the clock. "I was hoping the morning sickness would have you up at three a.m. to keep me company, but it's cool. I always knew you were selfish. So my delayed flight is now cancelled indefinitely, along with every other flight leaving New York. It's probably France with another strike." I stifled another yawn. "Anyway, I don't need you to collect me from Heathrow, so I will call you tomorrow when I get a flight out of here. Kiss Nick and baby bump good night from me. Okay, bye." With a heavy sigh, I hung up.

"For once, I don't think it was France." The voice startled me, and I looked up to see a woman standing nearby, staring up at the departure board.

"Excuse me?" I asked, looking at my deserted row of seats to see if she might have been speaking to someone else.

"The cancelled flights," she replied without looking round. Her British accent gave away that she was also likely stranded. "I think the French are innocent, for once. My money is on Iceland. They're just too nice." She turned to me and must have caught my puzzled look. "I'm kidding, of course. People from Iceland aren't even that nice." My bewilderment and silence caused her to elaborate. "The volcano erupting in Iceland probably had something to do with it. There's an ash cloud over the Atlantic that everybody is freaking out about."

I was trying to process her words but was too tired to get far. "What?"

"It's kinda on every single TV channel...in the world. And the internet too, but I imagine on a BlackBerry, you probably need dial-up to surf the net."

"Hey, BlackBerrys are cool, okay?" I got to my feet so she was no longer looking down on me. "And 'surf the net'? What are you, fifty?"

"Sixty actually," she replied, sarcasm dripping from every word. "But at least I have the wits to tune into the news, considering I'm in a departure lounge full of cancelled flights." She smiled smugly.

"Whatever." I dismissed her as I beelined to the desk for a flight update.

Two hours later, I was back in a New York hotel. The volcano story checked out, meaning that all flights to Europe were grounded until the air quality improved. But how long could an ash cloud really last? I looked around the lobby. At 12:30 a.m., I knew I needed something strong to get me to sleep, even though I was exhausted. I headed for the hotel bar.

"Vodka martini, please."

The bartender walked off to prepare the drink, but as he did, he revealed the only other person there. I let out a heavy, irate sigh when I recognised the girl from the airport, and that was when she looked up at me.

"Well, hey, look who it is. The last person who still uses a BlackBerry." The smug smile was back.

"What are the freakin' chances?" I said, wishing I'd left the hotel to find another bar.

"Probably as slim as an ash cloud cancelling three thousand flights over the next four days."

"Four days? You've got to be kidding me." I moaned into my hands as my martini arrived.

"She's probably going to need another one of those. Put it on my tab, Terry." She got up from her seat and took the stool beside me.

"I prefer to wallow and heavy drink alone, thanks," I said after knocking back the martini. I turned to look at her as she sipped what looked like a whiskey on the rocks. She looked no older than me, with short dark hair and eyes that playfully watched me over the rim of her glass. Her blue eyes managed to sparkle in the dimly lit bar, causing me to soften. She must have checked in and come straight to the bar, still wearing the professional suit she was wearing at the airport.

"Wasn't your flight also cancelled?" I asked. "How are you so okay with all of this?"

"This is my fourth." She swirled the contents of her glass. "So I'm a little drunk right now. I don't want to think about the fact that I'm missing my dad's surprise sixtieth birthday party tomorrow." She shrugged as I took a slow drink of my second martini.

The air turned quiet, and the guilt sank in. "I'm sorry about your dad. And about earlier. I was kind of a bitch."

"Yeah, but for good reason. I was being a smart-ass." She smiled before adding, "I've just spent the last three days trapped in a boiling hot conference room with a bunch of pretentious doctors."

"Oh, that's rough. I think you're entitled to be annoying as hell, then."

"Did I mention there were no windows?"

"Okay, now you're entitled to be annoying and a drunk for the next four days. Or for however long we're stuck here." I sighed, running my hand through my hair before coming across a foreign object. I yanked the oversized diamond brooch from my hair before rolling my eyes and tossing it to the side of the bar.

"Rough day?" she asked, watching my small tantrum. "Aside from the whole ash cloud thing?"

"My parents' thirtieth wedding anniversary was in the

Fairmont Hotel today," I said as I recalled the last conversation I had with my mother.

"Sounds posh. And by the look on your face, you had a ton of fun."

"It was a disaster. My boyfriend was supposed to come too, but we kind of broke up for the second time. She was berating me, as usual. Saying how I should settle down and get married. Guys like Tom don't grow on trees." A drawn-out sigh left me as I downed the remainder of my glass and winced as the liquid burnt all the way down my throat. "So I left her stupid party filled with fake morons, called a taxi, and went straight to the airport."

"Badass." She smiled as she too finished the contents of her glass before ordering another round. "Sounds like we both couldn't wait to escape. Strange, most people love New York. Shame I didn't see more."

"It was my first time here too, and what a waste it was." We shared a small smile. "Where are you…" I corrected myself with an eye roll. "Where were you supposed to be flying home to?"

"London. Gatwick, to be exact. You?"

"Heathrow." She returned my warm smile. "Do you live in London?"

"Yep, near Fulham."

"I live outside Chelsea. We're practically neighbours," I joked, evoking that same warm smile, the one that made her eyes dance. "Listen, do you think we can start over? Seeing as we will probably both be stuck in this hotel, and therefore drinking a lot at this very bar?"

"I'd really like that."

"I'm Elena." I reached out my hand, and she took it, revealing a warm and soft touch that caused an electric spark up my arm.

"Jax."

"You okay, Elena?" Cat peeked around the kitchen door.

"New York," I whispered as I read the JFK to Gatwick ticket stub with the name Keelin Jax on it.

"What?" she asked, stepping up beside me with concern in her eyes.

"I remember. I mean, not everything, but…" I trailed off as I held up the stub. "I met Jax in New York when my flight was cancelled." I smiled with relief that I could remember something. Even if it wasn't completely clear, it was still something. "We were both staying at the Bourbon Hotel. I remember. It was in Midtown, and we were there for almost two weeks. And we went to Central Park and Ellis Island, and oh my God, I remember." Cat hugged me tightly as my eyes filled with tears.

It felt like a dream, but I recalled our interactions over the course of the two weeks. Filled with laughter and excitement. However, there was also something else. A flirtation which could only be categorised as something more than platonic, and Jax couldn't be held entirely accountable. During our time in New York, I basked in the attention, and then the wave of fear of disappointing my parents crashed around me. Looking back now, it caused me to rethink my interactions with Jax as of lately. Was history repeating itself?

❖

Jax

"Sorry, I couldn't possibly cover for you on the Lord's day," Greg said as he typed his surgical notes into the medical tablet, and we walked toward the nurses' station.

"You're not even religious. Come on. Please? I need this weekend with my family." He remained unfazed, prompting me to resort to guilt. "We've been through so much."

"I would if I could, bro. But I've got stuff to do."

"What stuff? You don't have stuff." I leaned over the nurses' station, and Lynsey, the nurse on duty, passed my patient's chart.

"I do a lot of stuff, if you catch my drift."

I got the feeling his words were more for Lynsey's benefit

than mine. The air had changed when we'd approached her station, and more importantly, so had Greg. She was beautiful. I couldn't say I didn't notice. She was hardworking and smart and for some reason, laughed at Greg's bad jokes, so maybe she didn't have the best sense of humour, but he practically fawned over her. Greg's hair was always combed back perfectly when he knew she would be working, and he'd brought an extra coffee to work this morning, which was now miraculously on Lynsey's desk.

"I really don't get paid enough to care about whatever squabble you two are in right now." Lynsey turned her attention back to the computer as she seductively sipped her coffee, but she was very clearly eavesdropping.

"Jax, I can't do it, okay? You're just going to have to find someone else to cover you. I told you, I have plans." He emphasised the word "plans," which made me think this was all a front to entice Lynsey. "Maybe I have a hot date and want to have a lazy morning in bed with her," he said before he side-glanced Lynsey.

Okay, there was definitely something going on between these two. Usually, I would have cared for the details, but my mind was too focused on Elena and my own relationship.

"Yeah, sure, a hot date. Totally realistic," I said as I started filling in Mrs Andrews's appendectomy chart. "Seriously, though, I really need you to take my shift this weekend."

"You don't know. I could be dating someone. More than one person. I don't have to tell you everything, you know."

"You're not dating anyone because in order to be dating, you actually have to ask a girl out, and we both know that's impossible." I smiled smugly as I went back to my notes.

"Well, maybe I'd ask more girls out if my wing woman was there," he muttered under his breath. I threw him a challenging look over the top of my clipboard. "But I get it. You got your own shit going on."

"By own shit you mean, helping my roommate remember she's actually my wife and the mother of my child? Like that kind of shit?"

"Exactly." He nodded as I rolled my eyes, and Lynsey shook her head disapprovingly.

"Please cover for me," I begged again as he looked away. I was putting him in an awkward position, and I had already asked for cover last week, but I was desperate. "Please, Greg, I feel like I'm finally getting somewhere with Elena." He scratched his beard. "Please."

"Okay, fine." He sighed. "But I could have had a date."

"I know," I replied but contradicted myself by shaking my head at Lynsey, evoking a giggle she tried to hide.

"I could have!" We both handed our charts back to Lynsey and proceeded toward the emergency room.

"What was that about back there?" I asked once we were out of earshot.

"What was what?"

"Come on, Greg. You can hide from a lot of people but not me. Is there something going on with Lynsey?"

"*Pfft*, I don't kiss and tell."

"Since when?" I asked as we waited for the elevator. "Come on, spill."

"There's nothing to tell." His face changed from joking to serious as his eyes flitted toward mine. "Seriously, she's not into me like that."

"She looked pretty into you from where I was standing." I nudged him as we made it onto the empty elevator, and I pressed the ground floor button. "Why don't you ask her out?"

"Because she doesn't date trans guys." He sighed as he stared at his notes. "I overheard her talking to one of the nurses this morning."

A silence fell over the elevator, and I could almost hear the disappointment fill the small space. It was not the first time he'd been rejected for being trans. When it came to dating, Greg was always conscious that he was different, and every time something like this happened, it knocked his confidence once again. It used to infuriate and frustrate me no end because he was such an amazing person with the kindest soul, but some people just couldn't get past how he was born. In the wrong body. I just about managed to get out a quick "I'm sorry" before the elevator doors opened and another doctor joined us for the rest of the ride.

Greg masked his disheartened demeanour with a cool shrug. He was getting increasingly better at seeming as though this kind of rejection didn't hurt him as much it did.

"Plenty more fish in the sea, right?" He smirked. The response didn't fool me, but he clearly wanted to move on. "Anyway, what are you planning this weekend that you so desperately need the time off?"

"Not sure."

We made it out of the elevator and started walking down the hallway. Planning what to do with Elena was something that made me incredibly anxious. Before, I would never have thought twice about what to do on a free weekend, but with the new Elena…it was like planning a romantic date for someone that you literally knew everything about, but you had to play it cool so they didn't think you were a stalker. Part of me felt as if it should be something spontaneous, like a trip to Brighton or Cornwall, and then I remembered the unpredictable weather, which would no doubt leave us drenched and windswept. Maybe the cinema or shopping? No, Elena hated both of those things.

"You seriously have nothing planned?" Greg whined. "Then why do you need it off?"

"Because we barely see each other all week, and I need to stir up those feelings she has for me. That is, if she even still has them." The seed of doubt I'd been pushing down rushed to the surface again.

"She does, Jax."

"I don't know. What about before? The day she was in her accident?"

"I told you to stop thinking about that. It was a stupid fight. You guys would have made up later that day if…" He grabbed my arm so I would look at him. "It wasn't your fault. The accident was not your fault."

"Yeah," I sheepishly replied, but the gnawing guilt told me otherwise. "I know."

"Jax, she loves you, and you'll prove it by making those memories come back."

"Any ideas on how I should do that?"

"Well, actually I have." I narrowed my eyes suspiciously as we split to allow a gurney to rush past us in the hallway. "I read this study the other day about the senses being able to jog memories in amnesia patients. Figured maybe it could help you. Smell works best for memory recognition, of course."

"Well, she did seem to warm up to me after borrowing my cardigan. I guess it smelled like me."

"Exactly, and then there's touch. Touching is good, really good, if you know what I mean." He nudged me as I batted him away. "I'm sure taking her into the bedroom would definitely help."

"Do you actually have useful advice?" I barked, the sexual frustration from weeks on a single daybed taking its toll.

"Not all touching has to be sexual. But holding her hand or a massage or—"

"It's a little hard to do all that when we're just *friends*."

"Have you tried kissing her?"

"Yep, all the time, every day," I replied sarcastically as we approached the ER doors. "If I can't hold her hand without it being suspicious, how the hell am I supposed to kiss her platonically?"

"Who said anything about platonic?"

I spun around, a little more agitated. "Literally every single one of you said I should just be her roommate."

"Screw that. That was during the recovery, but she's doing

great. The chance of a mental relapse is extremely low, especially if she's back to work and into a normal routine. And with things coming back to her more and more, I'd say it's only a matter of time before everything comes back." I chewed on my lip apprehensively as Greg tried again. "You've done everything right. But now you have to kick it up a notch. Make her fall in love with you again."

"That's what I've been trying to do." I huffed as I attempted to walk away from the conversation and toward an ambulance that had just pulled up outside.

"No, Jax, you've been playing doctor," Greg threw back as I spun to face him. The look on his face told me that wasn't intended to be vicious but just to reinforce that he was paying attention. "You're still treating her like a patient, like she's fragile. Like you'll terrify her if you get too close, and she will run for the hills if she suspects you have feelings for her."

"You mean, exactly what happened eight years ago? When I told her I liked her? None of you get it. Elena is so deep in the closet, I don't even know if she's aware I'm flirting with her."

"Then try harder, Jax." he said. "This is your wife. The same wife who's been talking to her ex again. Quit taking up extra shifts and be with your family."

His words hit home. He knew exactly what I had been doing, just like my mother. Maybe I was keeping her at a distance, afraid that she wouldn't want me or that those feelings she'd once had for me were gone forever. Maybe friends was an easier option than to actually put myself out there and tell her the truth. However, making Elena acknowledge her feelings for me the first time, almost eight years ago, had been difficult enough. Maybe I didn't have the strength to go through that pain again.

"I don't want to sound like a dick," he said, softening his voice. "It's just, if you keep treating her like a friend, that's all she will ever see you as." I nodded, taking in his words before his mood lightened. "Besides, she's healthy now, and if I'm honest, she's never looked better. So why don't you start treating her like your super sexy and smokin' hot—"

"Watch it!"

"Delightful wife," he teased before grabbing the clipboard chart from the back of a patient's door. "Talk to Caterina. I think you're right. It's time she knows the truth."

Chapter Nine

The weeks had turned into months, and my accident seemed like a distant nightmare, and according to Dr Hall, or Greg, I was making great progress. My weekly doctor appointments were complete, and I was back to almost full-time working.

Professionally, most things had come back to me. Clients' names would just roll off the tip of my tongue, and I could pull files from the folders on my desktop as if I'd always known where they were. In my work, I was my old self again, and it didn't go unmissed by my superiors.

My life had really taken a turn, and although there was still so much I couldn't remember about my personal life, I found that small things would come back to me. Such as my time in New York. Or when I was picking up a few things for dinner one day, I lifted a can of sweet corn before putting it back. I'd forgotten Jax didn't like sweet corn, something that was old information. Even as we walked through the park another time, it felt familiar, as if this greenery and pond was a location I'd visited often.

"What duck was your favourite, Mum?" Jamie beamed up at Jax, pulling me from my thoughts.

We'd left the park and stepped out onto the streets of Chelsea. It was a rarity that Jax would have a Sunday free to spend the day with Jamie, and although the decision of what to do had been left in the hands of the five-year-old, I could have safely bet my life that he would choose a trip to see the ducks. Even with large raindrops beating off the umbrella we were all huddled under, he was always going to choose to visit the ducks. He had taken to holding mine and Jax's hand, using us as stabilisers for his puddle splashing.

"I like the one with the green neck. He was the quickest," Jax said as she attempted, and failed, to steer him away from puddles. "What was your favourite?"

"I liked him too," Jamie said, despite there being as many as a dozen green mallards in the pond today.

"The blue one was pretty cool too," I chimed in, only to receive an offended face from Jamie.

"He was so slow. He barely moved." Jax and I shared a look as he began a lecture in picking favourite ducks. My preference was clearly unacceptable.

"Come on, Jay," Jax said, "shouldn't everyone be allowed to have their own opinion, even if you don't agree?"

"I guess." He shrugged his shoulders defeatedly. "That's okay, Elena. You can think that. And it doesn't matter that you're wrong." I would have laughed at his bluntness if he hadn't sealed the line with a genuine smile, as if he meant every harsh word sincerely.

"Ouch," Jax whispered as I faked offense.

We walked in comfortable silence until out of the corner of my eye, I saw Jax glancing at me a couple times. I side-glanced to meet her eyes, but she nervously avoided mine. It was as if she wanted to ask me something but couldn't find the nerve, something that was very uncharacteristic of the Jax I knew, who practically oozed confidence.

A big jump followed by a loud splash between us broke the tension as water reached as high as my knees, and Jamie's giggling filled the street.

"Jamie, stop. You soaked Elena." Jax looked down at my jeans. "No more puddles. I mean it this time, or we'll have to go home." She mouthed "Sorry" at me.

"It's fine, Jax. Just a little bit of rain." I smiled, patting Jamie's head as he looked up with a toothy grin.

"We should probably get inside anyway. The sky doesn't look good." Rumbling thunder in the distance confirmed her suspicions of oncoming bad weather. "Want to grab a coffee with us?"

"I usually object to giving children coffee, but I don't want to tell you how to parent."

"Hold on, you don't love to watch hyper children?" she teased. "Does that mean you're not working today?" I shook my head. "This is a first. Alert the media, you're not working at the weekend."

"Very funny." I rolled my eyes.

"It's just nice to see you outside is all. You know, in the real world, away from your laptop."

"It's a bad habit, I know. I'm turning into my workaholic father. He always travelled for work when Cat and I were younger. We saw him like four times a year." Jax nodded, but I got the feeling she already knew about my relationship with Papa. "Did I work a lot before?"

"Yeah," she replied softly, almost sadly. "You did." The air turned thick around us as her eyes clouded over, and she stared down, avoiding my gaze.

"Maybe that should be one of the things I try *not* to remember." She looked at me with a soft smile. "Seeing as I'm trying to remember everything else." I shrugged just as she slowed and nodded toward a café a few doors ahead.

Jamie took it upon himself to lead the way as he took hold of my hand and pulled me toward the front door. Once inside, I shook off my wet coat and helped Jamie remove his jacket, taking in the puddles of water on the hardwood floor from other customers seeking shelter on this rainy Sunday. Large couches and armchairs were unorderly dispersed throughout the room. The bohemian coffee shop had vinyls mounted on the walls, some of which looked like signed editions, with soft 90s Brit rock playing in the background. Jax led us to a free couch in the back, taking us past students working on their laptops and an older couple reading a newspaper.

"Latte with an extra shot?" Jax asked, and with surprise, I simply nodded.

A small smile played on her lips while a glint in her eye followed quickly after. It was a look I'd seen before, an enjoyment she got out of knowing things about me before I could tell her.

"And Mr James, what'll it be today, my good sir?" Jax asked in an upper-class voice.

He put on his best posh accent. "I would like your best hot chocolate."

"I believe we have some of the finest in London, Mr James. Would you like marshmallows or cream on top?" I found myself grinning at the role-play as he thought deeply, caressing his chin as if there was a beard. "A tough decision, sir, please take your time." She shot me an exasperated look as I stifled a grin.

"Marshmallow, madam."

"The stickier and undoubtedly messier option. Very good, Mr James."

Jax curtsied before retreating toward the coffee counter, and I couldn't help but follow her with my eyes. Her jeans hugged her hips, showing off her slim yet toned legs, with her sweater clinging to her waist and chest revealing slight curves. Strangely, I found myself wondering about the body underneath.

"What are you looking at?" Jamie asked as I practically jumped in my seat.

"Nothing." I pulled myself back to him. "Just the pictures on the wall." I pointed to an infamous vinyl cover I knew far too well from my teenage years.

"You love that one about the wonder wall," he said.

"How on earth does a five-year-old know who Oasis is?" I put a hand on my hip and looked at him, decoding this cultured, beyond-his-years child.

"You play it all the time on the record player," he replied as he pulled out his colour book from the little backpack Jax had spent most of the afternoon chaperoning.

"Huh." My eyes gravitated back toward the coffee counter to continue my strange leering at Jax.

I was a little irked when I saw a young barista flirting with her. There was no concrete evidence that they were flirting, of course. I cursed the ambient tune of the Smiths, which my foot was still tapping to, as it meant I couldn't hear what was being said. The barista moved a few times behind the counter, preparing coffee, but her eyes remained glued to Jax, talking over her shoulder. The loud laughter from the blond twentysomething set my back teeth on edge as she moved to the till again and rang in the order. I shook the feeling, telling myself the barista was just being friendly, until she reached over and touched Jax's arm. My irritation redirected as Jax's head dipped bashfully, and she ran her hand through her hair, clearly enjoying the attention. Jax lifted the tray and began making her way back toward our table as I swallowed my aggravation and turned my attention to Jamie's drawings.

"Here we go." Jax smiled, handing Jamie his hot chocolate and taking my latte and a muffin to share off the tray.

He reached for the hot chocolate, which was in a rather large mug, and began slurping gulps of it, his eyes expanding as the sugar entered his system.

"Slow down, Jay."

"Leave him be, Keelin," I said, reaching over and smoothing his long wispy curls. "He's been out in the cold all day. But you do need a haircut, Mr Man. This hair is getting out of control. We should see if Trish can take him next week." I turned to Jax, and she looked at me as if she'd seen a ghost.

At that moment, I realised what I'd said and how I'd spoken to Jax, or rather, called her Keelin, which I'd never done before. At least, not that I could remember. In the next beat, I found myself apologising profusely.

"I'm so sorry. I don't know where that came from." Trish

owned a hair salon which opened a couple of years ago near the apartment, and just like that, I remembered her. "I'm sorry, I didn't...I didn't mean to undermine you. I have no idea why I said that."

"You're okay. Don't worry." Jax smiled playfully before she turned to Jamie again. "Elena lets you get away with everything." She winked at Jamie as he went back to drinking his hot chocolate, but my mind was still reeling.

"I...I don't know why I did that." I frowned shamefully. "I'm sorry if I..."

"Elena, it's okay." Jax placed her hand on mine, and an electric bolt leapt from her touch and ran up my arm. My eyes snapped to hers, and I could swear she felt it too. "You used to call me a fun sponge all the time. Maybe I should try to forget some things too."

Her eyes stayed on mine, and I couldn't break the hold as I felt her fingers stroke the back of my hand ever so slightly. Such a soft touch that was somehow affecting my ability to breathe evenly.

"I know you prefer Jax, usually," I said with a shaky breath.

"Usually, but..." She paused, her voice oozing confidence again while her eyes pulled me in deeper. "You can call me anything you want." Her eyes darted to my lips, and I felt my knees grow weak. Thankfully, I was seated. Otherwise, I would have been just another puddle on the floor. The trance she had on me was broken, and her touch vanished as we were interrupted—rudely, I might add—by the barista.

"One ham and cheese toasted sandwich." She placed the sandwich in front of Jax. "And there is no mustard. I wouldn't want a repeat of last time." She smirked at Jamie.

"Hopefully, there will be no waterworks this time," Jax replied as she nudged the already cut up sandwich toward Jamie. "Thanks, Cassie."

The barista didn't even bat an eyelid toward me; it was like I was invisible. And then my blood began to boil as she leaned down and whispered into Jax's ear. My mouth fell open in shock before Cassie pulled away and slipped a small piece of paper onto the table. She flipped her hair as she turned and retreated shamelessly back to the counter again. Jax read the note subtly before shaking her head in amusement and placing it in her pocket.

❖

Jax

I suppressed yet another yawn as I packed up the leftovers and put them in containers for Monday's lunch. After one final swipe of the kitchen countertop, I moved into the living room and found Elena on her laptop, engrossed in work.

"So you remember Trish, then?" I asked.

Elena glanced up at me before her eyes drifted back to her work. "Yeah, Jamie's hairdresser. Things like that are coming back a lot lately."

"That's good, though," I replied as the air turned awkward again. "And you remembered about that time we met in New York too." Elena nodded but remained silent. "Getting ready for Monday morning?" I asked as I tidied the living room of toys. Jamie was fast asleep in his room.

"Yep." Her curt tone told me I was in trouble, not that I didn't already know.

It was the same tone I'd experienced all evening. I retraced my steps, trying to figure out when I'd pissed her off; was it in the park or the walk home or maybe it was cooking dinner? Maybe I'd gone too far at the coffee shop, but she'd seemed to be flirting with me as well. Old me would have given up by now, knowing that eventually, my wife would tell me in great detail what I had done wrong, but this Elena was stubborn, and this could go on for days. However, with Tom in the picture again, I didn't have that kind of time. He went from calling once a week to every other day. I could feel it. He was sharpening his claws, readying them to dig deep into Elena the second she gave him a chance. While her memories were drip-feeding back, it wasn't fast enough. It was only going to make it harder when she learned the truth.

"What's wrong?" I folded my arms and looked at her from across the table. She shrugged as she opened her mouth, but I already knew the response. "And don't say nothing's wrong because clearly, there is."

"Nothing is wrong, honestly. Just a difference of opinion."

"You need to give me a little more to go on."

"It's cool, don't worry about it." She closed the lid of her laptop and slipped it into its bag, dismissing the conversation.

Vagueness, avoidance, and somewhat immature behaviour. What had I done to evoke these emotions? And that was when something clicked. I didn't see this side of Elena often. In fact, I'd almost forgotten what this "monster" looked like. After we'd gotten married, Elena's jealous side had disappeared entirely. Until now.

"Oh." I smiled to myself and tried to suppress the laughter in the back of my throat. "I get it now." Her eyes flashed a shade of fury and revealed I was onto a winner. I pulled the piece of paper from my pocket and held it up. Her eyes avoided it as if it was the sun, solidifying my theory. "You think I was flirting with Cassie."

"What?" She avoided the question before some immaturity followed. "Whatever. I mean, the barista was into you, so whatever, but I didn't think it was okay in front of Jamie is all." She slid the rest of her files into the laptop bag before leaving the dining table and making a swift exit toward her bedroom door.

"Care to read the note?"

"I really don't care." She turned to look at me despite every aspect of her body language telling me she did, in fact, care.

I unfolded the paper and began reading as I walked toward her. "Life is too short to wait for a hot guy to ask you out. Call me, Cassie. There's a smiley face too, and that looks like her phone number." I held the paper in front of her as she read it before frowning in confusion. "I usually go to that coffee shop on my work breaks with Greg." She began to blush as she joined up the dots. "He flirts with her every day but doesn't have the guts to ask her out. She asked me to give him her number." I folded the paper and put it back in my pocket and couldn't help but relish in the embarrassment radiating from her. "If I didn't know better, I'd say you were jealous."

"'Bittersweet Symphony' is the Verve's best song," she blurted out of nowhere. We had debated that on the way home this afternoon, which had turned into a slightly heated discussion. "I don't agree with what you said, that 'Lucky Man' is their best song."

This appeared to be her very poor attempt at hiding her jealousy, referring to that conversation as "the difference of opinion."

"It's okay, Elena," I said softly, moving one step closer. Her eyes found mine as I quoted our son from earlier. "You can think that. And it doesn't matter that you're wrong." The corners of her mouth twitched upward, and I couldn't help but mirror her smile. "I feel like someone important once said that."

"A prince, I think," she replied playfully as the room turned quiet.

"Thanks for coming out with us today." My voice softened, and the mood changed as I realised just how close we were standing to each other. "Jamie loves hanging out with you."

"And what about you?" Her question threw me, but she showed only confidence and an alluring boldness.

"What about me?" My eyes danced around her face as she gazed at me playfully. "Do I like hanging out with you? Well, I wouldn't be trying to defuse your jealousy if I didn't."

"I'm not jealous," she said, licking her lips nervously.

"My apologies, a difference of opinion."

"It's late," she whispered but didn't move toward her door, her eyes glued to my lips.

"Then I guess, this is good night." I looked from her darkening green eyes to her full lips. I wanted nothing more than to kiss her. But she looked hesitant. A second later, something resembling panic flashed before her eyes, and the moment was gone. Just like that, she took a step back, gave a weak smile, and closed her bedroom door, leaving me with no idea where I stood.

CHAPTER TEN

As soon as I emerged from the elevator and walked the short distance to the apartment door, I knew something wasn't right. Call it intuition or a gut feeling, but the air felt tense, colder, and I just knew trouble waited for me on the other side of the door.

I hesitated to put my key in the lock as I heard muffled voices arguing, but the curiosity became overwhelming, considering I was supposed to be arriving home to an empty house. Silence dispersed throughout the apartment as the jiggling of my keys in the lock seemed to rattle even the furniture. I crept into the hallway toward the living room, cautious to avoid the metaphoric eggshells lining the hardwood floors. Cat and Jax failed to compose themselves as the remnants of whatever they'd slung at each other hung in the air.

"Hey!" Cat spoke first while I stood frozen in the entrance to the living room as the tension oozed toward me. "How was work?" She stood and tightly crossed her arms like a protective shield, making me feel more uncomfortable.

"Fine. What are you doing here?" I asked, failing to see the point in pleasantries. "It's the middle of the afternoon. Don't you both have work?"

They shared a look before Jax spoke up. "Why don't you sit down?"

I narrowed my eyes as they led me toward the dining table

where a pot of tea was waiting. "Is this my intervention?" I half joked, shedding my coat. I was met with silence, which only caused my breathing to turn uneasy, panicked, and short. "What's going on, Cat?" I stopped before reaching the table. The atmosphere felt volatile and unpredictable.

"Sit. We'll explain," Cat said as she took a seat next to Jax, whose eyes were distant and glassy.

"Where's Jamie?" I asked, afraid. "Did something happen?"

"He's fine. Nick is collecting Jamie and the girls from school," Jax said, and I relaxed a little.

Cat gestured to the dining chair, and I reluctantly took a seat but remained on high alert.

"You both are freaking me out," I barked, causing them to share a look of concern. "What's wrong?" Neither conjured an explanation. Cat busied herself pouring tea and pushing biscuits toward me. "Will someone please tell me what is going on?"

"Just listen." Jax started. "After the accident, there were a couple of things we didn't…couldn't tell you." Her usual confidence seemed reduced to nerves. "Some things that might have hindered your recovery. We wanted to wait until you were better again."

"Okay," I replied slowly, watching their body language. Jax looked pale, clenched-jawed, and glassy-eyed while Cat fussed with her hair, bit her nails, and avoided all eye contact. "What don't I know?"

Jax gulped and looked to my sister, but she stood from the table and began pacing, creating a tenser air than before. "It's about Jamie."

"Jax, no," Cat said, shaking her head, pleading. "Let's just leave it, okay? It's too soon."

"I'm not doing this anymore, Cat. It's not fair. She deserves to know the truth," Jax said through a clenched jaw, almost in pain, before her soft eyes met mine. "Jamie is your son."

My insides froze, and my limbs turned to lead. Ragged

breaths filled the space, but it felt like white noise was filling my head as two concerned pairs of eyes watched my every move.

"What?" I said as my brain tried to process the new information. "Is this some kind of joke?" No one was laughing, prompting panic. "Wait, what? What are you talking about?"

Green eyes flashed across my mind, not mine but his. Jamie's eyes bored into mine countless times as I received glimpses of him, memories I'd misplaced over the last five years. Like a blur, showing me mere snapshots of his undeniable presence in my life. But my mind rejected it, too impossible to fathom.

"I'm so sorry I didn't tell you." Jax's voice dipped as she bit her lip. "We both are."

Cat took her seat again beside me, tears falling from her eyes. "We wanted to tell you but—"

"This is a joke, right? Jamie can't be mine. I think I would remember…" I trailed off, shaking my head. "He's your son," I said to Jax, short of breath.

"Elena, his eyes," Cat pressed. "His curly hair, just like us when we were his age. Look at the similarities with Abbey." Cat grabbed a book from the side table, placing it in front of me. "His school books." I read the name which had been on that table all week.

Jamie Ricci.

"But no. It can't be." Then I remembered what Tansy had said my first day of work. *Oh, he's Jax's son. I always thought you had him. He looks just like you.* Tears began to cloud my vision as I processed the indisputable facts. "You lied to me," I whispered as I ran my hand over the book. "Both of you did."

Jax stared at the table in silence. Cat began apologising, but I interrupted her, feeling nothing but betrayal. "Why couldn't you just tell me? Out of everyone, Caterina, you should have told me."

"I wanted to. Every day. You were just so fragile in the beginning. We were scared to tell you."

"We?" Jax growled, looking away from me.

"You wanted to tell me?" I asked as her eyes met mine. "Why did you pretend Jamie was your son?"

"I wasn't pretending."

Her chilling words hung in the air as I watched her carefully before turning back to Cat. She said nothing but wiped the tears from her cheeks as I felt my own eyes fill more. Jax reached behind her neck and unclipped a necklace. The same necklace she wore every day, but the pendant was always hidden beneath her clothes. As she pulled it out from under her jumper, she placed it on the table, allowing the two wedding bands to clatter off the hard surface.

Tansy's words sounded again in my mind. *Oh, he's Jax's son. I always thought you had him. He looks just like you.* Something more terrifying clicked in my mind. Jax's extensive knowledge of me and my history. Her frequent visits in the hospital, the concern, comfort, and familiarity. The flirting. The countless letters and mail addressed to both of us. Cat and Jax's close relationship, almost like family. My mind began to race, and I figured out what Jax was trying so hard to tell me without breaking down.

"I'm his mother too," she said.

"We're…I'm with…"

"I know this is a lot to process—" Jax tried, but I cut her off.

"Wait, I don't understand. Me and you are…" I couldn't even say it out loud. The words seemed preposterous. "And we both raise Jamie?" I struggled to vocalise my thoughts as they all jumbled together into a swirling mess. "No." Rejection rippled across my skin. "No. This is…this can't. I'm not gay!" The venom in my voice cut through the apartment.

"Elena," Cat warned as she side-glanced Jax, who could barely face me.

"None of this makes sense." My brain tried to process, and my chest tightened, making breathing a chore. "This can't be my life. This isn't me."

"Elena," Cat snapped.

Jax rose, stilling the room. "This has all been a lot for you." She spoke mechanically, keeping the emotion from her voice and refusing to meet my eyes.

"Jax, she's just in shock." Cat reached for her arm, but Jax shifted away from the touch.

"With time, I hope you'll understand why we didn't tell you." She gritted her teeth before continuing in the calmest of voices. "And that you'll find a way to forgive us." Jax glanced around the apartment as if she might never set foot in it again. "I think it would be best if I just go." She surprised me by turning to me with blurred eyes, revealing her pain. "Take as long as you need. Jamie and I will stay at my mum's."

"You don't have to do that." The guilt consumed me as I stared at someone I barely knew, who I was supposed to be married to.

"I think it's for the best. For everyone." She looked completely crushed but mustered a small smile. "If you need me, or anything, give me a call. I'll be there."

She left, and silence filled the apartment as Cat stared at the tea she'd never touched and waited for me to speak.

"How could you keep this from me?"

"To avoid this," she whispered numbly. "This complete mess. I love you, Elena. You are my sister, and I will protect you, always, but it's been a hard few months. For all of us."

"Even more reason why *you* should have been the one to tell me." Though I tried to keep my face neutral, the low tone in my voice tattled my humiliation. "I feel like a complete idiot. You let me walk around here completely clueless. Why didn't you tell me?" My voice became shrill as I replayed the previous months. "I've been spending time with Jamie without realising he's my…and I have been getting dating advice off Jax?" I groaned. "I can't believe this. All the lying, Caterina—"

"This isn't all on me, Elena. We all agreed that keeping Jamie a secret would be best. Greg was the one—"

"Greg is a doctor. He's not my sister." The accusation in my voice seemed to surprise us both, and I felt a lump form in my throat. "Out of everyone in my life, you're the one I turn to most. You're my family."

"I know," she said, sobbing. "But I was thinking about your other family. Jax and Jamie. I wanted to avoid this and wait until—"

"My memory came back? Seriously? What if it never did?"

"That's why we told you now," she argued as silence fell over us. "It was taking too long for the memories to come back on their own. Jax was worried they never..." She took a shaky breath. "It wasn't fair on you or Jamie. Your family was being ripped apart, and you had no idea."

"I can't believe...I have a son. I'm married." Each sentence seemed more ridiculous than the last.

"I'm sorry. I'm really sorry," she said. "I didn't want to upset you, I just prayed every day that your memories would come back, and the longer it went on, the harder it was to come clean." She wiped the tears with the back of her hand before her eyes softened even more. "I was just so happy you were still here to lie to." She made a slow exhale. "Don't forget, you nearly died, Elena. I would have lied my ass off a thousand times over if it meant I still had my baby sister around." She stroked the back of my hand softly. "But Jax. She wanted to tell you from the very beginning."

"She did?"

"She hated lying to you, and she was afraid of the effect it was having on Jamie."

"He's my son," I whispered in disbelief. "I don't remember. How could I not remember having a baby?" I groaned, frustrated, as Cat gripped my hand. "Even he lied to me."

"It's not his fault."

"I know. He's just a kid." I sighed before a thought occurred to me. I retraced the timeline and figured out a piece of the puzzle.

"He's Tom's son, isn't he?" Cat nodded slowly as my head fell into my palms. "Tom didn't say anything. Does he even know we have a son?"

"Of course Tom fucking knows." Her hand fled mine as a wave of anger crashed over her. "He left you when he found out you were pregnant, not before claiming it wasn't his baby, though." She huffed fumes of hatred.

"He's not the only one around here lying, so you can get off your high horse," I said bitterly.

"You're still defending that bastard. Do you have any idea what we've been going through? And all you can think about is him. What about your wife, Elena?"

"I have no idea who that person is," I shouted back. "You don't know what this feels like." I rose to my feet. "You sit there and tell me I have a wife and son and expect me to be fine, Caterina? I'm sorry I'm not living up to your expectations, but I can't accept this. I'm not gay."

In hindsight, my behaviour over the last few months had been utterly inconsistent. At times, I'd let myself enjoy Jax's attraction to me, never thinking it would be anything more than flirtation. A wave of fear crashed around me at the thought that I could be in a relationship with a woman. A perverse and unnatural relationship that was unacceptable.

"It's okay if you are." I stared at her in disbelief. "Think about it," she urged keeping her voice level. "Why you were jealous of the barista?" My entire body began to tremble, as if my nerves were rejecting her words. "You almost kissed that day I walked into your kitchen. You can't deny it. The chemistry—"

"I don't know what you're talking about," I shouted, but I struggled to conjure an excuse. What Cat was accusing me of, the person that she said I had become, created a tidal wave of shame and self-loathing to course through my veins. "That's not me. I'm not like that."

"There's nothing wrong with you." The way she said those

words caused an internal panic and had a profound impact on me, like a trigger igniting forgotten memories.

There is nothing wrong with you began to sound in my head, but it wasn't Cat's voice. It was a flashback, the memory of sitting in my psychiatrist's office. Dr Neill. Not only that one session but others before as the doctor said those same words. *There is nothing wrong with you.*

She pulled me from the flashback as she stood to be at eye level with me. "I know what they did." Taking a step back, I narrowed my eyes. "It took years for you to finally tell me what had happened. Why you transferred to high school in England." Bile began to creep up my throat as sweat formed on my brow. "Mama said it was your decision, but I know the truth now. What Mama and Papa did to you."

"I don't know what you're talking about." My vision blurred as she took a step forward to comfort me. "I can't deal with this right now. Don't you think I've enough going on without thinking about the past? Stuff that doesn't matter?" I backed away until the front door was in sight.

"You never dealt with it, Elena, that shame you feel."

"Stop it," I growled as I realised she knew about St Catherine's Boarding House.

"That's why you're struggling so hard to accept this. Even though deep down, you know you feel something for Jax."

The walls began to crash around me. "You don't know what you're talking about." But my head was spinning, coming undone. "I gotta get out of here," I managed to slur before I darted toward the front door.

"Go ahead, then," she called as I raced for the door, failing to grab even a jacket. "You've been running for most of your life." Her words stung, but I didn't wait around long enough to feel the full weight of them.

❖

Jax

That could not have gone worse. I pulled the car out of underground parking and began driving north. I replayed the conversation repeatedly, along with Elena's horrified expression. The betrayal and hurt in her eyes. Cat wanted to be the one to tell her about Jamie, but when it came down to it, she froze. I did too.

Sitting in rush hour traffic on my way to Cat and Nick's home to collect Jamie, I couldn't help but stare numbly at the string of cars held at the red light. I had planned out in my head how Elena might react when she discovered the truth. There were a thousand different scenarios, but none of them prepared me for the pain of how she'd truly responded. The complete and full body rejection of her life. Our life. If she ran away and never came back again, I wouldn't be surprised.

Doubts swirled in my mind: Had today been the right time to tell her? Should I have stayed? Could I have been more delicate in telling her about Jamie and our relationship? Had I lost her forever? The move to tell Elena today was a hasty decision, but I had to do it. It might have been the only way to save our family.

I'd arrived home earlier that day from a long night shift. No one had been awake at six a.m. as I tiptoed around the apartment, determined to make it to the dingy old daybed in the spare bedroom before passing out. That was until a foreign object stopped me in my tracks. A huge bouquet of flowers with a balloon reaching the ceiling had been placed on the dining table. On closer inspection, I could tell they were pricey, oversized, with a florist's card poking from the arrangement, professionally delivered. My stomach was already churning before I had a chance to read the card.

Dear Elena,

Your quick recovery is inspirational, and I'm very pleased you are feeling like your old self again. Though years have passed, I still take those canal walks in

Nottingham and think of you. Remembering the time we almost fell in! I can't wait to see you in person in a couple of weeks. It's been far too long.

All my love,

Tom

I could have crushed the card in my hand as I gritted my teeth. Not only was he constantly calling, now he was sending gifts, and next he would be visiting. My first thought had been of Jamie. He'd never met his biological father, and the thought of Tom being within a one-mile radius of this apartment had made me sick to my stomach. My chest had tightened, and my breathing had accelerated. My mind had clouded over as I'd felt panic. He was doing it. Sliming his way back into her heart, and what was worse, Elena was letting him. Tom was pulling her back in and maybe one day, Jamie too.

My phone had already been in hand, and I'd pressed Dial. A groggy Cat had answered the call, and just like that, the plan to tell Elena had been made. Cat had her doubts by the time she got to the apartment that afternoon. We'd argued, and she'd tried to reason with me not to tell her. "Wait and see if her memory comes back." But by that time, I might have lost her. She was already slipping away, but now, as I replayed Elena's reaction on a never-ending loop, I wondered if Cat was right.

I'm not gay. Elena's voice echoed in my mind, serving as a reminder of how different she was. *This can't be my life.* An ache rippled with every beat of my heart as tears rushed to my eyes. That was not *my* Elena. The woman I married was undeniably true to herself and confident in what she wanted. It had taken a lot of therapy to get her to face her demons, the past traumas she'd faced during high school, which had led to years of unacceptance, denial, and unhappiness. St Catherine's Boarding House, a boarding school in the midlands of England, specialised in conversion therapy and was Elena's punishment at fifteen when her parents had caught her in bed with her first girlfriend. Too ashamed to tell anyone, she'd suffered for years, suppressing her same-sex attraction. That led to a cycle of her chasing toxic relationships because she genuinely believed she deserved nothing more than heartache.

Elena had carried the shame of disappointing her parents for years, and the recent loss of memory meant she couldn't remember coming to terms with her sexuality. The complexities of Elena's past, and the massive amount of development she had done in the last eight years, had created an entirely different woman than who she was in her twenties. That, in a nutshell, had been the primary reason we hadn't told her about her son and our relationship. It was also the reason our flirting over the last week hadn't been able to progress. Elena was never going to allow herself to really feel what she wanted to feel. Not until she learned to accept herself.

"You've barely said a word, Keelin." Mum interrupted my thoughts, and I looked up at her face. Seated opposite me at the kitchen table, she gave a small smile, the crinkles around her lips multiplying. "Things will get better, love." She rubbed my hand softly. "But until then, you and Jamie can stay as long as you need."

"Thanks, Mum," I replied, tightening my grip on her hand.

"Do you remember what your da would always say after a bad day?" I felt myself well up, knowing exactly the phrase she was going to say. "It's always darkest before the dawn. Things look tough now, but they'll get better." I nodded along with her, even though that advice seemed unimaginable.

CHAPTER ELEVEN

I ran from the apartment with no idea where I was going. All I knew was, I couldn't stay there any longer after hearing the news. I had a son. I was married. To a woman. My mind was spiralling out of control with a thousand thoughts. It took me almost twenty minutes of pacing through the streets of London to realise it was raining, heavily, and I was umbrella-less and without even a jacket. My drenched jumper clung to my skin, but I was far too numb to feel the chill in the air.

I darted into a coffee shop to seek refuge only to realise it was the same coffee shop I had visited just last weekend with Jax and Jamie. The hardwood floors were darkened from customers trapesing in from the rain. Brit rock played softly in the background. Upon approaching the counter, I was surprised to be met by the same barista, Cassie, who had served us last week.

"What can I get you?" It took a moment before she seemed to recognise me, and a warm smile spread across her face. "Hey, I know you. You're Jax's wife, right?"

The question threw me as the news from today came crashing over me again, stunning me momentarily. *I am Jax's wife.* I couldn't find the words to reply, but thankfully, it wasn't necessary as Cassie continued her breezy chit-chat, oblivious to my internal meltdown.

"Let me see if I can remember your order. Hmm, a latte

with an extra shot?" I nodded, still unable to string a sentence together. "Yes!" She congratulated herself while starting to prepare the coffee. "To be fair, you guys are pretty regular in here, so it's hardly a challenge. And how's little Jamie doing?" Again, I couldn't respond, too bewildered to force politeness. "He's such a cute kid, I'm always praising Jax. You know, I get a ton of families coming in here, and it's always a mess when they leave, but with Jamie, he is so well-behaved. You struck lucky with him." She placed the coffee in front of me.

"Thank you," I managed to croak. I felt myself crumble inside because deep down, I knew he was the most important thing in my life. That was the effect Jamie had on me. "How much do I owe you?" I said before releasing I'd left the house without my purse. I frantically searched my pockets, but Cassie reassured me of humanity.

"It's on the house. You look like you need it." She smiled warmly. "Besides, Jax and Greg keep this place going with the amount of coffee they buy on a daily basis."

Sitting at a bench, I warmed myself beside the radiator while finally giving myself the time I needed to think. The afternoon ran through my brain on a continuous loop with more questions arising than I could keep track of. Hours must have passed. I heard the scraping of chairs being lifted onto tables, revealing I was the last customer. I waved good-bye to Cassie and walked home slowly, dragging my feet the entire way. Though I was dreading speaking to Cat again, I knew she would be the best person to answer the burning questions, even if it was going to be painful.

When I arrived at the apartment again, I found it empty. My sister was gone long ago. I'd never realised how big and empty the apartment felt when alone, almost lifeless.

"Jamie?" I wishfully called. A gentle push of his bedroom door revealed his absence. "Jax?" I found a quiver in my voice as I moved toward her bedroom. Silence followed, confirming she was gone as well.

I had never set foot in her room; in fact, I'd never seen the door open. I hesitated, not sure if I wanted to cross that boundary, but at the same time, perhaps it would reveal answers. With a flick of the light switch, the small space lit up, revealing her sleeping quarters. I wouldn't class it as a bedroom in its current state. It looked like more of a dumping ground, with barely enough room for a small daybed at one end and what I could only imagine was Jamie's old crib at the other end. Boxes were piled in the corner with old baby furniture crowding the space. Jax's clothes and scrubs had been thrown into the crib. She clearly had nowhere else to store them in here. Guilt swelled in my chest.

For weeks, she had lived without a proper bed or wardrobe and had managed to hide the fact that this room wasn't her bedroom at all. Perhaps Jax thought it would be more temporary, that she would soon return to the master bedroom. Other elements began to make sense, like why my wardrobe was half-empty. Because the person I used to share it with had to erase all evidence of her existence.

Countless picture frames had also been heaped into Jamie's old crib, likely removed from around the house. I reached for a handful in an attempt to gain greater clarity about the life I had forgotten and couldn't help but smile. In each photograph, I looked happy. Happier than I had felt in a long time. Some picture frames were playful, others even rejigged a hazy memory, but nothing was as impactful as seeing a snapshot of my wedding day.

My white dress was simple, inexpensive, and I walked on the beach holding my high-heeled shoes. The gown wasn't what I would have pictured for myself, but then again, I'd never really thought I would marry. Only people *in love* got married.

Jax was dressed in a pair of beige slacks with a matching waistcoat and pale blue shirt. She watched me with utter devotion, but she wasn't the only one caught in a daze. Jamie was also in the picture with an outfit matching Jax's, and he stared at me as if I was the most important person in the world. We looked unbelievably happy, walking, holding hands with Jamie in between us. Tiny droplets landed on the picture, confirming that my blurred vision was from tears as they rolled down the glass. I wasn't sure how long I stared at the picture, but one thing was clear, I had to speak to my family again.

Within an hour, I arrived at Cat's home, significantly drier after having remembered a coat and umbrella. Nick answered the door and smiled warmly. "Hey, kid." He pulled me into a bear hug. "I was wondering when you would show up."

I melted in his arms. The door closed behind us, but I continued to latch on to him, unaware of how much I needed that hug. The tapping of four feet moved down the hallway as Nick and I parted, and Marco, their golden retriever, began sniffing around my hands. I patted him on the head, and he looked up at me with soft eyes. Even the dog could tell I was a mess.

"You had your sister worried sick."

"Just my sister?" I raised a brow teasingly.

He grinned, not willing to admit how much he cared. Shuffling noises from farther inside revealed Cat's whereabouts.

"Do me a favour, huh?" he whispered as he nodded toward the kitchen. "Please go easy on her. There's no one in this world she cares more about than you." He warmed my heart and nudged me toward the kitchen as he moved back into the lounge to finish watching the football match. "Well, except me."

"You keep telling yourself that, Nick," I said, and he laughed to himself before disappearing from sight.

I walked slowly toward the kitchen and found my sister frantically cleaning. Standing on a dining room chair, half of her body disappeared into the back of one of the kitchen cabinets as she scrubbed. She was not a cleaner. The only time she fussed was when she was worried about something or someone.

"Need a hand?" I asked as she emerged, looking haggard and exhausted.

"I thought you'd be halfway to Albuquerque by now," she returned, but there was no malice.

"My flight leaves tomorrow," I teased as she climbed down from the chair and dusted herself off in avoidance. "Can we talk?" I sat at the dining table. "The place looks good, clean," I lied as my gaze drifted around the chaos and cluttered countertops.

"No, it doesn't." She closed the distance between us. "It looks exactly like how I feel." She took a seat. "Where'd you go?"

"I went to the Java Hut for a while. Walked about. Tried to make sense of everything."

"How'd that work out?"

"Why didn't you just tell me, Cat?" I asked, desperately needing clarity.

"I was scared. Really scared that if you found out about Jamie and Jax, you'd run." She shrugged defeatedly. "And you did." I stared at my hands, a little guilty until her voice pulled me back. "But you came back. That takes courage. Elena, you have to know, I only wanted to protect you."

"But you understand why I feel so betrayed?"

"Of course I do. Not telling you about them was wrong on so many levels. If I'd known your memories wouldn't be back by now, I would have never kept Jamie and Jax from you."

"Okay, I can accept that," I said. Cat visibly relaxed. "I'm just struggling so much with…Jamie is one thing but then…"

"Jax," she finished, and I nodded slowly. "I thought that might be harder for you to accept." She reached across for my hand. "Because of what happened."

"I told you about school?" She nodded. "When?"

"A few years ago. Your therapist recommended it."

"Dr Neill," I said, and she tilted her head in surprise. "I remember. It's a little blurry, but I remember talking with him. About my experiences. I guess I needed a shrink, huh?" I half joked, but she clearly didn't see the humour.

"It took a long time for you to come to terms with it." Her voice softened as she dipped her head to meet my eyes. "I'm so sorry I wasn't there for you."

"It wasn't your fault, Cat. You were just a kid."

"I was older than you."

"You didn't even know. I never told you what was happening at school. I didn't want you to know." I tried to lessen her guilt by clutching her hand, but she shook her head, dismissing me.

"I didn't want to know," she replied, clearly angry at herself as her eyes welled up. "For years, you were in that place. I could have helped you. I was in England too, remember?"

She had been accepted to the University of Oxford just months prior to me being sent away when I was fifteen. Oxford was just two hours south of my prison school. In Cat's first couple of years of university, we would text every other day but rarely called, so she had no idea how crushed my spirit was. We only saw each other at home during the summer holidays or at Christmas. My own sister had no idea of the hell I was living in. So many nights, I'd wished Cat would come and rescue me from the awful boarding school, but I was too ashamed to tell her why I was there in the first place.

"Getting drunk every weekend meant I didn't have time to check on my baby sister when you were—"

I gripped her hand tight and shushed her. "That was a long time ago," I told her, but the guilt she felt was still lingering in her eyes. "I know you would have done everything to help me if I'd been brave enough to tell you."

She nodded desperately, no doubt in an effort to reassure me. "I wanted to wait to tell you about Jax because of St Catherine's." I tensed at hearing its name aloud. I struggled to think about the school. My brain had seemed to develop a coping mechanism, preventing me from dwelling on that time in my life. "Those practises at St Catherine's are unthinkable." Hearing it again was like a trigger, a gunshot, causing suppressed memories to regurgitate in my head.

Same-sex attraction is an illness. We are here to help you heal.

The nuns would justify their actions. Forcing us to write essays about opposite-sex attraction and reciting the Lord's Prayer in the hope of healing our sinful thoughts.

You're a disappointment to your families.

You're very sick.

When you're better, you can go home again.

The voices swirled in my head as my breathing turned shallow and my vision blurred. All I ever wanted was to go home, but my parents said I couldn't until I was cleansed. I was only freed because they couldn't legally keep me any longer.

"Are you okay?" She scanned my face as I nodded slowly and forced down the demons for another day. Cat spoke again, pulling me back into the room. "I was scared that if I told you about Jax, you would lose it. Even the first time you realised you liked her, you shut down. Right after New York."

My brain began to race. "What happened in New York?" I thought back to the patchy memories I'd regained, but our interactions had been *mostly* platonic, and there was no memory of me "shutting down."

"You don't remember?" she asked. I shook my head. "Greg said that might happen. Your mind protecting itself from recalling more painful memories." She took a beat before continuing. "You had a *moment* together, and it caused you to address your past."

"A moment?" I asked. She raised a brow suggestively, indicating the not-so-innocent nature of the moment. "Oh, that kind of moment."

"After New York, you weren't yourself." The dip in her voice refocused my attention away from hypothesising about the so-called moment with Jax. "You came home and were more closed up than ever, even with me. You threw yourself back into a relationship with Tom, and for years, you and Jax never spoke."

"How did we…" I trailed off, still not entirely comfortable vocalising our relationship. "When did we start talking again?"

"That's something you're going to have to ask Jax," she

replied. I accepted her response. How my relationship with Jax progressed from friends to more was not my sister's story to tell. "Have you spoken to her?"

"How could I?" My reply was weak, full of regret. "After how horrible I was, she must hate me."

"Quite the opposite, Elena." Her words caused my mind to drift back to earlier in the apartment.

"I found a picture of my wedding day."

Cat's face eased into a wistful smile, and it was obvious she was recalling it. The blissful look on her face made me envious at first, jealous that she could remember what was supposed to be the best day of my life, and I couldn't.

I was overwhelmed with a surge of raw emotion. "Was it a nice day?" My voice trembled, revealing how lost I felt as the tears fell with no end in sight.

"Yes, Elena." She reached for my hand. "It was beautiful. You were so beautiful." I could barely hold back the loud sobbing as she continued. "We packed up the cars and drove down the south coast. It was a sunny day in June, and you got married in Worthing town hall. It overlooks the ocean, and Jamie gave you away because you said he was the only man you could ever rely on." Tears flowed freely, and she wiped them away as I listened, captivated. "It wasn't fancy. We had a picnic on the beach and stayed there all day. That's how you wanted it. There were only ten guests, maybe, and we drank champagne until dusk. You and Jax danced on the beach as the sun set. You said it was the best day of your life."

"It's not fair. I should know this. Know them."

"They're right here, Elena. Waiting." My eyes found hers. "Your amazing family is waiting to share everything with you all over again."

I nodded, as the need to speak to Jax overpowered all other thoughts.

❖

Jax

Mum set down another cup of tea. My body was too weak from the weight of today to do anything more than sulk. My phone buzzed on the table as the caller ID revealed it was Elena. My mother must have witnessed my wide eyes staring at the phone because she pulled me from the shock.

"Answer the bloody thing," she barked as I darted the phone to my ear.

"Elena? Is everything okay?"

"Oh, hi. Yes, I'm fine," Elena hesitantly responded. "How are you?" she asked in an extremely formal tone.

"I'm good. Well, fine, yeah," I returned as awkwardly.

"And Jamie?"

"He's good. Asleep at Mum's." I couldn't control the awkwardness as I overexplained. "I'm at my mum's house too. Not that you needed to know that. Are you at home? I mean, at the apartment?"

"No, I'm at Caterina's house. It was a little too quiet at the apartment. All by myself." Her response gave my heart a hopeful beat. I didn't know how to respond, though. Did she mean she missed us? Or perhaps she just wanted to be around her sister? Silence engulfed the line until Elena spoke up again. "Are you still there?"

"Yes," I almost shouted and then chastised myself for being so uncool. My mother hung on to every word as if trying to decode what was being said on the other line. "I'm here."

"I was hoping, well, wondering, if we could talk." I began nodding excitedly without actually vocalising. "Maybe tomorrow? Today was just a lot. I'm still trying to wrap my head around it all. And I feel terrible…about how I reacted."

"You have nothing to feel terrible about." My calming voice appeared in an instant, surprising me, Elena, and my mother. "Your reactions are valid." She was silent, prompting me to continue. "I'm here to help with whatever you need, but if you decide you don't need me, that's okay too. What happens next will be at your own pace. Whenever you're ready."

"Thank you, Jax." Her soft voice told me she was smiling. That knowledge gave me enough hope to breathe a sigh of relief. "Will you come home tomorrow? Jamie too. Only if you think it would be okay."

"Yes." I cut her off eagerly. "We'll be there. Looking forward to it."

"Me too," she finished before hanging up, and I slumped back into the chair with some newfound ease.

The next day, I drove straight to the apartment after leaving Jamie at school, unable to focus on work without speaking to Elena first. With no idea what she wanted to speak to me about, I was completely powerless.

Emerging into my darkened home, I followed the glow of light coming from the living room. Elena was at her laptop but quickly rose when she saw me. She looked exhausted and in the same clothes as yesterday, which told me she likely spent the night on Cat's couch.

"Hi." She sounded hesitant and followed my gaze to the laptop. "I decided to work from home today." I nodded, standing awkwardly in the middle of the room, unsure of what to do next. "Do you want coffee or tea?"

"Sure. Coffee, please."

She moved toward the kitchen and filled a cup. I removed my coat but stayed stationary, afraid to get comfortable. My hands shook as Elena returned from the kitchen and handed the cup to me, her hand brushing mine. Her eyes met mine fleetingly, but the uncomfortable shift in her demeanour caused me to retract my hand. Though I tried to hide the heartache I felt at how uncomfortable my touch made her, Elena must have spotted it.

"Will you sit?" She offered an olive branch as she led us toward the more informal setting of the couch. I followed her lead, conscious not to push her outside the confines of comfort, keeping a safe distance between us. "Is Jamie at school?"

"Yes, I dropped him off before coming home. Here," I corrected as she mirrored my nervous nodding. Silence settled around us, but it felt deafening, I couldn't stand it any longer. "Elena, I just wanted to say how sorry I am. I never meant—"

"Please don't."

Those words caused my mind to panic. I thought the worst. Elena would never forgive me; the trust was broken forever.

But she surprised me by turning to face me, showing nothing but remorse. "I should be the one apologising." Her emerald eyes softened as they met mine, and I could tell how raw they were from crying. "Yesterday was…" She trailed off.

"A lot. I get it. I'm not upset or anything. It's like I said on the phone, you don't have to apologise for your reaction. And we can do this whatever way you want."

"Do what?"

"With Jamie," I said, but she still didn't seem clear. "He can stay at my mum's so you can have more time to process. We both can. Or if you'd rather not live here anymore then—"

"No. I want him to be here. I want to get to know him. He's my son." She seemed to be almost reminding herself of that fact. "He should be living at home."

"Okay," I said slowly, painfully aware that I was left out of the arrangement.

Elena must have read my mind as she spoke up again. "And you should be here." My eyes collided with hers. "This is your home too." I was unable to keep my smile at bay. "Jamie needs you."

I desperately wanted to ask if he was the only one who needed me but instead mustered a neutral response. "Okay."

"But we have to change the sleeping arrangements," Elena added lightly, as if without great thought as she sipped her brew. She must have realised her wording as a crimson blush spread over her cheeks as she corrected herself. "No, not like that!" She coughed on the coffee before clearing her voice. "I meant, you can have your bedroom back. I will take that smaller room." She nodded toward my sleeping quarters.

"No, that's okay. Really, I'm fine sleeping in the spare room."

"That's not fair. Jax, that bedroom doesn't even have a wardrobe."

I narrowed my eyes, curious as to how she knew that.

"Seriously, I insist."

"No, it's okay. You have the master bedroom."

"Well, let's take it in turns—"

"Elena, really, I'm fine in the smaller room." She tried to argue again, but I silenced her. "Look, I can't sleep in there," I said. She seemed taken aback as my eyes drifted to our old bedroom door. "I can't sleep in that bedroom alone."

"Okay," she replied as her body tensed, and I immediately regretted my outburst.

The two weeks she'd spent in the hospital, I couldn't sleep in our bed. It felt so huge and empty that I slept on the couch or at the hospital to avoid the loneliness. But of course, I couldn't reveal that to Elena. I was about to apologise for the outburst when she spoke up first.

"Jax?" I locked eyes with her. "Why did we get married?" I stared back at her, stunned. What a loaded question, one that seemed obvious. "I mean, we waited years. Cat said that we already lived together, and you had adopted Jamie, so I guess, I just don't know why we got married."

My reply didn't require much thinking. "Because you asked me."

"I did?"

I nodded before adding, "You asked me to marry you in the exact same spot where you said I saved your life."

She furrowed her brow. "Well, now you're going to have to tell me." Her eyes danced around my face as she leaned back, getting comfortable. "You saved my life?" Her incredulous question caused me to chuckle.

"Not literally, but in a way, maybe." I leaned back as well. "It was a regular day, like any other. I'd just finished a long shift and was on my way home in rush hour traffic. You know how the Tube can be?" She nodded with a knowing groan. "I'd just about squeezed onto the train, and at the next stop, the door opened, and there you were." The memory came flooding back, as if it was yesterday.

"Elena?" I stared in disbelief at the ghost from my past.

"Jax?" Her voice cracked as relief washed over her beautiful features. I scanned her face, taking in the red nose and eyes with tears continuing to drop as she sniffled. "What are you doing—"

She couldn't finish as the warning sound of the Tube getting ready to close its doors interrupted us. I had three seconds to make a decision, stay put and perhaps never see Elena again or take a literal leap of faith. The door began to close, but her eyes pleaded, and in that moment, I knew she needed me. That propelled my feet to step off the train just as the door slammed behind me. The wind swirled around us as the train took off, causing Elena's hair and mine to dance together. We stood staring at each other in a trance. It had been almost two years since New York, that fateful night in her hotel room that had resulted in me turning my back on her. Despite having zero contact with her, I still thought about her often.

"Are you okay?" I asked once the train had passed.

"No, not really." She sniffed back the tears. "I had a fight with my boyfriend and I..." Her words seemed caught in her throat as she started crying. Without a second thought, I pulled her toward me, and her arms wrapped around my body.

"It's okay." I tried to soothe, but it seemed as if she just needed someone to listen. "Do you want to talk about it?" I asked as we pulled apart, and she nodded.

"Now? Are you sure?" she asked. "Aren't you going home?"

"Not anymore," I replied. A small smile appeared on her face. Though I was near exhaustion, the thought of leaving her in this state felt inhumane. "As long as you don't mind the scrubs." I revealed them under my jacket, but she didn't seem fazed at all, shaking her head. "Do you want to get coffee?"

We walked from Victoria Station to a coffee shop and talked for hours. The tears were gone before we'd left the station, and I had her laughing before we made it to a shop. Elena spoke as if she had known me her entire life. We shared stories and caught up on the last two years. I cancelled a date to drink bad coffee in a poorly run coffee shop with her, and I would do it again. I walked her home that evening, and it was on her doorstep that she told me I was a lifesaver. Before leaving, we exchanged numbers, vowing to remain friends. Of course, that didn't last long.

"Victoria Station?" Elena narrowed her eyes. "I asked you to marry me at Victoria Station?" She frowned in almost disgust. "And you said yes?"

"Always the romantic, Elena," I teased as she smiled back at me, the air around us feeling lighter. "We might have been a little drunk too, but I said yes regardless." I found myself staring at my left hand, spinning the wedding band on my finger. "So I didn't really save your life, but Victoria Station is where we ran into each other again after years of no contact." I shrugged before adding, "I guess that station is kind of special."

"And then what happened? After the bad coffee?"

"We remained friends. Got more bad coffee." She smiled as I continued carefully. "But then, a couple of weeks later, you found out you were pregnant. Then everything changed." The beeper in my pocket started buzzing, and I reluctantly checked the ID.

"Work?"

"Yeah. I'm late." I sighed, but when I looked to Elena, she

looked just as disappointed. "I've got to go." We stood at the same time and faced each other for a moment.

"That's a shame. The story was just getting good."

"I can finish it later." I added hesitantly, "If you want."

"I'd really like that." She smiled before she started walking me out. "Are you working late tonight?" I nodded, but before I could respond, she beat me to it. "Well, I can pick up Jamie after school. I kind of missed him yesterday."

"Okay, sure," I said before I remembered one important fact. "Except, he doesn't know. I didn't tell him that you know about him yet."

"Oh." She thought for a moment, stalling at the front door. "Maybe that's okay, for now, at least. If you think it's okay?"

"Yeah, that's no problem." I put on my jacket, rambling some more. "Whatever you think. Besides, I think he gets a real kick out of fooling you."

"Really?" Her eyes lit up excitedly.

"Yeah, it's just a big game to him. He keeps suggesting ways to make the story more believable. He even wanted to hide the quilt on his bed."

"Why?"

A small pang hurt my chest. She must have seen it on my face, as that excitement in her eyes faded and was replaced with guilt. "The two of you made it a few months ago. Took you both weeks of sewing to finish it." Her eyes dropped sadly, and I tried to lighten the mood. "But I explained to him that you wouldn't remember that."

"I wish I did. I really do."

Before I could stop myself, I reached toward her arm to comfort her. On contact, her eyes met mine, and I knew it wasn't a step too far. "There will be new memories, Elena. You're here and healthy. That's all that matters." My breathing picked up as she stared into my eyes. I was unable to break the trance she had on me. In that moment, she looked like her old self again. It was only a glimmer, though, before the buzzing in my pocket started again, bringing us back to reality.

"You really have to go." Elena smiled before adding, "But I will see you tonight, when you get home."

I left the apartment with hope, the polar opposite of how I felt leaving yesterday. The rest of the day dragged with my mind entirely focused on six p.m., when I would leave work and come home to my family.

CHAPTER TWELVE

"Mummy, Mummy, Mummy." The faint cries pulled me from sleep as the door was pulled open and Jamie raced in.

"What's wrong, Jamie?"

I couldn't understand what had happened through his uncontrollable sobbing. I tried to lull him as I pulled him up onto the bed and into my side. The alarm clock revealed it was 2:30 a.m., but the tears kept coming, Jamie clutching my side. He cried about monsters and the "bad men" while I rocked him back and forth, whispering soothing words. After his sobbing eased, I looked up as Jax moved into my room. Taking a seat on the bed, she threw me a small, apologetic smile before looking down at Jamie, who had yet to register her presence.

"He just ran in. He must have gotten confused in the dark," I said in the dim light as Jax nodded and rubbed his back.

"Another nightmare, Jay?" she asked softly as he pulled away and looked up at me.

Although he had calmed down, his eyes were wide and glistening with tears as he stared at me for a long moment, and everything stopped. Jamie watched my face as if searching for something he was unable to find. The mother I was supposed to be but had no recollection of. Then a small glimpse of panic appeared on his features, and he turned to Jax as a new wave of crying began.

"I'm sorry, Mum. I forgot." He sobbed, falling into Jax's

arms. His cries had a physical reaction on me as I watched him clutch his mother desperately. "I forgot, Mum. I forgot."

"It's okay," she whispered in his ear. She looked almost as devastatingly broken as him, leaving me feeling wretched. She lifted him up, wrapping his legs around her waist as he cried into her shoulder. "I'll get him back to bed." She retreated from the room, closing the door behind her.

My heart was broken as I thought about Jamie in the darkness. For some time, I could still hear his crying after Jax had taken him back to bed. It physically hurt hearing and seeing him so upset. It was just a dream, and children were naturally frightened by nightmares, but there was something more. The look in his eyes and devastation when he realised that I wasn't myself, the mother he desperately sought comfort from. Every time I pictured the upset on his face, my chest tightened again, and guilt washed over me.

My automatic, deep-seated feelings for Jamie were there, with the bond I felt and an overwhelming need to protect and care for him. I had never thought of myself as maternal, but he must have changed that in the last six years. How did I not realise it sooner? Of course he was my son. Though the worrying thoughts repeated on my mind often, I made a promise to myself to leave them behind when I got out of bed this morning.

Today was Jamie's birthday, and I wasn't going to let my guilt ruin it. While I was still hazy on the details of everything I had missed, over the last several days, we had all found some sort of routine. Jax and I decided it would be best to continue as if I didn't know he was my son until after his birthday. Besides, telling Jamie today could ruin the party Jax had worked diligently to organise. She had been meticulous with party games, decorations, and food, and I offered to bake the cake. I couldn't help but wonder if her enthusiasm for throwing his party was a distraction for Jamie or herself.

The toll my amnesia had taken on them was evident, and now that I knew the truth, I just wanted to relieve some of that pressure. Create some normality, for Jamie's sake. However, Jax had continued to give me the freedom to choose how integrated I was in Jamie's life, with the ability to take a step back if it all became too much. Her consideration and understanding had been never ending. It was her strength that fuelled my drive to be engaged. I wanted to be here. I wanted to be completely present in Jamie's life.

"Elena, could you pass me the duct tape?" Cat asked, pulling me back into the present. She stood on tiptoes, hanging "Birthday Boy" signs. "If we were just doing birthday decorations, this wouldn't take so long." She huffed as I passed the tape.

"You can't have Halloween and birthday decorations at the same time," I said.

Jax came up behind me carrying a box of Halloween decorations. "It's not his fault he was born the day after Halloween. You'd think you'd be used to it by now. It's not like you haven't been at his last five birthdays."

Cat let out an incoherent reply while taping down the edges of the red birthday banner to the living room wall. Jax was busy collecting decorations for Halloween while I helped hang the replacement birthday decorations.

"So what did you get Jamie for his birthday, Jax?" Cat asked while smoothing down the banner with another layer of tape. "He's six now. That's a big age. Next will be college, and with your parenting skills, probably prison."

"Cat!" I said, placing the end of the cobwebs in the box Jax was holding and meeting her gaze. "And he's going to love his new bike. You assembled it this morning, right?"

Jax threw me a look as if to say, "Of course I did." I mouthed an apology for asking yet again. Hosting parties had always made me a little anxious, but by her playful response, it was clear Jax knew that about me already. It wasn't just the upcoming party that had my heart accelerating; the intensity of Jax's eyes had to take some sort of responsibility. All morning, we had been doing this dance: few words were exchanged, and we were communicating in a silent language. Though Jax had moments of cautiousness with me, for the most part, she was starting to allow herself to become playful again.

Jax disappeared into her room to store the box of Halloween decorations as I slowly drifted toward my sister.

"Are you sure you're feeling up to all of this?" she whispered once we were alone.

"Yes, I'm sure," I replied firmly, recalling the numerous occasions I'd reassured Jax this morning. "I can handle it even if it is a little raw."

"Are things okay?"

"They've been oddly okay." I began to fill her in on the last few days since finding out the truth. "Jax and I are talking every night, going over what I've missed. And Jamie has been great, his usual caring self, but I hate lying to him. I have a newfound understanding for what you've all been going through these last few weeks." She nodded along, giving me her full attention. "Last night was rough, though," I whispered to avoid Jax overhearing. "Jamie ran into my room and cried in my arms. He had a nightmare and forgot the sleeping arrangement."

"Oh no." She sighed sadly. "I'm sure he was so disappointed in himself for 'slipping up.'" She used air quotes.

"You should have seen his little face. Completely distraught. I felt so guilty."

"I know the feeling," she replied as we shared a concerned look. "Are you going to tell him?"

"Jax and I plan to sit him down after the party. I don't want to ruin his day."

"Of course." She nodded before something thoughtful fell over her features. "You're a good mother, Elena." The compliment stunned me, and I felt my eyes sting at the corners. I smiled rather than let myself become overwhelmed, and Cat changed the tone to something more daring. "And I know you don't quite remember, but you used to be a good wife too."

"Cat." I shook my head, embarrassed to feel a blush. "I

haven't thought much about *that*," I lied. In fact, I thought a lot about *that*.

Last week, before I even knew the truth, I'd had a dream about Jax, and not the kind of dream I wanted to think too much about, especially at work. And it wasn't the first racy dream I'd had about her. Ever since my head rush in the kitchen, when I was caught with my legs around Jax's waist, my subconscious kept reimagining the scene.

The first dream was slow. Her lips grazed mine as her smooth hands crept up my thighs, causing my breath to hitch, but we pulled away, resting our foreheads against each other. I didn't think much of the dream because it was just a kiss, barely a kiss, really. The second, third, and fourth dreams only got more imaginative, until eventually, her head was between my legs as I gripped the countertop and screamed her name.

"Elena?"

"Ya!" I jumped out of the memory as Cat stared at me with a coy look.

"What were you thinking about?" she asked. I shook my head frantically. "Must have been dirty." I batted her arm, embarrassed. "It's okay to crush on your wife, you know." She wandered off, hanging balloons off various pieces of furniture across the living room.

"I told you, I'm not really thinking about that. We're taking it slow, focusing on Jamie, and then..." I sighed with no end to the sentence.

"And then?"

"Has anyone ever told you how nosey you are?"

"Nick. At least once a day." She steered the conversation back on topic. "You blush when Jax compliments you. You two communicate in this secret language that no one else can understand, you light up when she walks into a room, and you obviously fantasise about her 24-7."

"No, I don't."

"Hey, Elena?" My head whipped around as Jax appeared at

her bedroom door. "Can you turn down the heat in here, it's so hot." She removed her shirt, revealing her black sports bra.

Her bare toned abs and tattooed arms glistened as she wiped a light layer of sweat from her forehead. I could swear time turned still as I fixated. She was gone before drool could form, but my eyes remained glued to where her bare torso had been.

"I can see your boner," Cat whispered as she brushed past me.

❖

Jax

The collective soundtrack of Disney flooded my eardrums for the second time in a row as I wiped up spilled juice from the hardwood floors. Children, laughing and playing, filled the small space of my living room as a handful of friends and family mingled around the outskirts, apprehensive to get too close to the hyper youngsters in the centre of the room.

"Here, I've got the mop." My mum came up behind me and began cleaning the mess. "Why don't you sort out the cake? The candles are in my bag." I thanked her en route to the kitchen where I found Nick texting on his phone, most likely working, and Cat refilling the snack bowls.

"It'll be over soon." She let out a long breath. No doubt I looked as tired as I felt. It didn't help that I had been working nonstop the last few days.

"As long as Jamie is having fun, that's all that matters." I stared out the opening in the kitchen wall and into the living room. "He deserves a bit of fun after everything he's been through."

Jamie giggled at something Elena had just said as she pointed at his brand-new red bicycle. I couldn't hear their interaction, but I found myself captivated just watching from afar. He was using wild hand motions, pointing to the wheels as Elena returned his excited expression. She glanced up, her eyes locking with mine and knocking the air from my lungs. She was the only person who had this effect on me, rendering me completely useless under her attention.

"My little sister totally has the hots for you," Cat quietly sang in my ear, ruining the moment.

"Fake news," I muttered breaking eye contact and continuing my search for candles in my mother's purse.

"I don't know, mate. She's been checking you out a *lot* today." Nick chimed in as he munched loudly on the bowl of popcorn his wife had just replaced, never tearing his eyes from his phone.

"See!" Cat tapped my arm. "If my husband can notice that but not when I get my hair cut, then it's pretty obvious."

"Oh, you got your hair cut," he said. Cat glared at him. "It's lovely." He added a small apologetic smile, one which I tried to return to ease the tension, but she just looked deflated.

"Could you just go and make sure Kate isn't making a mess?" Cat asked, disappointment lingering in her eyes.

Nick looked apologetically at her, but she waved him off, unable to hide her dismay, something I bet he was getting increasingly used to these days. Nick looked just as annoyed with himself. Spending more than half his time in another country would do that to a marriage. They'd been fighting more, bickering even today; it made me worried. If a strong couple like them were in trouble, what chance did Elena and I have?

I tried to lighten the mood once Nick had left the kitchen. "He's just—"

She stopped me. "Not around to notice." Her eyes fixated somewhere in the distance. I wanted to say more, but she shook herself, and her eyes softened, turning to me. "But the good news is, my darling sister likes you."

"Not this again." I moved away to remove Jamie's birthday cake from the fridge.

"Yes, this again. You should ask her out. And not on a family day out to the park. On an actual date. A real date."

"It's too soon. I can't rush her," I replied before she could make an argument which would probably have been very valid, but it was my turn to stop her. "You remember the first time, right? Back in New York."

"Yes, I remember. Vividly. She thought she was falling in love with you and stupidly ran back to Tom. But she's not that girl anymore." I shook my head, unsure. "Okay, maybe in the hospital she resembled her old non-committable, in the closet, seriously insecure, twenty-year-old self, but now she's becoming more like the real Elena again."

"I can't afford to have her shut me out. I almost lost her. I have to think about Jamie."

"I know but—"

The sound of Kate screaming snapped both of our heads toward the living room. Cat rolled her eyes at the scene. Another little boy and Kate were both on the ground screeching, blaming the other for a fall. Nick was already in the middle of the squabble, trying to defuse the tears.

There was nothing worse than a domino effect at a birthday party, when all the children joined forces for the ultimate tantrum. We needed a distraction. Birthday cake; the thought seemed to pop into Cat's mind at the same time. She lunged for the matches while I inserted the candles. We were the perfect children-crying-crisis-control-duo.

Moments later, the tears were forgotten, the lights were dimmed, and everyone eagerly waited for Jamie to blow out the candles.

We sang in unison as I knelt on the floor and held his cake in front of him. "Make a wish, Jay." I smiled as his eyes sparkled while looking at the *Frozen*-themed cake with delight.

He thought hard for a moment before his eyes drifted to the right, to Elena. With a small nod and huge grin on his face, he blew out the candles. As the kids cheered and the adults clapped, Jamie leaned forward and whispered into my ear.

"I wished for Mummy to come back."

As if I didn't already know.

Ever since his nightmare, when he ran into Elena's bedroom—correction, *our* bedroom—by mistake, I'd had major concerns about the effect this arrangement was having on him. He had been so upset with himself because he'd almost spoiled the "secret" we were playing on his mother. He'd fallen asleep crying in my arms. I conjured up the best smile I could before kissing him on the forehead and making my way into the kitchen to cut the cake.

"Okay, before cake, let's play a game." Cat distracted the kids while I cut a few slices.

Elena was helping until her phone started ringing. She quickly excused herself and moved into the hallway. I didn't want to eavesdrop, but she was within hearing distance of the kitchen.

"Hey." She smiled. Even though I couldn't see her, I knew her smiling voice, and just like that, dread came over me. "It's good to hear from you too. Thank you again for the flowers. They're beautiful." Silence filled her end of the line for a moment before her voice raised an octave in surprise. "Wait, you're here? In London?" I froze on the spot, unable to move. "Tonight? Well, I don't know if I can meet. I'm…" She stuttered for a moment as if thinking, and my breathing stopped. "I'm at my roommate's son's birthday party."

She hadn't told him. He still thought she couldn't remember who Jamie was. They'd spoken a few days ago on the phone. I'd overheard them, but she'd neglected to tell him that she knew about Jamie. However, even something as innocent as "my roommate's son's birthday party" would be like alarm bells to Tom. He was a self-centred prick, but it wouldn't take him long to piece together who Jamie and I were.

"That's right, Jamie's birthday," Elena said, solidifying my theory that he was paying attention. "Of course I want to catch up, but I just…I'm not sure what time the party will finish. Are you here tomorrow?" she asked, and I prayed to a god I didn't believe in that he was busy. My hand lost control of the knife, and although I didn't feel the cold slice into my own skin, I saw the blood. "Flying to LA, huh? Sounds great. Well, if the party is over early, I can come meet you." I felt paralysed and numb. "I'll definitely see you in two weeks when you're back." The room muted, and all I could hear were my own ragged breaths and heartbeat booming in my ears.

"Jax!" I didn't realise Elena had called me until she was right in front of me, pulling my hand toward the sink. "Are you okay?" All noise came crashing back with a deafening bang. "What the hell happened?" The children's music and playful screams flooded my senses. "Jax!"

"I'm fine," I mumbled as I looked down at the back of my hand and registered the gash in the skin. "The knife just… slipped."

"What the hell is going on with you?" Elena asked, but she didn't sound annoyed. It was concern. "You could have really hurt yourself. Now who's working too hard?" She tilted her head disapprovingly as she reached for the first aid kit.

She cleaned and bandaged the wound. She was no surgeon, but she knew her way around. The crease that formed on her forehead, coupled with the concentration pout, had me in a trance. It was times like this when all I wanted to do was kiss her. She worked softly and delicately with the wound and glanced up at me frequently. All concern vanished, but a playful teasing lingered. The need to kiss her became even more overpowering as she bit her lip in concentration. With a final bandage on the cut, she brought my hand to her lips.

"Good as new." Sealing it with a kiss to my knuckles, she smiled at me as if I was the only person in the world, her eyes dancing around my face. "Are you sure you're okay? You look like you just saw a ghost." She raised her brows again, and that was when I knew I had to get out of there before I blurted out everything she didn't know about Tom. I couldn't ruin Jamie's party.

"I'm good. I'm just going to go and check on..." I trailed off with no end to the sentence, exiting the kitchen as quickly as possible. I couldn't bear being so close to her with the ache in my chest.

"Good cake." Greg's voice was barely audible as he shovelled another mouthful into his mouth.

I was unaware of his presence and the party in general as I zoned in and out, standing in the corner with a beer in hand. I had been dodging Elena like the plague for the last couple of hours, too unsure of my emotions around her and far too preoccupied with the newfound information that Tom was in London. She might see him today for the first time since she was pregnant.

"You make it?"

"Do I look like I bake cakes?" I muttered over the kids running around my apartment. "Elena baked it." I found myself gazing across the room at Elena, who was wiping Kate's face and hands to remove the chocolate. I couldn't help but smile while watching her, even though she was completely oblivious, and then the sinking feeling set in when I thought about Tom.

"You know who else bakes?" Greg asked.

"Who?" I asked, already knowing the answer, but I could barely focus on him as my mind spiralled.

"Cassie." He sighed, taking another bite of the cake as I rolled my eyes. "She bakes cookies, muffins, and I'm sure cake too."

It wasn't that I was unhappy that Greg was dating. I was thrilled for him, and usually, I would gush with him about someone new. The beginning weeks were always the most exciting, and he was clearly in a great place, but selfishly, my mind was elsewhere, consumed by the thought that Elena and Tom would meet again. They already talked and flirted on the phone; the odds of that chemistry being reignited face-to-face made me feel nauseous. Elena could only remember the love she'd had for him. I was no one to her. Engrossed in worry that my time was running out caused my mind to race.

"Cassie cooks too," Greg said, pulling me back into the heat of the party. "She made this amazing mushroom and truffle oil—"

"Risotto," I finished as I watched Jamie playing with another boy from his school.

"Yeah, risotto." He beamed. "How'd you know?"

"Because you've told me this story like six times."

"Jeez, sorry for having a hot girlfriend who can cook." He took another mouthful of cake before following my line of vision to Elena. "I didn't know she baked."

I couldn't look away from her. "She never used to."

"Glad to see my secret brain programming worked during surgery. She will also be able to have better orgasms now." He winked. "Not that you'll ever find out." I elbowed him in the ribs as his laughter became even louder. "It's true. What you're selling, she ain't buying." Usually, his banter would be met with a witty retort, but not today. My emotions were on edge.

"Dick," I grumbled through gritted teeth.

"No, that's what your wife wants, remember?"

"Shut up, Greg," I yelled, and his laughter disappeared immediately.

"Mate, I'm sorry, I was just joking."

"Well, don't." I chugged the rest of my beer.

Greg placed the plate of half-eaten cake on the table and took a step closer, lowering his voice and keeping his eyes on mine. "What's wrong?"

I gripped the bottle so tightly, I thought it might shatter. "He's here. Tom wants to see her. Tonight."

Greg's hand landed on my shoulder, all he could offer without drawing attention from the kids. "Fuck. Are you okay?"

"What do you think?" My eyes began to sting, the emotion rising.

"Hey, maybe we should get some air." He rubbed my

shoulder, but I shook him off. His touch only caused a swirl of unrest in my stomach. "Okay. Well then, how 'bout I kick his ass?"

"With your chicken arms? I think I'd do more damage."

He cracked a smile before turning serious again. "She can't really meet him. Not after everything she knows."

"I can't exactly stop her."

"But you could talk to her."

"What's the point?" I whispered in defeat.

"Because she's your fucking wife." His harsh words hung in the air for a moment, stirring a mix of surprise and shock. The surprise quickly faded, and a more dominating emotion was left in its place: anger. He sheepishly dipped his head. "Look, it's just—"

"Who the hell do you think you are?" Fury was building in my chest. "Do you think this is easy for me? Watching her fall in love with someone else? I wanted to tell her from day one, and you *all* insisted this would be better. 'Let her remember on her own.'" I mocked his voice. "You remember that?" He audibly gulped as his eyes darted around the room, silently warning me to calm down.

"Jax—"

"I have my kid wishing his mother will remember who he is for his sixth birthday." I could feel the tears forming in my eyes. "Do you have any idea how fucked up that is? For weeks, I have just stood by and done nothing because of you." I glared at him through blurry eyes. "And now she's going to see him again, and I can't do a damn thing about it."

"Lower your voice before she hears you," my mum said, appearing from nowhere.

I glared at her and saw only empathy. "What does it matter now anyway?" I began, frustrated. "I've already lost her."

"Is everything okay?" Elena asked, causing everyone to jump slightly. Thankfully, I had my back to her, so she couldn't see how upset I was.

"Everything is great." Greg took charge. "Delicious cake, by the way. We're out of beer, so I think we will just make a trip to the store. Right, Jax?" He placed a hand on my back, ushering me toward the door. I didn't look back at Elena, though I could feel her eyes on me.

Greg and I walked around the park for an hour to give me some time to compose myself. Thankfully, the party was almost over, so my abrupt exit was barely noticed by the guests. Greg lent an ear, listening intently to my fears of losing Elena. His reassurance helped break through the cloud in my judgement, reminding me Elena wasn't gone. In fact, she was still very much in my life. Whether or not she would remain there and in what capacity was entirely up to me and my actions.

We stopped by the store on our way home, and I noticed Greg buying wine, beer, and other snacks, much more than would be needed for just me tonight. His motives only became abundantly clear when I arrived home to my apartment, expecting to find only Jamie and my mother but instead, I was welcomed by a full house.

"What's going on?" I asked Greg as he nudged me down the hallway.

I found Mum, Cat, and the children playing board games in the middle of the living room. Nick emerged from the kitchen at that moment and gave a huge grin on his way to the living room, where he handed glasses of wine to Mum and Cat. He took his seat on the floor as Greg whispered into my ear.

"We thought you could use some company tonight."

My heart felt like it had grown in size as my mum winked at me from the couch and sipped her wine. I turned to Greg in amazement at the effort he had made to make me feel less alone. Frantically texting while we were in the park and the excess food and drink began to make sense. Unbeknownst to me, he was arranging my pity party while Elena chose to meet Tom. Greg turned to me again before I could utter my appreciation.

"No matter what happens, Jax, we will be here for you." He

pulled me into a hug and whispered in my ear, "And you will always have Jamie."

I let out a shaky breath, touched by the gesture of those closest to me. On a Saturday night, most, if not all of them, certainly had plans but cancelled them to be here. Greg released me from the tight embrace and led me to where my family gathered, playing games on the floor. Someone was missing, of course, but I tried not to dwell on Elena as I focused on enjoying this time with my son.

The front door swinging open surprised us all, as it was followed by Cat shouting, "Pizza's here!" The children ran in first to the kitchen, and I followed slowly, stunned to see that the delivery person was none other than the very person I wanted to see most.

I felt my heart rate accelerate the moment her emerald eyes landed on mine. A small smile graced my lips. "Hi."

"Hi." Elena returned the smile, gravitating toward me and into the living room where it was quieter. The frenzy that came with fresh pizza pulled everyone into the kitchen.

"What are you doing here?"

"I live here, remember?" she joked before she removed her coat and placed it on the coatrack. Her hands slid into her jean pockets as she looked up at me and inched closer.

"I know, it's just..." I trailed off, still surprised she was standing in front of me. "I thought you had plans tonight."

She bit her lip for a moment. She'd never divulged the call she had earlier with Tom, especially to me, but her response hinted that she knew I overheard: "I'm exactly where I want to be." I couldn't stop the smile that spread across my face as she gestured toward the kitchen. "Shall we?"

Chapter Thirteen

"Last quarter's results were fantastic," I announced to my small team as I clicked to the next slide of my presentation, revealing customer feedback. "We are now halfway through November, and I have no doubt we will reach our end-of-year target. And with me being off for basically September and a part-timer in October, I am so impressed with the hustle." Chuck and Sam high-fived each other as Tansy danced in her chair excitedly.

"Does that mean we all get bonuses?" Chuck asked.

"Do we get an office like yours?" Sam said before Tansy added, "How 'bout a company car?"

"How about lunch is on me?" My simple gesture was met by a sea of cheers in the small work space.

The loud vibrations from my phone on the table pulled my attention away from them, and I excused myself to take the call in my office. "Hello?"

"Hello, this is Morgan Ellis calling for Principal Gibson at Winton Primary School. Is this Elena Ricci?"

"Yes. Is something wrong?" I asked as the team watched me through the opening in my office door.

"There has been an incident with Jamie, and we can't seem to get a hold of Keelin Jax."

"She's in surgeries all day. Is Jamie okay? Is he hurt?"

"Jamie was involved in a fight with another pupil. Winton has a zero tolerance to violence policy, so he is suspended effective immediately. We need someone to come down to the school and collect him."

"Of course, I'll be right there." I grabbed my laptop bag, shoving whatever was scattered across my desk into it before I spoke to the team. "Jamie was in a fight."

"What? That doesn't sound like him." Tansy stood in shock, watching me helplessly.

"I have to go." I left no room for discussion despite my assistant looking hesitant. "Tansy, redirect all calls to my mobile phone." I sighed as I sent a text to Jax.

Call me, its urgent.

"What about your meeting with Alan Bishop?" Tansy called as I was about to dash out of our office.

"Reschedule for tomorrow, make something up," I replied over my shoulder as I rushed down the hallway toward the elevator.

I didn't hesitate to cancel despite me and Tansy preparing for it all week. This was more important. Jamie's school wasn't far from work, and I arrived not long after taking the call, a little short of breath.

"Hi, I'm Elena Ricci, here to collect Jamie Jax." I spoke to the younger man at reception, the same person I assumed had called earlier.

"Jamie *Jax*?" He returned, clear confusion in his voice. "Don't you mean Jamie Ricci?"

I rolled my eyes at my own forgetfulness. "Yes, Jamie Ricci." I clarified as the man stared, clearly sceptical. Perhaps surveying if I was an imposter since I was unable to remember my own son's name. "Sorry, it's been a long day," I remarked but regretted that excuse instantly, considering the clock above his head revealed it was barely eleven a.m.

He went back to shuffling paper on his desk as I strummed my nails anxiously on the mahogany desk. Most children were in class, so the hallways seemed derelict, hauntingly silent, though it made finding Jamie much easier. After spotting the bloody cloth, I raced toward him. Kneeling to his eye level, I tried to comfort the worry etched on his features.

"Are you okay? What happened?" I pulled back the damp cloth, revealing a cut to his lip which was oozing blood. He tried to speak, but it only caused more snuffling. "It's okay. I'm here." His eyes were full to the brim, and his cheeks were puffy from crying.

"Ms Ricci?" I turned to be met by a tall, broad, older woman who stood at a door behind me. "Join me in my office."

Her voice was stern and echoed, reminding me of the horrible nuns who used to teach in St Catherine's Boarding House. Past memories rushed to the surface. Facing Jamie's intimidating headmistress coupled with being in a school setting again was an unfortunate combination which made suppressing those memories near impossible. My breathing turned uneasy, and a cold sweat broke out along my neck.

Her fiery glaring eyes bored into my soul and caused me to shift back toward Jamie, and when I did, it was clear that he was just as frightened.

"You wait here, Jay." I patted his knee as I tried to conjure my bravest voice.

"I don't believe we have officially met." The demanding voice vibrated in the small and immaculate office once I'd closed the door behind me. The dated magnolia decor brought me back to boarding school again, an unnerving and debilitating feeling. The large crucifix positioned behind her head wasn't helping either.

"I am Principal Gibson." She informed rather than introduced as she sat behind the large desk. "Usually, it's not necessary for me to meet Primary Two parents, but here we are." Her brow peaked as she studied my standing, frozen figure. "At this school, where I am the headmaster and leader of these children, we do not tolerate bad behaviour. Especially the kind of behaviour I witnessed today."

"I'm just as shocked as you are, Principal Gib—"

"I am outraged that Jamie struck another six-year-old student, and I am holding you personally responsible." She pursed her lips, somehow looking down at me even though she was seated.

Her tone transported me yet again, and I found myself dipping my head as Jamie had done moments ago. If the daily torment wasn't enough, I remembered the other girls who used to pick on me. They'd been almost as bad as the nuns. Every day at lunch time, the girls would tease my broken English, my darker skin, my hair or freckles or backpack, anything at all. Then the teasing turned violent, and I finally stood up for myself. The months of bruises on my ribcage, arms, and legs meant nothing to the nuns because I had made the mistake of leaving a visible mark on my bully's face: a bloody nose.

The drawbacks of boarding school were simple, there was no escape, no respite. I had to face the wrath of the nuns and was put in solitary confinement between classes for weeks. For my own protection, they claimed. I remembered telling my parents, but to no surprise, they'd sided with the nuns. That was how things were handled in my parents' household. Why listen to the child when they could take the word of an adult they hardly knew?

I had tuned out the principal's voice as she criticised Jax and my parenting skills. Until I reminded myself that I was not that little girl anymore, dipping my head from the accusing tone of the principal. I didn't have to be like my parents and take the teacher's word. I trusted that Jamie knew better than violence. I might not have remembered everything about him, but I trusted his character and the person who'd raised him.

"Excuse me?" I said, cutting her off. She looked taken aback for a second, providing me with the ammo I needed to turn this crusade around. "From where I am standing, Principal Gibson, Jamie was physically assaulted under your supervision, and I am holding *you* personally responsible."

She looked flabbergasted, and I must say, it felt good, avenging myself on all the cruel teachers who'd ever wrongly accused me.

"I expect an explanation." I pursed my lips back at her.

"From the information I received"—she shifted papers on her desk—"it was Jamie who threw the first punch at another student in his class." Her tone was back to accusing.

It was like a trigger, causing an overwhelming need to defend Jamie. "He would never touch anyone. Why exactly did this fight start?"

"Well, I don't know the exact details. But the bottom line—"

"What do you mean, you don't know? You don't know the context of the assault that took place on your property? He's six!" I argued before moving toward the door to call for backup. "Jamie, come inside."

The old bat tried to insist that this conversation remain private. I dismissed her and waited until Jamie was inside the office.

"Did you hit the other student first?" I asked. I didn't even look at him, staring at the principal, waiting to see that righteous smile wiped from her face when she heard the truth.

"Yes." He frowned, still holding the cloth to his face as my head whipped toward him.

I knelt in shock. "Jamie, why?"

"You see. He lacks discipline. The child is clearly prone to violent outbursts."

"Shut up and let him speak." My voice seemed to shock her, and she stared with rage in her eyes, but I turned back to Jamie, ignoring her. "You know you are never to lay a hand on anyone," I said softly as he nodded, but his face was still scrunched angrily. "Why would you hit another pupil?" He looked at the principal with a glimpse of fear, prompting me to take his hand. "You can tell me."

With a big breath, he blurted, "Michael Peters said my mummy was a dyke, and she was gonna burn in hell." His hands tightened into little fists. "So I hit him." I couldn't hide the shock on my face as the harsh words hung heavily in the air. I nodded slowly before kissing him on the forehead, rising to my feet again.

"Please sit outside for two minutes, and we will go home."

When the door was closed again, I could feel the rage growing from the pit of my belly as my eyes turned on the principal, who looked a lot smaller behind her desk. "I was not aware of any conversations between Jamie and the other student—"

"How dare you? How dare you sit there and humiliate me and Jamie like that?" Her mouth bobbed open and closed, but she failed to verbalise her thoughts. "They are six-year-olds. Where the fuck do they learn words like 'dyke'? What kind of a circus school are you running here? And where is the other pupil from his class? Is he suspended too?"

"Ms Ricci," she calmly stuttered. "There appears to have been a mistake, a misunderstanding."

"You're damn right! I expect this suspension to be lifted immediately, or I will be writing a formal complaint to the education board for harassment and bullying of a student under your care."

"There will be no need for a complaint. This has all been a mix-up." She began to panic, wild eyes scattering around the room too ashamed to meet me. "My sincerest apologies for—"

"Keep your apologies for Sunday confession. I assume the *other* student's parents will be on their way to pick up their child for verbally and physically assaulting Jamie."

"I will be calling the other pupil's parents right away. This incident will be expunged from your son's record. I assure you, this is an inclusive school, tolerant of all family types—"

"How about you add the job of changing the word 'tolerant' to 'accepting' to your long list of things you have to do this afternoon. Right after you apologise to the young man sitting outside your office?"

She jumped from her plush seat, brushing past me, unable to meet my eyes.

❖

"That was so cool," Jamie said before wincing as the smiling irritated the cut on his lip. I too, found myself walking on a cloud as we exited the school grounds into the busy streets. "Mum is afraid of Principal Gibson. She never talked to her like that."

"Bitch needed to be put in her place," I said before checking myself. "And don't repeat that bad word to anyone." He nodded frantically.

"Are we going home?" he asked, jumping over a puddle as we walked toward the underground station.

"Do you want to go home?" He thought for a moment before shaking his head. "How about we go see a movie?" He jumped up and down with excitement. "Right after we get you a Happy Meal for being a big brave boy."

"You're the best, Elena!" He wrapped his arms around my waist and hugged me tight for a beat.

I felt a pang in my stomach, as I had every single time Jamie called me Elena. It didn't feel right since I'd learned the truth, particularly as Jax explained he would have always called me Mummy before the accident. Jax and I had agreed to tell Jamie, but we'd never put a timeframe on when. Jax was working nonstop lately, and we had barely spoken about it again. We were supposed to tell him after his birthday, but distractions cropped up, and days had now passed. I couldn't continue to lie to him.

Once seated in the food court, Jamie began munching on his fries, but I found my appetite was on hold until I got the truth off my chest.

"Jamie?" I asked hesitantly and played with the straw I hadn't inserted into the cup yet.

"Yeah?"

"You know the way…"

He stared at me, offering partial attention but focusing primarily on his chicken nuggets. "Yeah?" he repeated.

I inhaled, readying myself. "You know how… You remember I had my accident?" He nodded as his mouth was full. "Okay. And that I wasn't well afterward."

"You were in the hospital."

"Well, remember how we talked about me not remembering a lot of things."

"Yeah?" he replied, half listening as he began to shovel more fries into his mouth. Just like Jax when she was hungry. I could be saying anything and would have to repeat myself at least twice. "Yeah?" he repeated for the fourth time impatiently.

I must have zoned out thinking about Jax. "Well, I still can't remember a lot of things," I started again, looking at the straw, which I had bent and twisted to the point where it was no longer functional. "And so Jax, your mum, told me some things." He sipped on his juice, and I could take it no longer. "I know I'm your mummy too."

His eyes jumped to mine as he placed the cup of juice back on the table. "You know?" he asked cautiously, as if it was a trick.

"I know," I whispered as a silence filled the space, and he looked sadly at his food.

"Was it me?" he asked as I furrowed my brow in confusion. "Did I ruin the secret?"

"No, of course not. You didn't ruin anything." His face spread into a small grin, prompting me to continue my praise. "You kept it a secret. You were the best at hiding it. Very sneaky."

He giggled to himself as if he'd won the game. "It was hard."

"Really?" I returned the playful smile.

"Yeah! I almost called you Mummy like a hundred or maybe a million times."

"That many times, huh?" I gasped as he nodded, returning to eating his fries again.

"Yeah. Do you remember me?"

My heart ached as I shook my head slowly. "No. I'm sorry, Jamie. The memories aren't back yet." He nodded a little sadly. "But I want to get to know you again. I want to know everything. Will you help me?"

"Now?" I nodded before his brow creased in confusion. "But that will take all day. What about the cinema?" I stifled a grin at his list of priorities and opted to play along with his train of thought.

"That's right. Okay, how about you tell me later? After the movie."

"Okay, good. I was worried for a minute there." He exhaled in relief that I hadn't disturbed his afternoon plans. "What are we going to see at the cinema?"

I found myself smiling, pleased at how easy that turned out to be. Why was it that a six-year-old was so easily adaptable, but I had a minor meltdown? "Whatever you want. But you're okay?" He nodded. "You can also call me Mummy again too, if you'd like."

"Okay. Mummy." He smiled, and I returned the gesture and began eating my food, feeling significantly lighter with that off my chest.

❖

Jax

I paced the kitchen back and forth as I had done for the best part of an hour. My sneakers squeaked on the kitchen floor, keeping the apartment from deafening silence. I called Elena again, but her phone was still switched off. I had just hung up with Cat for the second time; she'd heard nothing. Tansy said Elena left before lunch to go to Jamie's school, but that was hours ago. It was dark outside, and they still weren't home.

I had been cleaning up after surgery when I listened to the voice mail from Jamie's school saying he'd been in a fight. I called them to apologise for running late only to be informed that Jamie had already left school earlier that day.

The key in the door pulled me from my pacing as Elena and Jamie walked in, giggling like two children. "Hey!" Elena smiled at me before putting Jamie's bag on the floor and removing his coat.

"Mum, you missed it. We went to the cinema to see—"

"Jamie, please go to your room right now. I'll be in there in a minute to speak with you." I used what Elena used to call my "bad cop" tone.

"But, Mum—"

"Now, Jamie," I yelled, louder than I meant to, and his bag of popcorn dropped as he ran into his room.

"Was that really necessary?" Elena huffed picking up the popcorn and walking into the kitchen.

"I have been calling you all afternoon. Where the hell have you been?" I demanded as I followed her.

"The cinema," she replied, shaking the bag dramatically. "I have the movie stubs if you don't believe me. I didn't get your calls because it's the strangest thing, but at the cinema, you turn off your phone. They even have that advert where it's like *please turn off*—"

"This isn't a joke, Elena. You don't just disappear with him, leaving me with no idea where he is. I get a voice mail from the school that he's been in a fight, and you reward him with a day out to the cinema?" I slammed my hands on the counter as Elena took a step back.

"Your son stood up to some snotty-nosed brat—"

"So we teach him it's okay to throw a punch when he doesn't agree? What excellent parenting skills!" I'd already registered my step too far when Elena's eyes turned fiery.

"And where the hell were you, Jax? Huh? Working. Big surprise, I didn't realise you had another child, the ER."

"Don't talk about stuff you know nothing about," I shouted as I felt a familiar sense of déjà vu. This wasn't the first time we'd fought about my intense work schedule. It was the centre of most of our arguments as a married couple. I just didn't expect this Elena to notice as much.

"You're one to talk, Jax. You know nothing about what happened to him today," she said just as loudly, and I gritted my teeth, ready to argue again, but she got in quicker than I did.

"Did you even stop to think why Jamie was in a fight? No, you didn't. Jamie stood up for *you* today." Her words shocked me into silence. "Both of us." She sighed as if she had just realised something more. "Some kid was teasing him about his mum being a dyke and that she was going to burn in hell."

I was taken aback like after a punch to the gut. I'd been called worse things than that, but nothing hurt as much as hearing someone bullying my son because of who I was. Hearing what happened to Jamie caused my shoulders to sink and guilt to wash over me.

"Violence is not the answer, and he knows that, but he stood up for himself. He stood up for *me* too. God, he's only six years old, and he's still braver than me." Tears filled her eyes and her voice cracked, but Elena seemed too angry at me to reveal her vulnerability. "You're in the wrong here, Jax, not him."

"Elena—"

She stormed out of the kitchen, leaving me alone with a mountain of guilt.

After I apologised to Jamie, he informed me that Elena knew she was his mummy again. I was surprised at first, but it was always going to be Elena's decision when she told him. And by the sound of it, they had a great day of bonding, which only made me feel guiltier. Jamie was happy he had his mummy back, even if she wasn't completely herself again. After hugging it out, I made the long walk to Elena's bedroom with my head hung in shame.

I knocked lightly on the door, but she didn't respond. After another louder knock, I was still met with silence. I leaned my forehead against the door and began my apology, knowing that she was too angry to face me.

"I'm sorry, Elena," I started as I stared at the bedroom door and tried to listen to any sounds from behind it. "Please talk to me. I overreacted. I was worried about him…and you when I couldn't get through to your phone. I should never have said those hurtful things. I'm grateful you were there and picked him up." I ran my hand through my hair, hoping she was listening, and I wasn't just talking to a door. "He told me you called the principal out on her bullshit, which is really something because she's bloody terrifying."

The door opened, and Elena stood facing me with her arms crossed.

"I'm sorry," I repeated as her face began to soften. But after years of marriage, I knew I wasn't forgiven just yet. "You were right, I should never have flown off the handle without hearing the full story." I sighed, taking a step closer.

Being at the door frame of our bedroom again stirred emotions I wasn't expecting. The room was barer than it used to be, but it still felt like *us*.

"I'm sorry." I tilted my head to the side and gave her my best puppy dog eyes.

She rarely stayed mad for very long when I brought out this move. A small smile tugged at the corners of her lips, and I knew she felt *something* for me. More than what could be pawned off as platonic. Daringly, I took a closer step, causing a grin to erupt on her face.

"Say you forgive me." She shook her head playfully and applied pressure to my shoulders, keeping me at a safe distance. "You're not gonna really stay mad at me, are you?" Her touch did nothing to slow me as I kept inching closer, causing her to walk backward, trying desperately to hold on to her icy façade, which was quickly melting. "I'm not leaving until you—"

Her back collided lightly with the wardrobe as my hands naturally found her hips, steadying her. My breathing hitched. Her eyes turned darker for a moment as they looked at my parted lips. The arms keeping me at bay relaxed a little, allowing me into her personal space as she bit her bottom lip. I could never resist it when she bit her lip. Her eyes invited me in, and I moved closer until we were inches apart, her hands intertwining around my neck, causing goose bumps on my arms. I could feel her breath on my lips pulling me closer until there was barely a gap. Her sharp inhale told me she wanted this as much as I did.

A loud ringing pulled me out of this trance. Our heads turned in the direction of the phone on the edge of the bed that flashed *his* name. For a few seconds, neither of us moved, breathed, or probably even thought. We just stared at the phone.

She broke first. Her arms dropped from around my neck, and she brushed past me, grabbing the phone and swiping to answer. "Hello."

I left to give her some privacy, though she caught my attention before I went out of sight.

"Jax?" She held her hand over the receiver as I turned from outside our bedroom door. "I forgive you." She smiled, and my heart swelled a touch before she returned to the call. Then she moved to close the door, and my heart shrank back down to size.

CHAPTER FOURTEEN

The phone ringing in my pocket startled me as I left Baker Contracts on my way to meet Cat. Large raindrops beat down as I attempted to open my umbrella while answering the call.

"Yeah?" I threw the phone to my ear.

"Elena?" Mama said. "Are you all right? Is it raining?"

"Hi, Mama. I can't really talk right now." I tried to brush her off as I hurried down the street, dodging puddles, already late. "Can I call you back later?"

"I've sent you a few links for properties in London. Affordable too and we will help with the deposit. Do you want a three- or four-bedroom house?"

"Mama, I'm not buying a house," I replied sharply. "And I said I was only looking for something temporary until I figured things out."

The moment I told Mama about my confused feelings for Jax, she encouraged me to take some space. After a long discussion with her last night, we agreed I should move out for a few weeks to clear my head. Something which I reinforced to her would be temporary. Honestly, I'd barely thought about moving out since our call, but from her tone, it was clear Mama had thought of nothing else.

"What's to figure out?" she asked, a little agitated. "You're seeing Tom tomorrow, aren't you? I know he's dying to get you back."

Tom was travelling to London tomorrow for the weekend, and we had made arrangements to meet weeks ago.

"It's more complicated, Mama."

"But he's Jamie's father." I found myself stumble as I tried to conjure an excuse.

"I know but—"

"Surely you would want to reconnect them. Do you want Jamie to grow up without a father?" I gulped, unsure as that disheartening thought played on my mind. "Do you want Tom to never know his son? Could you really live with yourself?"

"Tom broke up with me when I was pregnant," I tried to argue.

"Is that what Jax told you?"

"No, Caterina told me that."

"She never really liked him though, did she?" That was true. Would Cat have embellished the truth? "Even if he did, he was young. Everybody makes mistakes. He wants to be involved now, doesn't that count for something?"

"It does count." I found myself agreeing in a small voice. "And that's why I'm still seeing him this weekend. Maybe he has changed."

"I'm sure he has, bella." Her voice turned almost elated. "And you can finally tell Tom you know about Jamie. You can both work out some kind of routine." I sighed as she attempted to sway me.

"I don't know about that, Mama. I haven't spoken to Jax about it yet."

"She's not his mother. You're his biological mother."

I found myself wanting to argue, but the more she pushed, the more I found myself bending to her will. Like I had done all my life. "I know, Mama. It's just hard. I don't want to hurt her."

"But you're only going to hurt Jamie in the long run. Growing up without a father."

Plenty of children grew up without a father, but did I want that for Jamie? The guilt of keeping him apart from his father coupled with my lingering feelings for Tom should be explored. At least, that was what I was telling myself. Though I knew for a fact that not everyone would accept it.

"I have to go, Mama. I'm late for a meeting," I lied as I waved at Cat through the glass window of the café.

"Okay, but please think about what I said. You don't want to have to live with disappointing your family." Her tone darkened. "*Ciao*, bella."

The thought of disappointing my parents caused my hands to tremble, though I blamed it on the cold weather. However, the temperature wouldn't explain why the blood also drained from my face, and the overwhelming need to do whatever Mama wanted consumed me.

"I'm sorry I'm late." I forced an upbeat tone as I neared Cat. "My meeting ran on, and I have to be back soon before another meeting starts," I said as I removed my coat and scarf, throwing my drenched umbrella somewhere on the ground beside our table.

"No need to apologise." Cat smiled as she took a sip of her latte. "You're always late." I faked a gasp of surprise, which only seemed to goad her, and I already felt my mood lighten. "Even when you've lost your mind, you still remember to be late. Which is why, as the delightful big sister I am, I took the liberty of ordering for you, knowing that you will have scheduled a meeting for directly after lunch." She beamed at me as a chicken wrap and salad was placed in front of both of us.

"Thanks, Cat." I smiled before starting to eat slowly, the thought of Mama's disappointment having had a lasting effect on my appetite. "Well, we meet every other Thursday at this very spot. I'm surprised the staff don't know our orders by now."

"They do but politely pretend they don't. It's the ultimate British politeness that I love about London."

"Still trying to talk Nick out of moving to Paris?" I tilted my head as she rolled her eyes. Nick had been travelling a lot to his law firm's sister company in Paris, a company they wanted him to manage, but he couldn't do that unless he moved, something

Caterina was not happy about. "Is it better that he continues to travel every other week?" I asked, already knowing the answer.

"No, he works late when he's here, and then he's gone the other half of the week." She frowned as she twisted her wedding band and stared at it bitterly. "When he's here, we argue, and then he stays away longer because he doesn't want to come back."

"Did he say that?"

"No." She huffed. "But it feels that way." I nodded, trying to understand how difficult it must have been raising two children alone. "I hate that he's missing things. Things with the girls that he can never get back. Like Abbey's dance recital or Kate's blue belt in taekwondo. You remember what it was like when Dad used to travel so much. He would come home for a few weeks and not even know what school year we were in." I nodded as my mind drifted back. "I don't want my girls to know what that's like."

That thought ignited my feelings of guilt when it came to Jamie's life. It brought back exactly what Mama had said. Perhaps she was right: Tom deserved a place in Jamie's life. I remembered the loneliness of barely seeing my father. I couldn't imagine what it must feel like to not have a father at all.

"I just wish he would fight for us a little more." She sat up straight and let out a long exhale. "Enough about my sad marriage. I want to know about you. It's been a couple of weeks since we last spoke." She cleared her throat, and her features seemed to harden as if I was about to be scolded. "How's things?"

"Fine."

"Just fine?" The tone was neutral but with purpose, conjuring a tension.

"Yeah, it's fine. Nothing new to report." I focused on my plate and changed the topic. "How's work going? Did you sign that new author you wanted?"

"Don't change the subject," she snapped. "Did something happen?"

"No." I pushed my plate away, my appetite disappearing.

"What's going on with you, Elena?" She squinted, studying me.

"Nothing. Why are you asking so many questions?"

"Because you're not answering any of them." She cocked her head.

"Let's be real, Cat. Why don't you just ask whatever it is you really want to know? Rather than tiptoeing around me all the time."

Her nostrils flared as she let out a frustrated breath. I didn't expect the conversation to take a turn like this, but if I was being honest, an unspoken tension had been brewing for weeks. Cat had become more invasive than usual. She must have known Tom was visiting this weekend. Why else would she be digging? Mama must have overshared.

"Fine," she said. "Why didn't you tell me you're talking to Tom again?"

And there it was. "Why ask when you already know?"

"Is that why you're looking for a new apartment?" Her accusatory question threw me and caused a swirl of unease in my stomach. I looked at my half-eaten plate, trying to piece together an excuse. I'd never wanted her to find out through someone else, especially our mother.

"I was just looking."

"Right. Where is it? The apartment you're *just looking at*." Her frosty expression told me an argument was brewing.

"There's a couple, but they're a little bit farther out of town," I said as I scrolled through my phone, not wanting to look at her. "It's hard to afford rent by yourself."

"Where is it?"

"North London, but still close enough that—"

"Where?"

"Luton."

"Luton!" The sound of her cutlery chiming off the plate pulled my gaze to her mask of horror. "That's over an hour away. It's basically Northampton."

"Don't be dramatic. It's still technically London, just more northern."

I told myself her response was an overreaction, even though deep down, the distance didn't feel right to me either. I understood why my sister was upset, but I wasn't planning on leaving for good. But, like Mama said, I couldn't live with Jax any longer *and* explore things with Tom. How was I supposed to know what I really wanted when I was forcing myself into a mould that didn't quite fit anymore? I wasn't the same person I had been before the accident. What if there was something still there with Tom? These were the questions I needed to uncover, and I couldn't do that living with Jax. It filled me with dread thinking about being that far from them, but that was exactly why I had to go.

"What about work?"

"It's not that much farther than I already travel, and they said I can work from home a few days a week."

"What about Jamie? Are you really going to take him away from Jax?"

"I haven't figured it all out just yet."

"Why now? Why so far?"

"It's not that far," I tried to argue. "Look, Luton is cheaper, quieter and—"

"Closer to Tom," she deadpanned. "You're actually serious?"

I should have been able to face my own sister, who I had always shared everything with, but I couldn't even begin to explain the tornado of emotions swirling inside. She wouldn't understand. She wasn't broken like I was. As I drifted closer to Jax, the feeling of guilt and self-loathing grew, a reminder that my feelings were wrong. Why else would I have felt that shame for wanting to kiss Jax unless it was wrong? Everything would be easier if I was with Tom. I could hold his hand walking down the street without feeling under scrutiny. My son wouldn't be bullied if I was *normal*. It was clearly what my parents wanted.

Everyone would be better off, even Jax. She could find someone else who was actually brave enough to love her back.

"It's complicated." I knew it was weak, but I had to at least try to be *normal*, even if it killed me. The pathetic response only caused more tension. "I just can't stay there anymore."

"Well, neither can Jax. She couldn't afford that place by herself."

"She can get another roommate."

"You're not just a roommate!" Cat's eyes were fiery. "That's your wife." My chest tightened, but I breathed through it, pushing down those feelings. "Don't you get that? Can't you see you're making a mistake?"

"You're the only one who thinks that. Mama actually thinks—"

"Oh, wake up, Elena!" The volume of her voice shocked me. I checked around to make sure we weren't drawing too much attention, but there were a handful of spectators nearby. "Don't you see what she's doing? Our spiteful mama. That woman has got her claws firmly into you, her precious bella."

"What's that supposed to mean?"

"Oh my God, you literally can't see what she's doing. She's pushing you toward him and away from your family." There were tears in her eyes. Cat's reaction caused my chest to ache, and deep down, I knew my mother was manipulating me like she always had, but I couldn't stand disappointing them. Cat's frustration was written across her face as she stared at me, enraged, as if she had no idea who I was. It hurt to see. "Other than our vindictive mother, who else knows about the move? Does Jax even know?" I avoided her gaze, though it only seemed to fuel her rage. "Don't look away, enlighten me. Let me guess, the douchebag from up north is thrilled. He's talked you into this, hasn't he?"

"This is exactly why I don't talk to you about Tom."

"Because I'd tell you what a fucking idiot you're being, Elena."

"I don't have to listen to this." I rifled through my bag, snatching some notes.

Before I could put them on the table and walk out, she stood. "No, you know what? Keep your money. You'll need it in Luton," she spat as she handed the waiter a couple of bills before exiting the café.

The rest of the day, I thought of nothing else. I knew Cat would never be on board with me meeting Tom again. It was precisely why I had kept her in the dark. I foolishly thought that if I could see Tom again without the pressure of anyone knowing, I could see how I felt. Maybe he had changed; perhaps he regretted how we left things. Wasn't it worth at least exploring our relationship? For Jamie's sake if nothing else. Then if I discovered I didn't have those feelings for Tom anymore, I could finally put it to rest and move on.

Later, I found myself on the tube on the way home from work as I replayed my argument with Cat. It repeated like a broken record until I felt my eyes start to close over, exhausted from the day.

Craning my head to the left and rolling it around to the right again allowed my muscles to contract, offering some respite from the long day at work. Dealing with invoicing, data analytics, and general incompetence left me feeling ten years older. After kicking off my heels, I reached around to unzip my fitted dress, but the clasp was caught. With a groan, I tried reaching again with the other hand but failed miserably.

"Need a hand?" A voice behind me gave me a startle. "Here, let me."

Their hot breath on my shoulder caused me to relax, and I felt the zip slide effortlessly down my back, halting at the base of my spine. Feeling free of the tight fabric, I let out a long, exasperated sigh as I felt warm, soft hands caress my hips and waist. The same hands roamed the length of my back, feeling every curve on their journey. The softness in his touch evoked a low moan as my head eased back slightly, resting on his chest.

"You're so tense," Tom whispered in my ear as he massaged my shoulders.

His working hands resulted in the perfect combination of pressure, comfort, and ease, rousing a heat in my core as I relaxed onto his front. My eyes closed, and I felt myself enjoy the sensual sensation. A soft kiss to my neck only caused my breathing to accelerate. The hands continued to work on my shoulders, drawing another low moan from me before he removed the capped sleeves. The dress breezed down my arms and puddled around my feet as a trail of kisses laced my neck.

"You smell so good," he whispered as his hands dragged up and down my sides, causing a fever across my skin.

My bra was removed in record time while hands travelled south and teased along the waistband of my underwear. I became impatient, my ragged breaths filling the silence. Sensing my arousal, the same hand which had contributed to my frustration plunged underneath my underwear and between my legs. The circular motion was agonisingly slow at first as I rocked my hips into the crotch behind me.

"You feel so good," she said huskily. It wasn't Tom.

When I spun to face her, Jax's lips were on mine instantly. The connection caused her to moan as I crashed my almost naked body into hers. I unbuttoned her shirt clumsily while our kissing grew hungry. Her hand continued to expertly draw pleasure from me, and I found myself gasping for air, resting my forehead on hers.

She pulled away from me, taking a step back. Swollen lips, untamed hair, and lust in her eyes caused a rush between my legs, and I needed to kiss her again.

"Wait!" She stopped me. "What are you doing?" The glint in her eyes was gone as she stared at me coldly.

"I..." I realised just how vulnerable I was, practically naked. "I'm...I don't know what happened."

"You kissed me," she blasted, almost blamed. The reversal

of circumstances alarmed me. Nothing short of blind terror and fear pulsed through my veins. "Are you gay?"

"What? No."

"You're disgusting." Voices surrounded me as my bedroom walls began to crash around us. "What's wrong with you?" A sea of voices taunted me, and to add to the torture, Jax had disappeared, leaving me alone to face judgement. "You're a sinner. Disgusting! There is something *very* wrong with you." My vision blurred, *and all I could hear was a string of allegations and hurtful slurs.*

My eyes shot open, and a teenage girl with oversized headphones stared at me as if I was a lunatic. The screeching tube tracks of the underground must have woken me. The young girl seated opposite gave a strange look, prompting me to exit the tube a stop early. The horrific dream replayed continually on my longer-than-usual walk home. However, the fresh air helped ease my temperature and nausea. The fabric of my grey dress felt suffocating and itchy as I struggled to shake the remnants of the nightmare.

I entered the apartment, expecting to find it empty, but I was mistaken.

"Hello, love." Bridget, Jax's mother, smiled from the kitchen as she poured hot water into a mug. "How was work? Would you like a cuppa?"

"Think I could do with something a little stronger," I said before kicking off my heels and removing my coat, which was still wet from getting caught in the rain earlier today.

"I'm sure we can arrange that," she replied, rifling through the fridge. I stretched my arms and moved into the living room just as Jamie bounded from his bedroom, crashing into me.

"You're home!" He hugged my waist, and I felt the hard shell I'd created around myself melt. His smile was so wide, it caused his green eyes to crease and almost disappear. I ran my hand through his hair lazily. “Grandma said I can play motorcars. Will you play too?”

“Sure. I’ll even beat you this time. You go set it up.” He gave an excited fist pump before running into his bedroom to set up the game.

As I turned, Bridget sat at the round dining table with two clear fizzy drinks. She smiled before pulling out a chair for me to sit. Though I had been around Jax’s mother a couple of times, we hadn’t spoken at any great length. Usually, she left once I got home, but today she seemed keen to stick around. I pulled up a seat and took a gulp of the drink, which turned out to be mainly gin with a splash of tonic, resulting in a coughing fit.

“That’s a real drink,” she said happily. “The kind that almost kills you.” I offered a weak smile and rotated the glass in my hands. “Rough day?”

“Just long,” I said in a voice that didn’t sound like my own, devoid of energy and a little lost. “Back-to-back meetings, and then, I had an awful argument with my sister at lunch. It’s just not been a good day.” I trailed off, not wanting to get into what happened.

“Sisters fight all the time. I nearly murdered my sister once. I’m sure it wasn’t as bad as you think.”

“It was pretty bad,” I replied, getting lost in my thoughts. All I felt was hopelessness and confusion about my life. I was torn. My feelings for Jax were complex. I couldn’t deny the connection to her, but I was struggling to accept it. I hadn’t allowed myself to have feelings for another woman since I was a teenager, and look how that turned out.

I’d spent years hating myself. Men were just easier, in every way, and it wasn’t like I didn’t enjoy being with them. My feelings for Jax felt as if they emerged overnight, whereas with Tom, we shared this long history. We had a son together, as Mama said. That was surely grounds to explore things further. I couldn’t deny the passion and attraction either; he was the last person I remembered being intimate with. I wished I had more time to figure things out, but the reality was, Tom was coming to town tomorrow, and I had agreed to see him.

Bridget watched me until it seemed she'd had enough. "You know, Elena, maybe it's not my place, but do you want my opinion?" she asked rhetorically because she was going to say what she wanted regardless. "You don't seem like yourself." Her words caused a wave of guilt. "And I'm not talking about today. You were always such a smiley girl. Happy." Tears rushed to my eyes. "I always loved that about you. I don't remember ever seeing a frown on your face. Well, I guess that was before."

A feeling of failure washed over me. "I'm different, aren't I?" I asked, my voice small as she sadly nodded. "Was I happy? Before?" My voice cracked, and my vision blurred as I met her caring eyes.

"Oh, immensely."

"I don't know why I can't..." I trailed off, trying not to break down in front of someone I barely knew. "I don't remember who I was, but she sounded pretty great." She looked at me thoughtfully but showed no judgement. "No one has said it, but I can see the way they all look at me. Like I should be someone else. Someone better, braver maybe, happier."

"What are you afraid of?"

My lip began to quiver, and tears started to fall. "That I'm never going to be that person again. That I'm disappointing everyone."

Keys twisting in the lock interrupted us, and I shifted my back to the door, shielding the upset on my face. I knew who it was, but I couldn't face her, not in this state. Bridget came to my rescue, greeting Jax instead, but not before she squeezed my shoulder and whispered, "You'll be okay."

The words helped me compose myself enough to reach my bedroom before I broke down any further.

❖

Jax

I welcomed Mum into a hug, searching over her shoulder to witness Elena retreat to her room. The way she rushed off, her hand on her cheek, had me thinking the worst.

Mum caught my eye. "She just needs a minute. Long day is all."

"Is she okay? Did she say something to you?" I asked unable to hide my concern. "Should I go speak to her?"

"I think it's best to give her some space, love." She rubbed my arm soothingly before she pointed to Jamie's bedroom. "He's in his room, homework is finished, and I gave him his dinner."

"Thanks, Mum." I sighed contentedly, tired from a day of surgeries. "What would I do without you?"

"Probably starve," she said before reaching for her coat. "When was the last time you went grocery shopping, huh?" I pecked her on the cheek as she lifted her handbag. "I left half a lasagne in the fridge for your tea, and don't bother calling me this evening."

"Why not?" I asked as she gave me a shrug, but the smile on her lips piqued my curiosity. "What are you up to? Wait, do you have another date with Trevor?"

"It's not a date. Christ, Keelin, at my age, I'll be lucky if he doesn't keel over during dessert." But her face told me she didn't mind the attention.

"I'll not bother you then on your *not-date*," I teased before saying my good-byes.

Sometime later in the evening, I read Jamie's favourite bedtime book. I turned to the next page, which I could have recited from memory, only to glance over and find him peacefully asleep. I slowly got up and switched off the light, tiptoeing into the living room and closing his door behind me.

"Was it *The Tiger Who Came for Tea* or *The Hungry Caterpillar* tonight?" Elena asked from the kitchen as she filled a glass of water from the tap.

"The tiger," I said.

She shook her head. "I could have bet money it was going to be the caterpillar. There's always tomorrow." She glided toward the bedroom, wearing her short dressing gown and revealing toned calves that I couldn't help but take in. She had stayed in her bedroom all evening, while I had been gathering the courage to speak to her, and this was probably my last chance.

"How was your day?" I asked, chickening out from what was really on my mind.

"Shitty, if I'm honest." She stopped and looked at me, and I registered her worn-out features. Her green eyes looked almost grey and dull with puffy red eyelids, evidence of crying. Her hair was pulled back into a messy bun, though strands had escaped, and the oversized T-shirt told me all she needed was comfort this evening. How I wished more than anything I could provide that comfort for her.

"You can talk to me about it, if you want."

Her hesitance made it obvious I was the last person she wanted to speak to. "It's okay, but thanks."

Watching her walk away prompted some newfound bravery to emerge. "Are you free tomorrow night?" I blurted, and I held my breath in anticipation. She stopped when she reached the bedroom door and turned back to me, curiosity etched on her features. "I was just wondering if you wanted to do something? Get a drink? Dinner or whatever you want?" She looked at me as if intrigued but remained speechless, which only caused me to continue rambling. "I'm off work, you see, and that doesn't happen very often. Greg said he can watch Jamie, so I just thought, I don't know, maybe we could go out. Together."

My babbling was humiliating. I had never showcased such a woeful attempt at asking someone out. Even I wouldn't have said yes to that display of no-confidence. The sheer embarrassment coupled with Elena's silence caused me to regret my decision, and I almost started to backpedal.

"That sounds really great. Perfect, actually." Elena smiled brightly, the first smile I'd witnessed all evening, but it was short-lived. "It's just. I can't tomorrow night. I've a friend visiting."

"A friend?" I asked, but her inability to make eye contact confirmed my suspicion. "Tom." I had forgotten he was visiting this weekend. It was impossible to hide my disappointment.

"Yeah," she said, looking a little guilty. "But it's not what you think."

"What do I think?" My reply sounded snide as I struggled to keep my emotions at bay.

"It's just dinner." I nodded, choosing to hold my tongue and bury my fears. "I just have to figure things out!" My failure to speak seemed to ignite something as she proceeded to take her frustrations out on me. "Can everyone please just try and understand? It's all so confusing."

"Join the club," I returned, equally frustrated. "You know, you're not the only person who's confused here. I have no idea where I stand, Elena." I sighed as her eyes pleaded with me, begging me not to ask her to choose, but I couldn't go on any longer. Not like this. "Do you want to be with him?"

"It's complicated," she said quietly. The air caught in my throat, and it hurt to breathe. Finally, she was being honest.

"Well, when you figure it out, maybe you could let your wife know." The bite in my tone was glaringly obvious.

"That's not fair."

"I'm being unfair? You're practically having an affair, Elena."

"I can't cheat on a marriage I don't remember." But the look on her face revealed how much she regretted the harsh wording. "I didn't mean—"

"No, I think that's exactly what you meant. Finally, you're being straight with me."

She narrowed her eyes. "Is that supposed to be a joke?"

"Trust me, no one is laughing here. This is just my life we're talking about. And Jamie's, of course, but I guess that's asking too much for you to think about him."

"Don't you dare, Jax," she yelled back. "Jamie is separate from this."

"This? What is this?" I gestured between the two of us. "Who am I to you?" I asked bluntly for the first time after weeks of living in limbo. "Am I your friend? Your co-parent?" Tears filled her eyes as she stared at me. "Or am I just your plaything when you want attention?"

"I'm sorry, okay?" She sobbed loudly. "I'm sorry I'm not her." My brow furrowed for a moment. *I'm not her* hung heavy in the air between us as I watched her battle those internal demons. "That woman you fell in love with. I wish I could bring her back because who I am now is such a disappointment." Speechless, I watched as tears rushed to my own eyes. "You're not a plaything. I care about you, Jax. You mean so much more to me than…but I can't…" I inched closer to her. Seeing Elena this distraught had a physical reaction on me. "I'm so lost. What I'm feeling inside doesn't make sense in my head. I'm trying to please everyone and letting everyone down at the same time. Trying to be the perfect daughter, sister, and it's just so…" She sniffed back the tears as I took another step closer to her.

"Exhausting," I finished for her as she let out an exasperated breath. Remaining a safe distance away, I said, "Elena, you can't keep doing this to yourself. You do not have to please anyone. Not your parents. Not Caterina or Tom or even me. Just be happy and be happy with the person you are."

"What if what I want isn't what everyone else wants?"

"Fuck them."

She watched me intently before the corner of her lips started to twitch. "Fuck them?" She stifled a laugh.

"Don't let anyone tell you what to do." She watched me thoughtfully, and how I wished I could read her mind in that moment. "You're not a disappointment. Not to me, at least. I just want you to be happy, and if that's not with me then…" She nodded, so thankfully, I didn't have to finish that sentence.

With nothing more to say, we took one final look at each other before going our separate ways. Lying in bed, I was filled with regrets, and countless times, I thought about going to her. There was so much that remained unsaid, and I couldn't help but feel I was losing her. Regardless of how torn Elena was, I couldn't force her to be with me. To choose our family. She had to fight for our marriage, and until she was ready to accept herself, she would continue to suppress those feelings.

CHAPTER FIFTEEN

The next day, I was still berating myself for how I'd left things with Jax. Guilt had consumed me as I tried to fall asleep last night, knowing I was too much of a coward to tell her how I really felt. She'd asked me out on a date, and I'd passed it up for what? An ex-boyfriend? My phone buzzed on the dresser as I continued to rifle through my wardrobe for something to wear. I let it go to voice mail, but the caller was persistent, and it started to ring again and again.

"Hello?" I sighed, frustrated.

"Darling," Mama cooed on the other side. "Getting ready, bella?"

"Mother." I smiled through gritted teeth. I found myself conjuring a fake cheerful voice, which only added to the anxiety I'd had all day. "I didn't expect you to call so soon. We talked just yesterday." And the day before that.

"I know darling, but I just wanted to wish you good luck on your big date tonight."

"It's not a date," I argued as a nauseous gnawing feeling came over me. "We're just catching up."

"Elena, this is your ex-boyfriend of three years and Jamie's father. People change, you know, age matures everyone. Wouldn't you want him to be a part of your son's life? A boy needs his father." Her go-to method of persuasion that usually worked like a charm on me. "Thomas truly is a delightful man with a very good job, able to support and take care—"

"I can take care of myself, Mama." This conversation felt like another attempt at manipulating me. Mother was pushing me toward Tom. Cat was right. I was just sorry it took me so long to see it myself. "As for Jamie, he has two parents already, and it's not like Tom has shown any interest before."

"He never stopped caring for you, Elena. Why else would he be travelling to see you this evening?"

"Well, thanks for checking in, but I should get going."

"Just make sure to wear something pretty." That demanding tone returned. "A dress, perhaps the black dress I got you last Christmas. It probably still has the tag on it."

I could feel my grimace as I stared at the dress on the bed, which did, in fact, still have the tag on. In the cull of my wardrobe, it was the first thing I'd given a hard pass to. Frills were never my thing, and the low-cut style meant my breasts would probably fall out during the entrée.

"I will leave you to make yourself beautiful. Give my love to Jamie." She mustered a cheery response. "*Ciao*, bella. Call me tomorrow."

"*Ciao*, Mama." I threw the phone onto the bed.

My mother was beyond pushy, borderline obsessive. Recommending what I should wear so that I looked pretty? The pressure to see Tom again and rekindle our relationship was unbelievable.

I settled on an outfit, a simple navy dress, and checked myself over in the mirror. My makeup was light, but I never was a fan of heavy foundation.

Don't cover up your freckles, a voice whispered in my head as I was transported back into a memory.

"Put down the foundation, Elena, I mean it. I'll break the bottle," Jax said as she tied her shoelaces. I rolled my eyes and squeezed a small blob of liquid onto a brush. "Elena, don't do

this. Think about the children," she teased as I began applying the makeup to my face. "That's it!" She threw up her arms dramatically as she grabbed a blazer from the wardrobe. "You've done it now. You're hideous." She sighed as she stood beside me, looking into the mirror.

"Thank you, that's the sweetest thing you've said to me all day."

"The day's not over yet," she said huskily in my ear before pecking my cheek. I reached for the blush brush, but she snatched my hand, halting me. "You don't need blusher. You're already blushing," she whispered in my ear, sending shivers down my spine. "I'll just keep whispering in your ear all night."

"Why are you so against makeup?"

"Because you're so naturally beautiful. You don't need to cover up your freckles or the dark circles under your eyes."

"You noticed the dark circles?" I swooned sarcastically. "I made sure to only get three hours of sleep just for you."

"Well, I think you're beautiful. Just the way you are."

I was pulled from the flashback with a force that left me weak at the knees. Using the dresser to steady myself, I looked into the mirror. In the flashback, I was standing in the exact same spot, but I looked like a completely different person. My reflection showed insecurities and unfamiliarity, but the old me was carefree and filled with happiness. I longed to know that woman again, the one on the receiving end of so much love.

My eyes drifted to the jewellery box. I pulled out a necklace. In the flashback, I was wearing the same necklace, and after placing it round my neck, I felt calmer somehow. I'd admired the simple rose gold before but hadn't felt the desire to wear it…until now. The pendant landed neatly over my heart. I slipped on a pair of heels and grabbed my bag.

As soon as I stepped outside my bedroom, I felt a pair of eyes watching from the kitchen. I didn't look around as I walked farther into the living area and scrolled through my phone that was charging on the dining room table.

"Going out?" she asked even though she knew perfectly well I was.

"Yep." My response was short. I couldn't help being cold. It was the only way to minimise the gnawing in my tummy.

"You look beautiful." Her voice was much closer, causing me to jump slightly.

She stood at the other side of the table and stared into my eyes. My breath turned unpredictable under the intensity. It felt as if she was digging into my soul, and it only caused the gnawing to become sharper, like a clenching on my insides.

"Your necklace is tangled at the back. Can I?"

I nodded, granting her permission to fix it.

I turned my back, and a shaky breath escaped when her hands brushed my hair to the side. Though I tried to resist, my mind replayed the dream from yesterday, the way her hands expertly moved across my body as if she knew every curve by heart. Her fingers were soft and warm on the back of my neck as she fixed the necklace. A shiver erupted across my skin from the intimate contact.

"Perfect." The word was soft, and although she didn't whisper it in my ear, her breath lingered on my neck as I turned.

Drowning in blue eyes, there was no escape. The gnawing in the pit of my stomach finally stopped, and my heart began to race. The rhythm in my chest made me feel as if I was breathing for the first time, as if my heart had woken up from hibernation. Her close proximity, the intensity in her eyes, the crease on her forehead, her breath on my lips…all of it overpowered my senses. I had never wanted anything more in my life than to kiss her. My breathing picked up, and I felt myself leaning in.

Beep.

Like the same irritating beep that pulled me from my coma in the hospital bed, the buzzer sounded loudly.

Beep.
Beep.

❖

Jax

Her eyes bored into mine a moment longer, and I thought maybe she wouldn't answer the door. Thoughts like that made it hurt all the more when she pulled away and moved toward the buzzer. She pressed the unlock button on the intercom, and I knew then that I only had seconds.

"Elena?" She was still facing the intercom, her back to me. "Elena? You don't have to do this. Stay." My pleading caused her to turn slowly, and in her eyes, I saw the same conflict from last night. "It's okay to feel the way you feel."

My words hung between us, and I knew it struck a dark chord in her, the shame she struggled with and always had. It was why she couldn't properly deal with her feelings. She'd been conditioned to believe our love was wrong. Tears were in her eyes, and all I wanted to do was comfort her and wash away all her fears, the pain and suffering she'd faced the first time she'd tried to accept who she was.

"There is nothing wrong with you, Elena."

A knock on the door interrupted us, but no one moved. It was like playing a game and watching an hourglass that only had a couple of grains left. Everything slowed except the players' heart rates as they silently wished for more time. Except this wasn't a game.

She turned and opened the door, and I exhaled in defeat.

"Hey, you." Tom wrapped his arms around her waist and pulled her into a hug. "You look more beautiful than ever."

I watched his hands roam across her back while his face sank into the crook of her neck. The intimate embrace brought bile to my mouth. After every shitty thing he'd done to her, it killed me to watch their interaction. As they pulled apart, he smiled down at her. I'd only seen a handful of photographs of him, and even then, Elena had always been in them, so my eyes would gravitate toward her. I wouldn't consider him handsome, more boyish in features. He was a fair bit taller than Elena with light brown, perfectly styled hair. His eyes met mine as he quite literally invited himself in like an intruder inspecting our home for a heist.

"You must be Jax." He addressed me while moving farther into the living room. Elena trailed somewhere behind. "Elena's told me a lot about you."

Tom knew exactly who I was even though we'd never met. I recalled Elena telling me years ago how threatened he had been by our friendship in the beginning. He thought that I was only pretending to be her friend to seduce her, ironic considering his long list of infidelities.

"Hmm." I gave a tight-lipped, barely there smile. I would have put on a better show for Elena, but she wouldn't even look at me.

"I just have to use the bathroom, and then we can go," she said as she moved to the bathroom, leaving Tom and I watching each other from a safe distance.

"Nice place," he said awkwardly as he swung his arms a little.

"I'd ask you to sit, but I don't want you in my home."

He smirked. "I get it. Can't say I was expecting the warmest of welcomes, but she reached out to me so…"

"So you just thought, what? You'd give it another go?" I crossed my arms.

"Why not?" I shook my head, flabbergasted at his response. He narrowed his eyes. "Look, I always regretted the way things ended with Elena—"

"The unplanned pregnancy or when she found out you were cheating?"

"You're just mad, Jax. She's actually into me, and there's

nothing you can do about it." I gritted my teeth as he spoke up again. "I was surprised to hear from her, in fact. The last I heard, you two were married."

"We are."

"Well, shit. This must be really awkward for you." He made a poor attempt at covering his grin as my hands tightened into fists. "So where is he?" Tom craned his neck, looking around the apartment. My eyes shifted to Jamie's closed door, and I prayed he didn't come out.

"Do you even know his name?" I challenged as his eyes darted around the room, avoiding mine. "How about his birthday, huh? I'll give you a clue, it was recently. Or his age? Come on, why don't you give it your best guess?" I rolled my eyes as he stood quietly. "You're such a waste."

"Look, she wanted to see me," he said in a hushed voice. "I didn't go looking for her, so you can hate me, but if there's even a chance she has feelings for me, I'm sticking around to find out."

"Oh, this time you're sticking around?" I raised a brow. "Makes a change from the last time." I narrowed my eyes, loathing every inch of him. "I can't wait for her memories to come back, and she remembers what a dick you are."

"That's if you're still around." He looked me up and down. "By then, she'll be in Luton."

"Luton?"

"Oh, she didn't tell you." He grinned, and I felt my chest tighten. "She's viewing an apartment in Luton. Getting her own place. Let's see, that's an hour away from you and, well, an hour closer to me." He inched closer as I tried to retort, but I couldn't think of anything. "And when the time is right, you better believe I will make sure Elena knows the truth about Jamie. That he's *our* son, not yours." But Elena already knew the truth.

The click of the bathroom door pulled him out of his taunting, and he swung around to meet her again. "Jax was just recommending this great pub near the restaurant. We should go for a drink first," he said pleasantly as I resisted the urge to gag.

"Sure," Elena replied as they made their way to the door, his hand on her lower back making my blood boil. "I won't be back too late. Kiss Jamie good night for me?" she asked over her shoulder but didn't make eye contact. Just like that, they were gone. Perhaps forever.

Chapter Sixteen

Jax played on my mind the entire stroll to the pub, even as we waited for our drinks, and Tom filled me in on his day. He'd met some partners in London to go over an expansion opportunity and proceeded to tell me all about it in detail. I'd become a master at seeming interested in something I cared very little about.

With Christmas approaching, soft festive music played in the background, but I wasn't feeling all that merry as Jax stayed at the forefront of my mind. Her asking, pleading with me to stay. I didn't want to leave her, not when she looked so small. Thinking about it now made me feel sick to my stomach. I should have stayed, but I was afraid.

Natural relationships are between man and woman, as God intended. Same-sex attraction is a disease, it should be treated as such.

My mind flashed back to St Catherine's, one of the many lectures I was forced to sit through. The flashbacks were happening more often, coincidently as I found myself falling more for Jax.

It is a disgusting sin echoed in my mind as I took gulps of my wine, washing down those demons to steady my breathing again. I smiled at Tom as if I was still paying attention to his work woes as I ridded myself of those thoughts.

I had been weak and ashamed back then. I still was. I'd been ashamed of the way I felt about Jax for weeks. Pushing down those emotions, telling myself she was just a friend despite knowing these feelings ran much deeper, like nothing I had ever felt before.

Love is between man and woman. My mind repeated the words drilled into me for years, and I drank more wine, in need of escape from my own past.

It didn't matter how I felt about Jax, none of it did. I wasn't supposed to feel that way. Those feelings weren't normal. I wasn't normal. She was better off without me.

"Would you like another?" Tom asked, pulling me from my thoughts. I looked down at my glass, seeing it was empty while Tom had half a pint of beer left. "You must have been thirsty." He grinned, calling over a waitress.

The waitress approached, and as if on cue, Tom's eyes raked her from head to toe, tapping into that shameless charisma. She masked a polite smile but side-eyed me, perhaps uncomfortable that she was being quite obviously ogled while I sat idly by. After taking the order, she left us, Tom studying her curves as she walked away.

I remembered this side of him. We'd fought about it all the time when we were together. He couldn't help but look at anything with a heartbeat, and the constant flirting with every woman hadn't helped either. Although I'd never vocalised it, I'd always wondered if Tom's eyes could drift so easily, could he stray just as quickly?

"Ha. I know that look." He grinned. "Still the jealous type, even after all these years." He threw a wink at me before I felt his hand on my knee. The gnawing feeling shot up through my body again as I studied the hand, which he removed.

"I wouldn't say jealous. I'd just rather you didn't objectify women every ten minutes," I said as the waitress came by with another round of drinks. "Like a quota."

"Such a feminist now," he said as I took a large gulp. "It's sexy."

I had always been a feminist. I'd just kept my mouth shut

more when I was in my twenties. It was times like these when I wanted to confront Tom about what Cat had said. How he'd left me when he found out I was pregnant. When I'd asked why we'd broken up, he cited the breakdown in our relationship being because of clichés such as work, lack of communication, etc. Vague reasons that seemed to frequently change. It only made me think there was more that he was hiding.

"Drink up, we're going to be late for dinner," he said, reaching for his coat.

The wine had started to kick in as we left the pub and made our way out into the wintery night. The streets were busy as they normally were on a Friday night in Soho. People in suits fell out of bars while young couples wined and dined, and groups of students staggered their way in heels to a club. As I looked around the cobbled and bustling streets, I couldn't help but feel out of place. The usual Friday night for me was sitting curled up with Jamie, eating takeout and drinking wine with Jax while watching the new Disney movie of the week until he fell asleep and we could put on Netflix. As boring as it sounded, it was something I looked forward to at the end of the working week.

Walking beside him, no doubt looking like any other couple, I couldn't help but feel that meeting him was a mistake. The answers I thought I needed to know didn't seem important anymore. And more importantly, the love I thought I'd feel for him was long gone. My gut feeling had been to cancel, and I should have done that rather than trying to please my mother. Tom was not the person I remembered, and I was not the person I used to be.

We were just walking past Soho Square Garden, and I was about to excuse myself when Tom grabbed my hand and stopped us in our tracks.

"Look." He pointed to the sky. The moon was bright as it sat nestled amongst a handful of stars. "Look how orange the moon is."

The volume and colour weren't what surprised me. It was that I could see it at all in London. Usually, the stars and moon were disguised behind the amount of light pollution. It had been a long time since I'd witnessed a more beautiful evening. And to think, I was sharing it with the wrong person. The person I wasn't *in love* with.

"It's amazing."

"No, you're amazing." Tom looked at me for a moment before he leaned in, and his lips grazed mine.

I was caught in shock when he kissed me, but by the time I realised what was happening, I became overwhelmed by something much more powerful. In that moment, everything came back to me in one striking jolt. I remembered each day from the last eight years, four months, and fifteen days. Every monumental piece of my life flooded back to me until the very second I'd stepped off the curb. Every happy moment and all the hard days, every laugh, every tear, and every smile replayed in my mind, reminding me of who I was. And more importantly, who I was not. Just as Greg had said, my memories would come back all at once, and all it took was a kiss.

The wrong kiss.

He pulled back and gazed into my eyes. I didn't even register what had happened until the slapping sound echoed off the cobbled streets, and Tom let out a howl. My palm stung from where it had collided with his cheek, but God, it felt good.

"What was that for?" he cried, gripping his face.

"For being a misogynistic asshole," I shouted as angry adrenaline spread throughout my chest. "For cheating on me five times, two of which were with my friends, as far as I can remember, and yes, you better believe I remember." He gulped audibly. "For the three years I wasted with you, for the six months I cried over you, wondering why I wasn't good enough." And then I remembered. The memory caused me to shove him, and his back collided with a metal railing. "For trying to bully me into not going through with the pregnancy." I stared at him with intense rage.

"You remember," he whispered. And remember I did. He cowered away from my gaze. At least he felt remorse, not that it prompted any sort of sympathy. "I'm sorry, Elena. I never meant to hurt you."

"You're sorry? After all the horrible things you did to me, how could I ever forgive you?"

"I'm so sorry for everything. I was immature. Stupid," he said, believably too. If I had been twenty-four again, maybe I would have listened. "I have never loved anyone like I love you, and I just want a chance to make it up to you. I just got you back after all these years, and I want to be the man you always thought I could be, for you and our son."

"He was *never* your son."

He looked stunned and a little outraged, as if maybe thinking I'd been unfaithful to him. Of course his mind would jump to that conclusion rather than really think about what it meant to be a parent.

"He was always Jax's son. Every step of the way, she was there for him in a way you could never have even come close to. He may share DNA with you, but trust me, he is nothing like you."

The thought of Jamie filled my mind and caused my heart to expand in my chest as I remembered the day he was born. The first time he'd wrapped his hand around my finger, his first steps, and his first words. All the memories I'd misplaced came rushing back as I looked one last time at Tom.

"And do not misunderstand, you will never meet him. You lost that right the day you said you wanted nothing to do with him." He stared at me, disappointed, but I couldn't care less. "I have to go." I turned and started running.

Racing through the streets while crashing into passing pedestrians did nothing to slow me. I was a woman on a mission with my destination in sight.

❖

Jax

The TV was on, but no one was home. That was what Elena used to say whenever I'd stare off into space, deep in thought. My mind was elsewhere as I regretted everything over the last couple of months. I should have told her from the instant she'd woken up rather than lie to her for weeks. I should have been braver once she knew the truth, but the time to make a difference had already passed.

Jamie shifted against me, fast asleep. After checking the clock, I realised it was past his bedtime. Rising slowly from the couch, I carefully lifted him and moved toward his room to tuck him into bed.

"Good night, Jay," I whispered with a kiss to his forehead before retreating.

As I closed his door, the apartment front door closed too. I didn't bother to look back at Elena, too afraid Tom was with her. I walked toward my bedroom, unable to face her. I just wanted to be alone.

"Keelin?" Her voice was so small that I almost missed it. I hadn't heard her say my name since…

I turned slowly, and the second I saw her, I knew it was my wife. She threw her keys in the bowl like she used to do, and before I even had a minute to register, she was running toward me. I closed the gap just as fast, and she jumped into my arms.

"I remember," she whispered repeatedly in my ear.

I held on to her, resting my head in the crook of her neck, breathing her in. She held on just as tightly, most likely creating bruises until she pulled away. I didn't realise I was crying until she wiped the tears from my face.

"I'm so sorry." Tears filled her eyes.

Words couldn't articulate the joy I felt as I leaned in and

captured her lips. She kissed me with just as much passion. Her hands found their way into my hair, tugging slightly, as I gripped her hips and pulled her closer. Soft moans surrounded us, and occasionally, we'd break apart for air, but in those moments, she would look at me as if it was the first time she was seeing me. I guess, in a way, it was.

"How much do you remember?" I pulled back breathlessly.

"Everything," she breathed, leaning her forehead against mine. "All of it came back in the blink of an eye. I'm sorry I didn't remember."

"No, I'm sorry," I whispered. "I'm so sorry."

"Why are you sorry? I should be the one apologising. After what I put you through?"

"No," I tried, but the sobbing made it hard to get the words out.

"Keelin, what happened?" she asked, placing light kisses on my cheeks, removing the tears that had fallen, but more tears were en route as my emotions took over.

"I'm sorry for what I said to you. The last thing I said to you before…" My mind cast back to the moment that was still so prominent, the centre of all-consuming guilt that hadn't left me for a moment.

"Jax?"

I stirred out of the exhaustion which had possessed my limbs.

"Jax, wake up. Keelin?" I opened my eyes to find Elena fully dressed in her navy suit, which I'd dubbed her "I need to make a good impression" attire. "Do you want me to take him?" she whispered, motioning to Jamie lying in my arms.

I had fallen asleep on the couch after coming home late from work. A ten-hour shift hadn't ended with collapsing into bed like it should have. Jamie had caught a bug from school a few days ago, and it had been all hands on deck for another night of hourly puking.

"No, it's okay," I replied, lifting Jamie cautiously so as not to wake him.

I placed him in his bed and pulled a sheet over him to ensure his fever didn't rise any higher. After checking his forehead, I felt a small touch of relief that his temperature had dropped compared to during the night. I pulled the basin closer to the side of his bed in case he was sick again before collecting the vomit-covered sheets and leaving his room. My vomit-stained scrubs were the first thing I shed as the smell of dried sick wafted every time my hair fell from behind my ear. I put the clothes and sheets in the washing machine before I dragged my exhausted body to bed for a quick nap before my next shift.

When I returned to the living room, I found Elena at the dining table typing on her laptop. I tried to bite back the frustration swimming to the surface at seeing her working yet again, but alas, my temper got the better of me.

"Elena, give it a rest. It's the middle of the night," I barked grumpily.

"It's six a.m.," she replied just as crabbily, failing to tear her eyes from the laptop. "I got nothing done yesterday with Jamie throwing up every ten minutes, and I have an investment meeting first thing." She rubbed her forehead tiredly.

"I told you, surgery ran on."

"That's a first." The sarcasm was evident, and I felt another argument brewing.

"Not now, okay. I'm running on about three hours of sleep." I dragged my feet toward the bedroom.

"Well, you can catch up on it today when you're watching him."

"What?" I turned angrily to face her.

"Look at the state of him. He can't go to school."

"I'm back at the hospital at ten. I can't stay home with him today."

"I stayed home yesterday to take care of him, and I can't

miss another day at work." She sighed as she closed the laptop and began packing up her work.

"So just like that, discussion over?"

"Yes. This is not up for debate. You're watching him. I told you, I can't afford to miss another day."

"No, Elena, I can't afford to miss work because people actually die when I'm not there."

"Oh, I forgot your work is more important than mine." She threw her hands up in the air dramatically. "Let me just get back in the kitchen to be a good little housewife, shall I?"

"That is not what I meant, and you know it."

"My work is just as important as yours, Jax. And let's not forget whose job contributes more to the bills."

"And you never let me forget it," I barked before her eyes sparked a fury she rarely unleashed.

"You know what, I really don't have time to get into this argument again with you. Okay?" She let out an exacerbated sigh. "I can't stay home another day, or I could lose my job, so you have to pick up the slack. And don't even think of calling Caterina. I know she covered for you last week."

"Why am I not surprised?" I rolled my eyes, feeling the betrayal. "Of course she would have told you. No secrets between you two. Heaven forbid she'd help me out without ratting me out. What do you want from me? I'm in my final year of residency, every surgery counts toward my finals, and if I don't put in the hours—"

"This is such bullshit, Jax," she shouted before adjusting her voice so as not to wake Jamie. "I've heard this speech a thousand times. It's always been this way with you, even when you were interning, and it'll be this way when you become an attending physician next year. Work always comes first, followed by us. I knew this even when I married you, but when it mattered, I thought you'd put us first."

"I did," I yelled back. "I was put forward for residency

supervisor months ago, but I turned it down. For you, for Jamie, but it's too much, it's all just too much. I can't do it anymore."

"Do what?"

"This," I shouted. "All of it. It's already chaos with Jamie, do you really want to add another one?"

The air turned silent as Elena stared at me in almost horror. "What are you saying?"

Our hurtful words hovered in between us, making me feel as if I'd never been further away from her than where I was standing right now. Worlds apart. The silence lingered between us as we looked at each other like strangers.

"We're supposed to be trying for another baby, and if you're changing the game, you need to tell me right now, Keelin. Do you want more kids?"

I wanted to say yes, but the exhaustion made it impossible. Between double shifts, Elena's promotion, paying the endless sea of bills, and Jamie's bug for the last few days, every day was a struggle with no end in sight. I was exhausted, losing myself and all memory of happiness. Even in the darkest of days, I'd always had Elena, my beacon of light. We were strong, at least we had been. Like an oak tree, but recently, the roots felt tired. Ties to the ground were fraying, and rather than stand tall in a storm, we were swaying and breaking down. Arguing every day or not speaking at all had its consequences. Disappointment and loneliness replaced the home of happiness and joy which had once flourished until eventually, I barely recognised the person lying beside me.

"Do you even want me?" she asked in a whisper.

That moment, that very second was my biggest regret of all. In that moment, I had stopped fighting for us. It was only for a second, in utter exhaustion, but I'd stopped fighting for us, something I'd agreed to do every day of my life when I'd said, "I do." I'd watched her heart break in front of me and did nothing.

My head had rolled forward tiredly into my waiting hands, my legs had swayed, and I was unable to look into her eyes.

And then she'd left.

"And you said," she whispered now. The same heart-wrenching emotion I remembered so vividly appeared again. The look on her face that had caused me so much guilt warped her expression, and my tears began to fall freely.

"I didn't know if I wanted more kids?" My voice trembled, and I tried to get the words out through my sobbing. "I was tired and angry, and I'm so sorry. I love Jamie more than life." She wiped away my tears as my hands found her waist, urging her to listen. "Of course I want more of him, more little people just like you."

"I know you do. It was just a fight."

"I love you," I said, looking deep into her eyes, willing her to listen. "I thought I'd lost you and I would never get to say it again. I love you so much. I have never for one second not wanted to be with you, and I'm sorry if you thought for even a fraction of a second that I didn't want you. Want us, our family. And if it was because of what I said that you weren't thinking and stepped off that curb…" I lost my voice.

She kissed me deeply, washing away my guilt. "It wasn't you. I promise, you are not to blame. I remember why I was distracted on my way to work that morning," she said. "It wasn't because I thought you didn't want me. It wasn't you at all." I stared at her as she took a deep breath as if readying herself. "Dr Shapora called me that morning. They'd received the sample from the donor. She'd said that when I was ready, I could arrange an appointment for insemination. I was so happy." Her eyes lit up, turning glassy at the memory, and she gripped my forearms that were still glued to her waist. "That's when I stepped off the curb."

"We got the sample? We can have a baby?" I whispered in disbelief, my mind flashing back to the endless nights spent searching for the perfect donor. The countless disappointments of trying to get pregnant in the months leading up to Elena's accident. "And that's why you..."

"I was so happy, I forgot where I was and just walked. It was so stupid. So stupid. I don't know what I was thinking." She sighed before her frustration seemed to turn to elation, and her fingers laced in mine. "But we can do the insemination whenever we're ready. And when I'm ovulating." She held her breath for a moment. "That is, if we still want to."

I captured her lips, unable to form words as she kissed me passionately back. "Of course I want to. I want everything with you."

Her lips were on mine again as the back of my legs collided with the dining table. She pushed me onto the surface, causing her work files to fall onto the floor.

"Mum?" The small voice came from inside Jamie's room, and we pulled apart, but Elena continued to stand close, still latching on to my shirt.

How could we forget? In our little reunion, we'd somehow forgotten about the most important person. The door creaked open, and Jamie appeared, squinting in the dimly lit living room. I couldn't take my eyes off Elena as she stared at him as if he was on display in a museum. A prized possession too fragile to touch, and it seemed as if she was falling in love with him all over again.

"What's going on?" he asked behind the hand shielding his eyes. His confused expression had me looking to Elena for an explanation, but she was speechless, seemingly in awe of him.

The tears were already forming in her eyes as I spoke for her. "Remember your birthday wish?"

Jamie thought for a beat before he gasped. Delight passed in front of his eyes, and he seemed to hold his breath as if unable to believe my words. His eyes met with Elena's, and like me, he instantly knew. One look was all it took. It was bizarre. Elena had looked the same, with all her old mannerisms, but she hadn't been herself, barely masking an imitation. The Elena who had been living with us for the last couple of months was a shadow of the woman I'd fallen in love with. Her eyes didn't shine like they did now. That intoxicating happiness in her eyes was reserved for the love of her life, Jamie.

"Mummy?" he asked as he looked hopefully at Elena. Before she could respond, he was running toward her. She dropped to her knees as he fell into her arms, gripping her tightly.

Chapter Seventeen

A light kick to the stomach stirred me. I had to blink a couple of times to adjust to the sunshine streaming through the window. In all the commotion last night, we must have forgotten to close the blinds. Another kick came, this time nudging me in the thigh as I pulled back the covers to reveal the culprit.

Jamie slept a little restlessly, not surprising considering how late we'd stayed up last night, basking in our reunion. He was nestled up against Jax as both snoozed peacefully. It was rare to see them both so still and beautiful. Although they weren't biologically related, the string of similarities made their bond irrefutable.

How had I not known them? How could I have forgotten who they were to me? Countless times, I'd almost uncovered their secret. For one, Jamie had my eyes and swarthy skin; he looked identical to my younger self. It was a little comical now in hindsight. The bills that had tumbled from the cupboard had mine and Jax's name on them. I'd read the title of mortgage letters and bank statements addressed to both of us, but I'd never put two and two together. So what was my excuse? Was I really that oblivious, or was I just too scared to believe the obvious? It was not the first time I'd tried to hide from my feelings for Jax.

I thought back to the moment I knew I liked her, that I could fall in love with this woman. It was in New York, and even though my mind had gifted me with the memories of how we'd met and had spent two wonderful weeks together, the flashback had left something out. I had suppressed our final night together in the city that never slept. Now it made sense why I couldn't recall the night we became more than friends.

"Wow, those whiskey sours were strong," Jax said with a stumble into the elevator of our hotel. "Or was it the margaritas?"

"I think it was the tequila shots that tipped me into drunk territory," I slurred as I leaned against the mirror in the lift while propping myself up on the railing.

"Oh no, we had tequila shots, didn't we?" Jax asked. I couldn't contain my giggling. "That's it. I'm never drinking again."

"You said that yesterday after the Brooklyn pub crawl," I replied and watched as she slapped her head with her palm. "I thought the Irish could drink."

"I'm half-Irish, and we can, just clearly not as well as the Italians. Don't tell my ancestors." I laughed as the elevator doors opened on my floor. "This is your stop." She flashed a dazzling smile, casting a bit of a trance over me and resulting in a rather unflattering stumble. I almost fell, but she managed to catch me. "Maybe I should walk you to your door," she said as her cool yet sweet breath lingered on my face, sending a wave of butterflies to my stomach.

"I tripped. I don't need an escort," I said as she walked down the hall with an arm of support around me. Feeling her arm around my waist sent shivers across my body as we both swayed down the long hallway. "You're way more drunk than me."

"I agree. But unlike you, I don't like to wallow and heavy drink alone." She smirked as we reached my room.

"I haven't drunk alone in the last ten days, thanks to you. Oh, I still have a little bit of Scotch left. Care for a nightcap?" My speech slurred as I fumbled in my bag for the room key.

"Why break our nightcap tradition now? It is our last night." She swayed on the spot before following me inside.

I threw my jacket onto the floor and staggered to the table where the fifth of whisky sat. Jax plonked onto the bed and let out a big sigh as if relishing the plush surface.

"I can't believe we walked all the way from Greenwich Village. Why didn't we just call a cab?" she asked as she lay at the foot of the bed.

"You said it was a great night for a stroll, and I think you wanted pizza," I said as I poured two hefty measures of whisky into the complimentary plastic cups.

"That was good pizza." She sat up when I sat next to her.

"The best pizza in all of New York." I handed her a drink. "To pizza." I toasted into the air, and she nudged her cup against mine, and we drank.

"I'm gonna miss this." She looked at her cup. "Who would have thought the mean girl from JFK would turn out to be such a cool dude?"

"Who would have thought Eavesdropper Sally would turn out to be…well, you're just okay." She elbowed me, causing my giggling to return. "I'm kidding. It's been a blast, Jax. I mean, my life savings are shot…"

"Completely annihilated," she said for me as I looked at her. Her glassy eyes still shimmered despite the amount of alcohol we'd both had as she swept her wavy hair back behind her ear. "But it's been a lot of fun."

A new air surrounded us as she looked at me, really looked at me, and it was like she could see everything. The intensity should have scared me, but it didn't. In fact, it awoke something in me that I had been feeling since the moment I'd met her. A strange tug had been pulling us slowly together for days. In this light, her blue eyes were captivating, darting between my eyes and lips. She looked as if she was about to say something, but I couldn't let her take away this moment. I reached up to her cheek and revelled at the softness in my hand. Her eyes connected with mine in surprise, but she leaned into the touch, telling me she wanted this as much as I did.

To my surprise, she closed the gap before I could. Her lips grazed mine, sending a jolt throughout my body. Scotch lingered on her lips, acting as an encouragement to deepen the kiss further.

There was nothing slow about this kiss. The more my hands roamed, the more hurried we became. My breathing was ragged, out of control. The moment I felt her hand on my thigh, I knew I wanted more, and next thing I knew, I was straddling her hips as my black dress crept up increasingly high. I wouldn't have noticed if Jax's hands weren't hot on the exposed skin, like a fire moving across my thighs. I clawed at her back and neck as she quickly removed her jacket before kissing me again. A fire was growing in the pit of my belly and, more importantly, between my legs as her hands explored my body. I started to unbutton her shirt, but as I got about halfway down, I heard her voice.

"Wait." I barely heard it as I continued to kiss her neck, but the second time she spoke, her voice was clearer. "Elena, wait."

I pulled back, panting, a dark shade of desire in her eyes connected with mine. The sight alone caused another wave of arousal. My lipstick was smeared on her swollen lips, and her hair was a little wild as she looked up at me. I thought she was going to capture my lips again and with any luck, rip off my clothes, but something changed. Her face softened. We were caught up in a moment earlier, but now, the way she stared made me feel so vulnerable. Like she could really see me. See everything I'd tried for years to hide.

"I like you." Her words were barely a whisper, pure and full of truth. "I really like you."

Those words caused my heart rate to accelerate because the truth was, I liked her too. Jax was just braver. My mind raced through the declaration, and it overwhelmed me. Optimistically, I thought we could make this work. We both lived in London, we were both single, and she made me happy. The only thing stopping this fairy tale from becoming a reality was…everything.

The pressure of the meaning behind those words became unbearable, causing a swirl of emotions inside my stomach. The vulnerability in her voice made me feel sick as guilt washed over me. I couldn't be the person she wanted. I was damaged.

In a flash, I climbed off her and moved to the table to steady myself. "Why'd you have to ruin it, Jax?" I said angrily, taking a swig of whisky.

"What?" The confusion in her voice only filled me with more frustration.

"I told you, I'm not gay. Why couldn't you just fuck me without making a big deal out of it?"

"Because I would never use you like that." The way she delivered that line, I knew my words had hurt her. She wasn't using me. I was using her. The raw, choppy sea of emotion in the room made me feel as if I was drowning, meaning that Jax was forced to break the silence.

"I get that you're scared, but I know you feel the same way."

"You don't understand. My parents would flip if they found out I was doing this again." I yanked the lid from the whisky and guzzled it straight from the bottle.

"Again?" Jax asked as I winced, not just from the burning liquid sliding down my throat but also from the overshare.

"It doesn't matter. You should go." I took another swig, keeping my back turned as I tried to force down the dark demons from my past.

"I'm not leaving you like this." Her voice was a whisper but startled me as I realised she was right behind me.

She touched my shoulder, and the warmth caused me to turn to her. Once my eyes collided with hers, I felt it again, that magnetic pull. Everything about her pulled me in. From the moment I met her and every minute we'd spent together over these last few days.

We had been forced into a circumstance when our flights were cancelled as a result of the Icelandic ash cloud. To anyone else, it was a nightmarish inconvenience, but I'd never been happier. I'd never laughed so much or had more fun or as many thought-provoking conversations with anyone. She challenged me in ways no one ever had, and she did it with a smile I couldn't help but return. Every time Jax smiled at me, my body tingled with warmth. Like she was heating up my cold heart frozen from years in the dark. Years of feeling as if I didn't deserve what others called love. Slowly but surely, and without me even noticing, she found her way behind my walls, making me feel something that I swore I would never feel for another woman.

"It's too much. I can't do this." My voice cracked as I fought back tears. Jax's eyes gave away her heartache as she moved closer and soothingly rubbed my bare arms.

"It's okay to feel this way, Elena." She watched me intently, and I knew then I could very easily fall in love with her. Perhaps I already had. That thought alone terrified me. Jax was getting too close. Pushing her away was best, best for everyone.

"I don't feel anything for you." I pulled my arms forcefully away. "I don't even like you like that." The hurt in her eyes was gut-wrenching, but I persisted heartlessly. "I have a boyfriend, okay?"

"You don't even love him. Those are your words." Her brow crinkled. "Talk to me, Elena. This isn't like you." She tried to step forward, but I took another step back.

"You don't know me. You've known me a week, Jax. You know nothing about me."

"I know you feel something for me," she replied honestly. "Why are you being like this?"

"Because I'm fucking broken, okay?" I grabbed the bottle of whisky, needing the distraction. "Is that what you want to hear?"

"You are not broken. I can help you."

"The only thing I needed help with was a good screw. But seeing as that's sure as hell not gonna happen anymore, you should just go." She didn't budge. It was what forced me to hurt her as much as I did. "Look, it's been fun. We laughed, we drank, but now it's over. Tomorrow, we both go back to our separate lives and forget this ever happened."

The look on her face was like a dagger to the chest. She

picked up her jacket and walked straight out of my room without a final word. With the loud bang, *tears began to fall freely and I collapsed onto the bed.*

I had been so afraid to love her. How I'd felt about her had scared me so much, I'd run back to a man I'd never loved. I was terrified to the point where I spent the next two years in a long-distance relationship with someone who treated me like shit because that was easier than facing what I was really feeling. Being alone meant I'd have to face my feelings, feelings that were unnatural and perverse. At least, that was what had been continuously drilled into me.

I had always been attracted to men and women. In fact, I had been in love with one of my best friends. We were fifteen, she was the prettiest girl in my class, and although all of the boys tried to court her, she would spend her Friday nights with me. One day, my parents caught us in my bedroom. They were furious. The very next day, I was put on a plane and sent to a boarding school in the midlands of England.

Well, boarding school was where I'd told my sister I was. It was hard to believe St Catherine's Boarding House was allowed to call itself a school at all. During my three years of residency, I'd learned the ins and outs of conversion therapy, which, as anyone could imagine, had a damaging impression on my life.

Only after years of actual therapy in my late twenties did I come to terms with what I had gone through. How the nuns at the boarding house had taken great pleasure in lecturing me in all the ways my thoughts were disgusting and shameful. The classes I had been forced to sit through, describing what "normal" and "acceptable" sexual relationships were. The years of verbal abuse were what forced me to bury such a huge part of myself for so long. That was where I spent some of my most vital teenage years until I'd turned eighteen and I got the hell out of there. I went to university, returning to civilisation, and hoped I would forget all about St Catherine's. But by then, the damage had already been done. St Catherine's followed my every step and repeatedly "scared" me into staying put in toxic relationships. For so many years, I'd never explored those feelings again until someone had finally taken the time to see past the façade I'd spent years building.

Even after I'd learned the truth about who Jax and Jamie were to me, I still couldn't accept the facts. Living with amnesia, I found myself so disconnected from my current life because twenty-four-year-old Elena could never fathom being happily married to a woman. The years of therapy had helped me to accept myself, and I'd slowly learned to stop being afraid of disappointing my parents. I'd stopped pleasing others and allowed myself to become the person I wanted to be.

A smile crept onto my face as I watched Jax sleep. I wondered, would I have ever truly accepted myself if it hadn't been for her? I was a different person in 2010. Jax barely knew me, and even then, it was a scratch to the surface. I didn't even know who I was. So full of shame and unsure of myself. It was why Jax had treaded lightly during these last few months, never pushing the boundaries without being certain I was comfortable. It was why I fell in love with her in the first place. Despite all my self-loathing, she was still able to see the real me.

❖

Jax

My eyes slowly fluttered open, and I caught Elena watching me. A small blush crept onto her face, and I remembered that she was herself again. Lying in our bed, I finally breathed a sigh of relief, knowing that I was home again. Her memories had come rushing back last night, restoring our family.

"Hey, beautiful." I smiled but tried not to move to avoid waking Jamie.

“Hi.” She sighed as her eyes glistened with tears.

“What’s the matter?”

“Nothing.” She shook her head, but a tear had already escaped. I was about to comfort her, but she spoke again. “I’m just happy.”

“I missed you.” My voice was quiet as she bit her lip. The look in her eyes told me she wanted alone time with me. She glanced at Jamie and motioned toward the door. “I’ll take him,” I said, replying to a question she didn’t even need to ask.

With a careful lift, I carried Jamie to his own room before making my way back to Elena. “It’s so nice to be back in my own bed again.” I beamed as I climbed back in.

“That daybed must have been dreadful.” The guilt was written across her face as she snuggled next to me. “Why didn’t you swap with me when I offered?”

“I couldn’t be in this bed without you,” I said. “Those days you were in the hospital were horrible. The bed felt so large and empty.”

“I felt that way too when you weren’t here.”

“Really?”

“Yeah. I mean, initially, I didn’t know why the bed felt empty because, you know, I’d lost my mind, but when I learned the truth, sometimes I thought about having you in here with me.”

“Huh, if I’d known that, I wouldn’t have waited so long. Maybe my kiss could have brought back your memories rather than that dick—” Elena’s lips on mine cut the ranting short.

“Can we agree never to talk about Tom in our bed again?”

I nodded before eagerly accepting her lips again, a heat stirring between us.

The buzzing of Elena’s phone interrupted us. She leaned over to her bedside table. “Gross. It’s my mother.”

“But you love your biweekly calls with your mama these days.” I smirked as she turned off the phone.

“That manipulative dragon.” Elena practically seethed.

"Please can I be there when you tell her you got your memories back?"

"I would have to speak to her again for that to happen." Elena curled back into my side. "Of course she would use my temporary amnesia as a way to push me back toward Tom."

"I thought we were never talking about him again," I reminded her as she began planting small kisses to my neck.

"Right. Let's not talk about Mama either," she said between kisses. "I'm still sorry that you had to sleep in the spare room."

"It was awful. Truly terrible. You will have to make it up to me."

"Is that so?" She propped herself up on her elbow so she was looking down on me as she began to caress my arm.

"Yes. For all of the trauma I've experienced these last few weeks." She threw me a playful look, telling me that she wasn't buying any of this. "I've been through so much."

"Really? And what will make it better?"

"Well, first off, some kissing," I said as she leaned down and planted a soft kiss on my lips before I continued. "Your cooking, like, every day, breakfast, lunch, and dinner. And you should probably take care of the cleaning and driving Jamie to school. Because I'm traumatised. Oh, and a lot of sex. For a while, maybe even years." She bit back a smile as I exhaled a content sigh. "I'm so happy you're back."

"Me too," she said before she lowered herself and kissed me.

Her tongue brushed my lower lip as she deepened our kiss without hesitation. Months of a lonely bed had left Elena's patience almost as thin as mine, it seemed, as she effortlessly found her way on top of me, straddling my hips.

"Is this the start of you making it up to me?" I asked huskily, sitting up and relieving her of the restraints of her T-shirt.

"This is just a warm-up," she teased as she pushed me back down into the mattress.

I caressed her back as she repositioned herself between my legs. The temperature began to rise as we shed the rest of our clothes, and she planted wet kisses down my neck. She didn't stop there but continued to travel down. Although she stopped briefly at my chest, it was clear where her end destination was. My underwear was removed, and she began her promise to make it up to me. Elena always kept her promises.

CHAPTER EIGHTEEN

"A text message, really?" Cat said over the phone. I heard the sound of honking horns and passing cars in the background. "Is that really all I am worth?"

"You're lucky you got that at all," I replied, throwing Jax a seductive look, which she seemed to immensely enjoy. I popped another grape into my mouth as I sat on the kitchen countertop, half listening to Cat but watching Jax in my oversized shirt as she poured some coffee.

"Well, I am pleased you've pulled yourself from the throes of passion long enough to tell your only sister that your memories are back."

"I knew you would drive straight over here once I told you. Had to buy myself some much-needed alone time," I said.

Jax closed the gap between us, moving in between my thighs and planting a kiss on my lips…one which lingered.

"This has Jax written all over it." Cat's loud voice caused us to break apart for a beat.

"Does not," Jax said as I placed my hand over her mouth to silence her.

"You just wanted to roll around in the hay all day," Cat said, seemingly more to Jax than me, but it fell on deaf ears as Jax kissed my neck, drawing in my pulse point and biting. "Do you need anything from the shop?" My eyes rolled back as I pulled Jax closer, making concentration on the phone call impossible.

"I think you're going through a tunnel, Cat. You're breaking up." I began to make static noises as Jax started to kiss my lips. Chaste kisses at first, which slowly began to deepen. "Gonna have to call you back."

I didn't have a chance to set the phone down before Jax gripped the back of my knees and wrapped my legs around her waist. Her hands dipped under my shirt, moving along my back and sending a shiver down my spine. She silenced my moans with kisses, and I tightened my thighs around her waist, begging for more contact.

"You have no idea how much I've thought about this," I said in her ear as I tugged at the nape of her neck, pulling her closer.

She moved away from my breasts despite my breathless protests and down to the waistband of my sweats. Her hand dipped under the hem, and I braced myself for contact.

The vibration of the phone derailed my concentration. With a quick swipe, I barked, "For the last time, we don't need milk, Caterina."

"Elena?" My mother's incredulous voice caused me to yank Jax's hand away.

"Mother."

Jax's eyes went wide before amusement set in.

"That's no way to answer the phone," my mother said, setting my back teeth on edge. "I'm just calling to find out how your date went."

My nostrils flared, and Jax gave me a "calm down" look, which did nothing. How could Jax be so calm when this woman was responsible for so much confusion and pain.

"It went terribly, Mother, and you want to know why?" I jumped down from the counter, shifting Jax out of the way despite her warning eyes. "Because I am not interested in Tom. Why? Because I am with Jax. I am in love with her, a woman. Hard to believe, I know. It's only been eight fucking years." The rage pulsing through my veins kept me pacing.

"You remember?" Her voice, which usually carried a punch, even on the phone, was quiet.

"Yes, Mother. I do. How could you...I can't believe you would..." I groaned, unable to even finish the sentence. The longer I was on the phone, the more I was getting worked up. "I can't believe you would do something like this. Push me toward him again when you know I'm with Jax. We have a son, a family, and you tried to destroy that, you monster."

"Bella...listen..." My mother tried to interrupt, but the anger pulsing through my bloodstream meant I couldn't stop. I was like a steam engine train travelling beyond capacity, ready to derail.

"Don't *bella* me. You're a manipulative bitch," I spat. "I am married. Happily married. Unlike you and Papa. After everything Tom did to me, and somehow, you thought he is still better than my loving, amazing, successful wife? What kind of a person does that?" Jax gave me a small smile over her coffee, and I began to calm just by looking at her.

"Elena, let me explain." The only reason she got a word in was because I was running out of breath. "After your accident, it was like a silver lining. Tom is Jamie's father. I just want to see him in my grandson's life."

"You're unbelievable," I shouted with my hands wild in the air. Even Jax had fled, knowing how angry my mother made me when she pulled out the nuclear family card. "Tom is not Jamie's other parent. He forfeited that right when he slipped me an envelope of cash to get an abortion. Jax is and always has been Jamie's other parent. We have the adoption papers to prove it." She tried to interrupt, but I wouldn't give her an opportunity this time. "This has absolutely nothing to do with Jamie. This doesn't even have anything to do with Jax. You can't accept that I like women, that I've shamed you."

"Elena, I won't listen to this again."

"It's always been about that, and it will always come back to it. You can't accept who I am. I spent years trying to be the perfect straight daughter, and you know what? That still wasn't good enough. It doesn't matter the circumstances. You'd rather I be miserable than with a woman." I sighed as the line went quiet. I wasn't even sure if she was still on the call. "Well, you know what? Jamie is better off without Tom in his life, and now, we will be better off without you." Tears were in my eyes as I grinded my teeth together to get out the words without a shaky voice. "Good-bye, Mother."

With that, I hung up before gripping the countertop and exhaling slowly.

"Proud of you." Cat smiled from the kitchen side entrance with a look that told me she'd heard a good chunk of the conversation. She might have heard all of it. I hadn't noticed her come in. I smiled back sadly and within seconds, her arms engulfed me from behind.

"Thanks, Cat." I leaned into her embrace, and we were quiet for a beat.

"You sure told her." Cat chuckled as she began to pull back. "But you should have said something about her botched nose job. Really hit her where it hurts."

"Goddamnit." I sighed sarcastically. "Next time. How long do you think it will be before she calls you?"

"Ten seconds," she replied just as her phone started ringing from her back pocket. "Or less." She let it go to voice mail, of course. "You look like you again."

"I feel like me again." I returned her smile.

With her in tow, I moved into the living room toward the dining table, but I didn't get far before I realised Jax wasn't alone in there.

"Mummy," Jamie called from his spot beside Jax on the couch.

Both their heads turned at the same time, hair unkept and messy, but they both smiled, melting my insides as I drifted toward the couch. He must have woken up while I was on the phone. Cartoons were playing on the TV, but by his excited expression I knew it was just a distraction until I finished my call.

"Hey, baby boy." The words left my mouth naturally as I reached the back of the sofa and kissed his forehead and then proceeded to plant a soft kiss on Jax's head.

"Come on, Jay. Let Auntie Cat speak to Mummy for a minute." Jax stood, ushering Jamie into the kitchen.

"How over the moon was Jamie when you told him?" Cat asked once we were alone, and I'd sat across the table from her.

"I didn't even need to tell him, he just knew."

The corners of my mouth turned upward as I looked at my coffee. I recalled the hours we'd sat up having a slumber party. Cat's left hand wrapped around mine and squeezed it comfortingly, and though she was about to speak, something caught my eye.

"Your ring," I said as I realised she was wearing her engagement ring again. She hadn't worn it in months. She sometimes didn't even wear her wedding band, usually after a bad argument with Nick.

"Snap," Cat replied as she nodded at my left hand.

It was one of the first things I'd wanted to return to normal again. My hand had felt weightless without the rings. After Jax had placed my engagement and wedding ring back on my hand, she'd sealed it with a kiss. Smiling, I remembered our reunion last night, but my attention sprung back to Cat as she was beaming down at her own ring, a sight I hadn't seen in a very long time.

"Something's changed?" I wondered aloud as her delighted eyes met mine. "Something good?"

"Something great. He quit the firm." I gasped as she nodded, blissfully and unapologetically happy. "His plane was delayed yesterday, and he missed Abbey's play. We had both spent weeks getting her costume perfect. She had a solo dance and everything. Abbey was so devasted that he couldn't make it. I was furious when he got home, but that all melted away when he said he quit his job. No more travels, no more missed occasions, no more weeks away." Her eyes glistened, and she seemed unable to hide her smile. "He did it for us. He quit."

"He quit?" I said in equal disbelief.

"He really quit."

"Who quit?" Jax asked, appearing back in the living room with a bowl of cereal. Jamie followed her.

"Nick." Cat rolled her eyes but smiled regardless.

"Uncle Nick quit his job?" Jamie said as he launched onto my lap, his hands wrapping around my neck.

"Uncle Nick quit his job," Cat repeated.

"What now?" I said.

"With all his free time?" Cat asked. "I guess he's taking care of Christmas dinner this year, and becoming the go-to, stay-at-home dad. Think of all the weekends he has been away. I think we all deserve a night on the town, don't you? Leave Nick with the little ones."

"You read my mind." I giggled with her, pleased and relieved to have my life back again.

❖

Jax

"Grab the cranberry, will you?" Elena called from the living room just as I was picking up the extra serving spoons.

I frantically searched the fridge, and after some almost mishaps with tumbling jars, I found it "strategically" placed at the very back. With everything shoved back in the fridge, I darted back into the living room. Christmas lights twinkled above the dining table, which was overflowing with food while soft music played in the background.

"What took you so long?" Mum asked, taking another gulp of red wine, her second glass. "Turkey is getting cold."

"You don't eat meat, Ma."

"She's only saying what the rest of us are thinking," Greg said as he clinked my mother's glass with his. My mother threw him back a wink.

"Do I have to separate you two again this Christmas?" I said as I sat between my mother and Elena.

Her hand crept onto my thigh, reminding me to take a deep breath. Elena threw me a coy smile with a look in her eyes that made me forget about the rest of the room. Her warm touch on my thigh stayed longer than it should have.

"Do we have to separate you two?" Nick said, causing Elena to remove her hand and me to curse every single person around my dining table. "Who's hungry?" Nick asked as he stood to carve the turkey.

"Me," the room cheered in unison, the three children the loudest.

Our apartment was small, but for some reason, hosted the majority of these gatherings. This was our third year hosting Christmas dinner, and although we didn't have the best silverware or the most lavish dining room, we made it work. Mum, Greg, and Cassie were already on their second glasses of wine and heading toward their third at the head of the table. Cat, who hadn't taken a seat yet, was micromanaging dinner—as always—placing the first small carvings of turkey onto Kate's and Abbey's plates before moving to Jamie's. Nick looked truly happy for a change as he carved the turkey. He and Cat shared warm looks as they made the perfect team, passing slices across the table. Elena was almost as involved as she started passing bowls of sprouts, roasted carrots and parsnips to the other end of the table.

I sat, utterly useless, completely incapacitated at how everything had turned out. This time last month, I had worryingly begun to make arrangements to have a Christmas dinner for four with my mum, Jamie, and Greg while Elena had discussed going back to Italy to spend Christmas with her parents.

Thankfully, that plan was shot after Elena's argument with her mother. Stefano and Maria Ricci were proud people, never the type to ask forgiveness, but even they'd registered how much they'd fucked up. We'd received a Christmas hamper last week, flowers a few days ago, and a big box of expensive presents yesterday. Even I got a couple of pricey items, which was a testament to how much they were "trying," in their own morally bankrupt way.

Christmas was as it should have been: surrounded by family eating overcooked turkey and lumpy gravy, and with the kids complaining about sprouts.

"A toast," Cat announced as she raised her glass in the air, and the table followed suit. "To my sister and her wonderful family"—she coughed—"minus Jax." It got a couple laughs. "I'm kidding. You guys are hashtag family goals."

Half the table groaned, including her children. "Don't say hashtag, Mum," Abbey said with a look of mortification. "It's really weird."

"Everybody says hashtag," Cat said. "I can pull off hashtag."

"No, you can't," several voices argued.

"Irrelevant," she sang, silencing everyone before her eyes landed on Elena. "This has been a particularly tough year for you and well, for all of us." She softly scanned the room. "And when I look around the table, I see the absence of some special people. We remember them most at Christmas."

I reached to take my mum's hand, and she smiled sadly but didn't meet my eyes, no doubt thinking of Dad. I could tell she was tearing up, and any eye contact with me would only cause her to lose the small grip she had left on her emotions.

Cat's voice pulled everyone from their own thoughts and back to her. "But today is not the time to dwell on the negatives. Like how Elena overcooked the turkey."

"Nick overcooked the turkey," Elena tried, but Cat barely stopped for a breath.

"Today is a day to celebrate family, friends, and the return of people's memories." She nodded in Elena's direction.

"Cheers to that." Greg beamed, his eyes on me. "Because I was about to get my ass kicked if your memories didn't come back soon."

"Language," my mother scolded as the children giggled.

"You might still get your ass kicked," I muttered low enough for only Greg to hear before raising my glass one more time. "Cheers to Elena." Before I could turn to look at her, she planted her lips on mine as the faint sounds of glassware clinked and chimed together.

CHAPTER NINETEEN

Exactly one year later from the day my memories had come back, a day filled with so much love and happiness, I was back in the hospital. But for a very different reason.

"Is Mum ready to try feeding again?" a nurse asked as she came into my room with a small bundle.

I must have dozed off, and by the look on Jax's face and the drool, she had just woken up too. It was a wonder we could close our eyes at all with the sunshine beaming through the window.

"Sure, why not." I groaned as Jax helped prop me up with pillows. "It's not like I haven't been awake for the last twenty hours."

Jax planted a soft reassuring kiss on my forehead. "Unfortunately, I can't breastfeed for you. But what I can do is turn over the channel so *Coronation Street* isn't on anymore."

"My hero." I sighed.

"I think she might warm up to you this time." The older nurse smiled as she handed me our baby girl.

I cradled her close to my chest and watched her for a moment. Her eyes hadn't opened yet, but the prominent frown told me all I needed to know about her strong-willed character. The short wisps of dark hair surprised me. Jamie had been so fair when he was born, but there was still an undeniable resemblance. Jax joined my side and stared at her in awe. We could have been like that for minutes or hours. Time was irrelevant when she was in my arms.

"She's so beautiful," Jax whispered, clearly mesmerized. "Which means she's probably going to make our lives hell." I giggled as I tried to get her to latch. "The cuter the baby, the harder they make your lives."

"Jamie was pretty cute too and he's—" I cut myself off after a moment. "Okay, maybe there is some truth in your theory. Remember his terrible twos?"

"That lasted until he was four," Jax said before stroking the baby's head. "Jamie is going to seem like a walk in the park. I mean, just look at her. She is going to break a lot of hearts."

"All while curing cancer," I said quickly.

"No, she will be building rockets to space or fighting for world peace," Jax argued. "Or who knows, we might fail as parents, and she will become a conservative."

"Mama would be thrilled," I said until I felt something. "Wait, she latched. She's doing it." I smiled at the nurse as she nodded, offering a small rub to my arm before she left me and Jax to bask.

"I told you she would," Jax said thoughtfully before she leant down and kissed me. "When she's ready. Just like her mother. No one tells a Ricci woman what to do." She stared at me for a moment before she became distracted with something very loud outside the room. "Not even your sister."

"Excuse me, I'm her sister." Cat's voice echoed through the hallway as hushed whispers were heard arguing with her. "This is just my voice. It doesn't go any lower." More whispers of protest came, but it did nothing to slow her down. "Trust me, she wants to see me. Elena?" she called as I shook my head at her gumption. Cat stormed into the room with an assortment of helium balloons. "I'm here," she sang as she batted the balloons out of her line of vision. "Just about. It's like Fort Knox in this place."

"Cat, it's not even nine o'clock in the morning," I argued. "Visiting hours don't start until—" I cut myself off as I noticed some of the balloons. "And why did you get 'Baby Boy' balloons?" I raised a brow, considering we'd known about the sex for months.

"And 'Get Well Soon'? And...is that a 'Happy Birthday' balloon?" Jax added.

"It's all the gift shop had," Cat said before placing the balloons on the side table and moving to my free side. "You work here. You should really talk to someone about this."

"I don't work in the gift shop," Jax argued.

"And what ever happened to it's the thought that counts, huh?" Cat said before she pointed her finger at Jax. "You were supposed to call me once the baby was born."

"I thought you'd want some sleep."

"A text does not suffice when it comes to my sister, Jax. You know better."

"The baby was born in the middle of the night."

"Can everyone be quiet?" I said. "She's finally feeding." The room turned silent as all eyes stared at the little bundle.

"She's so tiny," Cat breathed as she slid onto the bed next to me. "She looks just like you, baby sis." She nudged me. "Jamie doesn't know he has a new baby sister yet, figured you'd want to tell him. I could barely get him into bed last night he was so excited. Nick will bring him over whenever you two want."

I let out a contented sigh, unable to tear my eyes from the baby in my arms.

"Nick's on call? Interesting. Some of the perks of being a freelance consultant?" Jax asked.

After quitting his job last year, Nick had become a free agent. He managed his own schedule and worked around Cat and his kids. In the end, he'd decided to choose his family over work. A brave and difficult thing to do, I knew from experience.

During the last year, I'd reined in my workaholic ways, and so had Jax. The laptop was rarely opened on the weekends now, and I'd made conscious efforts to stay no later than six p.m. at the office. I no longer missed bedtimes with Jamie, and I'd found the energy to work on my own health and wellbeing. Yoga a couple of times a week and a more active sex life, which Jax was thrilled about if not struggling to keep up with. Some things in life were just more important.

"Nick is basically a stay-at-home dad, and I've never seen him happier." She rubbed her swollen belly.

Cat had found out she was pregnant not long after I did, a pleasant surprise for her and Nick. To think, our kids would once again grow up together, just as Jamie and Kate had, no more than six months apart in age. It shouldn't have surprised me that we were both pregnant at the same time, again. We did everything together, always had.

"Do you have a name yet?" Cat broke the silence as we watched the sleeping girl in my arms.

"Oh crap, we have to name her." Jax looked panicked.

"You really didn't have any names picked out?" She turned to Jax.

"We did. We picked names. Didn't we?" Jax asked me as she rubbed her tired face.

"This is just the beginning, you know. You have two kids now. That's a whole world of fun and tears," Cat added.

"I know her name." I smiled at her. With a shaky breath, I looked up at Jax and found my eyes starting to well up. "The day we found out we could have her became one of the worst days of my life." My voice trembled as I thought back to the day of my accident. "I lost sight of who I was, who I am today, and the ones I love." Jax's eyes glistened, but she didn't look away. "She will not be remembered for that day because she is and always will be, the dawn of a new chapter. Our new beginning." My eyes turned back to the baby in my arms as I leant down and kissed her forehead.

"Aurora."

About the Author

Emma L McGeown is an Irish writer and author of the new novel *Aurora*. Professionally, Emma does very little except for distracting her co-workers from deadlines. In her free time, she has spent much of her twenties traveling and reading queer fiction, including fanfiction, though she will never voice it out loud. Her main characters are almost always LGBTQ because why not? Positive representation has never been more important, and the three-dimensional folks she creates in her writing try to offer a unique voice with heart, flaws, and of course humour.

Books Available From Bold Strokes Books

Aurora by Emma L McGeown. After a traumatic accident, Elena Ricci is stricken with amnesia, leaving her with no recollection of the last eight years, including her wife and son. (978-1-63555-824-1)

Avenging Avery by Sheri Lewis Wohl. Revenge against a vengeful vampire unites Isa Meyer and Jeni Denton, but it's love that heals them. (978-1-63555-622-3)

Bulletproof by Maggie Cummings. For Dylan Prescott and Briana Logan, the complicated NYC criminal justice system doesn't leave room for love, but where the heart is concerned, no one is bulletproof. (978-1-63555-771-8)

Her Lady to Love by Jane Walsh. A shy wallflower joins forces with the most popular woman in Regency London on a quest to catch a husband, only to discover a wild passion for each other that far eclipses their interest for the Marriage Mart. (978-1-63555-809-8)

No Regrets by Joy Argento. For Jodi and Beth, the possibility of losing their future will force them to decide what is really important. (978-1-63555-751-0)

The Holiday Treatment by Elle Spencer. Who doesn't want a gay Christmas movie? Holly Hudson asks herself that question and discovers that happy endings aren't only for the movies. (978-1-63555-660-5)

Too Good to be True by Leigh Hays. Can the promise of love survive the realities of life for Madison and Jen, or is it too good to be true? (978-1-63555-715-2)

Treacherous Seas by Radclyffe. When the choice comes down to the lives of her officers against the promise she made to her wife, Reese Conlon puts everything she cares about on the line. (978-1-63555-778-7)

Two to Tangle by Melissa Brayden. Ryan Jacks has been a player all her life, but the new chef at Tangle Valley Vineyard changes everything. If only she wasn't off the menu. (978-1-63555-747-3)

When Sparks Fly by Annie McDonald. Will the devastating incident that first brought Dr. Daniella Waveny and hockey coach Luca McCaffrey together on frozen ice now force them apart, or will their secrets and fears thaw enough for them to create sparks? (978-1-63555-782-4)

Best Practice by Carsen Taite. When attorney Grace Maldonado agrees to mentor her best friend's little sister, she's prepared to confront Perry's rebellious nature, but she isn't prepared to fall in love. Legal Affairs: one law firm, three best friends, three chances to fall in love. (978-1-63555-361-1)

Home by Kris Bryant. Natalie and Sarah discover that anything is possible when love takes the long way home. (978-1-63555-853-1)

Keeper by Sydney Quinne. With a new charge under her reluctant wing—feisty, highly intelligent math wizard Isabelle Templeton—Keeper Andy Bouchard has to prevent a murder or die trying. (978-1-63555-852-4)

One More Chance by Ali Vali. Harry Basantes planned a future with Desi Thompson until the day Desi disappeared without a word, only to walk back into her life sixteen years later. (978-1-63555-536-3)

Renegade's War by Gun Brooke. Freedom fighter Aurelia DeCallum regrets saving the woman called Blue. She fears it will jeopardize her mission, and secretly, Blue might end up breaking Aurelia's heart. (978-1-63555-484-7)

The Other Women by Erin Zak. What happens in Vegas should stay in Vegas, but what do you do when the love you find in Vegas changes your life forever? (978-1-63555-741-1)

The Sea Within by Missouri Vaun. Time is running out for Dr. Elle Graham to convince Captain Jackson Drake that the only thing that can save future Earth resides in the past, and rescue her broken heart in the process. (978-1-63555-568-4)

To Sleep With Reindeer Justine Saracen. In Norway under Nazi occupation, Maarit, an Indigenous woman, and Kirsten, a Norwegian resister, join forces to stop the development of an atomic weapon. (978-1-63555-735-0)

Twice Shy by Aurora Rey. Having an ex with benefits isn't all it's cracked up to be. Will Amanda Russo learn that lesson in time to take a chance on love with Quinn Sullivan? (978-1-63555-737-4)

Z-Town by Eden Darry. Forced to work together to stay alive, Meg and Lane must find the centuries-old treasure before the zombies find them first. (978-1-63555-743-5)

Bet Against Me by Fiona Riley. In the high-stakes luxury real estate market, everything has a price, and as rival Realtors Trina Lee and Kendall Yates find out, that means their hearts and souls, too. (978-1-63555-729-9)

Broken Reign by Sam Ledel. Together on an epic journey in search of a mysterious cure, a princess and a village outcast must overcome life-threatening challenges and their own prejudice if they want to survive. (978-1-63555-739-8)

Just One Taste by CJ Birch. For Lauren, it only took one taste to start trusting in love again. (978-1-63555-772-5)

Lady of Stone by Barbara Ann Wright. Sparks fly as a magical emergency forces a noble embarrassed by her ability to submit to a low-born teacher who resents everything about her. (978-1-63555-607-0)

Last Resort by Angie Williams. Katie and Rhys are about to find out what happens when you meet the girl of your dreams but you aren't looking for a happily ever after. (978-1-63555-774-9)

Longing for You by Jenny Frame. When Debrek housekeeper Katie Brekman is attacked amid a burgeoning vampire-witch war, Alexis Villiers must go against everything her clan believes in to save her. (978-1-63555-658-2)

Money Creek by Anne Laughlin. Clare Lehane is a troubled lawyer from Chicago who tries to make her way in a rural town full of secrets and deceptions. (978-1-63555-795-4)

Passion's Sweet Surrender by Ronica Black. Cam and Blake are unable to deny their passion for each other, but surrendering to love is a whole different matter. (978-1-63555-703-9)

The Holiday Detour by Jane Kolven. It will take everything going wrong to make Dana and Charlie see how right they are for each other. (978-1-63555-720-6)

A Love that Leads to Home by Ronica Black. For Carla Sims and Janice Carpenter, home isn't about location, it's where your heart is. (978-1-63555-675-9)

Blades of Bluegrass by D. Jackson Leigh. A US Army occupational therapist must rehab a bitter veteran who is a ticking political time bomb the military is desperate to disarm. (978-1-63555-637-7)

Hopeless Romantic by Georgia Beers. Can a jaded wedding planner and an optimistic divorce attorney possibly find a future together? (978-1-63555-650-6)

Hopes and Dreams by PJ Trebelhorn. Movie theater manager Riley Warren is forced to face her high school crush and tormentor, wealthy socialite Victoria Thayer, at their twentieth reunion. (978-1-63555-670-4)

In the Cards by Kimberly Cooper Griffin. Daria and Phaedra are about to discover that love finds a way, especially when powers outside their control are at play. (978-1-63555-717-6)

Moon Fever by Ileandra Young. SPEAR agent Danika Karson must clear her werewolf friend of multiple false charges while teaching her vampire girlfriend to resist the blood mania brought on by a full moon. (978-1-63555-603-2)

Serenity by Jesse J. Thoma. For Kit Marsden, there are many things in life she cannot change. Serenity is in the acceptance. (978-1-63555-713-8)

Sylver and Gold by Michelle Larkin. Working feverishly to find a killer before he strikes again, Boston homicide detective Reid Sylver and rookie cop London Gold are blindsided by their chemistry and developing attraction. (978-1-63555-611-7)